Welcome to the Fae World

 "THAT'S NOT POSSIBLE," I whispered to myself.

"I would tend to agree." The deep voice came from right behind me, a warm presence wrapping around me in a cloak of reality.

I blinked, realizing he must have been standing there for quite some time for his heat to have seeped so deeply into my skin. "Uh…" I glanced over my shoulder, half expecting him to be an invisible figment, and gasped at the sight of a stunning male.

Holy Fae…

His blondish-brown hair fell in waves to his non-pointy ears. And he boasted a high-fashion look about him that models would kill for—the type of male who fit a suit perfectly and wore it with a regal flair that made others bow at his feet. Yet it was his eyes that held me captive.

Because he possessed the most hypnotic multicolored eyes, framed by long, dark lashes.

Beautiful. Too beautiful. Almost distractingly so.

"Hello," he greeted, that single word containing an incredible amount of sensuality. This was the kind of man who killed women with his beauty, his features almost surreal, and distinctly inhuman.

Shit. I swallowed. "I, uh…"

"You were busy reading," he finished for me. "Yes. I've been watching."

I almost asked him to tell me how long he'd been watching, but I wasn't sure I wanted to know. "It's engrossing material."

"I have no doubt that's true," he agreed, canting his head to the side. "You're welcome to take it back to your room, Camillia. In fact, I strongly encourage it, as curfew passed by over an hour ago."

Hell Fae Captive

USA TODAY BESTSELLING AUTHORS

LEXI C. FOSS   J.R. THORN

Hell Fae Captive

Editing by: Outthink Editing, LLC

Proofreading by: Katie Schmahl

Cover Design: Covers by Juan

Cover Photography: Wander Aguiar

Cover Models: Sophie, Alex, Philippe, Forrest & Camden

Title Page Design: Luminescence Covers

Published by: Ninja Newt Publishing

eBook ISBN: 978-1-954183-47-6

Paperback ISBN: 978-1-68530-107-1

To those who root for the rebels and don't like playing by the rules, this devious little tale is for you.

#WhyChoose

Welcome to the Hell Fae Realm, a place where only the strong survive.

My parents made a deal with the devil, and now I'm a Hell Fae Captive.

Enslaved. Owned. Thrown to the Hellhounds and expected to survive.
Because only survivors earn their mates.

It doesn't matter that I don't want to be a bride.
I'm a Halfling. Part Hell Fae and part girl-who-doesn't-give-a-shit.
But because of a bargain, *he* owns me.

Lucifer. The Hell Fae King who created this godforsaken realm.
Also known as the orchestrator of these deadly bride-trial games.

Okay, Luci, I'll play.
By burning this whole kingdom to the ground.

Assuming I don't get caught in the hot Midnight Fae Warden's web first.
Or ensnared by the brooding Hell Fae Commander lurking outside the gates.
And don't even get me started on the Hell Fae King's favored prince. That sexy lunatic won't stop sending me gifts.

No amount of hotness or sensual persuasion will keep me here.
I'm not bride material.
I'm a menace.

You made a deal for the wrong girl, Lucifer.
Prepare for the fight of your life.

A NOTE FROM LEXI & JEN

Welcome to the Hell Fae world. It's dark. It's deadly. And it's riddled with nightmares. There may be scenes that make the reader uncomfortable, but everything is done for a reason. Reasons that may or may not be defined in book one.

Hell Fae Captive introduces the infamous bride trials. Therefore, there are strong sexual undertones, violent scenes, and themes of dubious consent. There are also several strong male-on-male relationships in this world, and these men absolutely like to fuck each other. But they'll be inviting Cami to join them... once she proves her worth. ;)

However, Cami isn't the type of heroine to bend over and take it. She'll fight until the bitter end.

Her mates have a lot of work ahead of them.

As well as some groveling to do along the way.

Their journey won't be easy. But it'll be deliciously sinful.

So step into the Hell Fae world. Be careful who you trust. And watch out for the infamous mirages.

Nothing is what it seems.

Just like our Hell Fae King…

Love is for the weak.
Hate is what keeps me alive.
And fate is a promise worth breaking.
—Cami

CAMI

WHAT THE HELL?

I squinted. Blinked. Shut my eyes. Then squinted again.

Because no. No, that did *not* just happen. That big, fluffy black dog did not just grow three heads before turning into a man with sharp, pointy ears.

He grinned, his teeth a slash of white against his dark skin. Obsidian orbs glistened with malice in his gaze, his expression radiating violence.

"Hello, Halfling." His gravelly voice reminded me of grating rocks, his low growl an ominous promise of death.

Hellhounds loved to intimidate their prey.

Unfortunately for this asshole, I didn't scare easily.

"What the fuck do you want?" I'd run into fae of all kinds on Earth. Midnight Fae, Fortune Fae, and Paradox Fae being the most common, but lately, it'd been mostly hellish beings stepping into my path.

This mutt probably thought I was his future dinner.

As I wasn't all that inclined to be munched on, I'd have to change his mind.

He snarled, his lips dripping with saliva.

I merely cocked a brow. "Need a bib?"

He released a growling, snarly noise that would probably cause a normal human to run.

I yawned instead.

Having a Hell Fae for a dad made me rather accustomed to the bullshit supernaturals of the world. Of course, my mortal friends didn't know about them. Had this genius attacked me at the party a few blocks over, we'd be having a very different conversation, one that involved the violation of the interrealm treaty—not that the Hell Fae ever seemed to respect the rules.

But he'd waited until I was alone and walking back to the dorm, so maybe he didn't want to deal with bureaucratic bullshit after all.

Good thing my roommate, Allison, had decided to stay with Benji at the party. As a mortal with no idea that fae existed, she'd be freaking out right about now.

"Seriously, what do you want?" I asked, bored by his posturing. He was the third beast-like fae to attack me this week, and I was really tired of stabbing them. Perhaps I could talk this one down and save another outfit from bloodstains. Not to mention my dwindling weapon supplies.

"I have orders to take you in, Halfling."

I rolled my eyes. "Yeah, the last guy said that, too. My answer is still the same—no."

I had no idea where these assholes wanted to take me. I'd tried calling my parents about it three different times, but they'd never answered or returned my messages. They'd probably changed their phone number and had forgotten to give it to me. *Again.*

My mom and dad weren't exactly up for the Parents of the Year Award. They preferred the "she'll survive on her own" approach to parenting. It'd worked all my life for the most part, so why change anything now?

"You think you have a choice?" the thing grated out, his voice scattering goose bumps up my arms. Because *ouch*, it sounded like it hurt for him to talk.

"I think life is all about choices," I informed him seriously. "For example, you have the choice to walk away now and leave me the fuck alone. Or you can try to attack me and see what happens. Personally, I suggest option one. It'll be much less painful for you."

Hellhounds weren't particularly fond of silver.

And I had a blade tucked into my boot for an instance just like this.

My parents had at least taught me general self-defense as a kid. While normal seven-year-olds had received clowns and cartoons for their birthdays, my parents had introduced me to a game of grenades instead. When I'd turned ten, they'd upgraded grenades to knives. By thirteen, I'd had three guns to my name.

And so the training continued. For all I knew, my dad was probably sending these jerkwads as some sort of new test.

They told me I could never be too prepared for the fae of the other worlds.

Well, they weren't wrong.

Mister Slobber grinned, his anticipation thickening the night air and eliciting a sigh from deep within me.

What was it with these guys? They never saw me as a threat, always interpreting my five-foot-four, slender frame as a weakness. Being petite made me fast, not inept. It served as a strength against a being of his size because it allowed me to duck his hands and go for the balls.

Unless he shifted again.

Then I might have to run.

But he predictably lunged for me instead.

I ducked, my body moving on autopilot as I snatched the blade from my boot and plunged it upward into the Hellhound's groin.

He gaped at me, his shock palpable. These assholes always underestimated me, thought I was an easy target, and like all the rest, he lost before the fight even began.

He collapsed to his knees with an agonized sound that had me shaking my head.

"See? Life is all about choices," I told him. "And you just made a bad one." He'd also cost me my last silver blade. I could go digging and try to pull it out of his junk, but then I risked being splattered with his acidic blood, and that shit burned.

My shoulders sagged as I realized a trip home was required, not just to replenish my weapons stash but also to ask if my parents knew anything about these strange visits. Three in a week was a lot.

The Hellhound started to smoke, his teleportation ability kicking into gear.

I jumped back and watched him disappear into a cloud of ash.

That was probably why they always tried to grab me—they wanted to whisk me away in that whirlwind of soot.

"Never gonna happen," I said, spinning around to resume my path back to the dorm and walking face-first into a hard male wall instead. I frowned, confused. "What—"

"That was a neat trick," a deep voice informed me, his hands clamping down on my hips to hold me in place. "Of course, Payan is going to be pissed that I set him up just so I could watch you work, but after the last few incidents, I was intrigued. I had no idea silver could do such a thing to a Hell Fae."

I looked up into a pair of obsidian irises rimmed with deep blue flames, set in a face that caused the air to still in my lungs.

Most fae were alluring.

This one was stunning in a rugged, masculine, take-no-prisoners kind of way. He had a devilish smirk about him as well, one that said he found my antics amusing more than terrifying, and he would absolutely be cocky in a fight.

The problem was, unlike the others, I suspected this wall of muscle might win because he boasted an aura of power around him that defined him as clearly *other*.

Not a Hell Fae.

But a Midnight Fae.

Vampiric in nature. Deadly. With an aura of magic around him that flickered and burned and dared me to defy him.

I swallowed, my heart skipping a beat. "What do you want?" Most of them just wanted a bite, to imbibe a little blood and run back to their realm.

However, none of them ever chose to snack on me. I wasn't fully human. If they bit me, they risked mating me.

And no one wanted that.

"I want a lot of things," he said softly, his fingers combing through his thick, dark hair as he studied me. "None of which you can give me." A hint of darkness lurked in those words, his expression hardening with a past defined by pain. I recognized it because my mother frequently wore a similar expression, her history one I wouldn't wish upon anyone in the world.

An orphan, abused for two decades until my father had saved her from certain death.

I was their mistake—the child they'd never wanted.

So on some levels, I understood loss, and on others, I didn't, because I'd never had a family around to really lose.

But this being wore his pain as a shield, the lines of his past etched into his hard features and crystalizing the sapphire edges of his eyes.

"Well," he continued, his voice hushed. "No blade for me?"

"All out, I'm afraid," I told him, waking up to my situation once more. "But I can give you something else?" I phrased it as a question, an offering, curious to see what he would say.

His lips curled, revealing a subtle scar over the bottom left curve of his mouth. "I do love gifts."

"Then you're really going to enjoy this one," I replied, my voice deceptively sweet.

I brought my knee up between his legs in the next breath, only to find my thigh trapped between his as he arched a brow.

"Do you always go for the jewels on a man?" he asked conversationally. "Or is that just your natural response to fae males? Because I do think that might help you in the trials. Hell Fae men like their females feisty and ready to fondle."

"Trials?" I repeated, trying futilely to yank my knee out from between his legs. Aside from a minor wince, he seemed to hold me with ease, his strength dwarfing mine and forcing me to remain balanced on a single foot.

"Hmm, yes. Bride trials." His gaze dropped to my lips, then he cocked his head. "I think they'll quite like taming you, Camillia."

I gaped at him. "*Bride trials?*" He had to be joking. "What the fuck are you talking about? And how the hell do you know my name?"

"Had you accepted the previous invitations, you would already know. But you chose to stab them all instead."

"Invitations?" Apparently, I'd turned into a parrot who

could only repeat words. "You mean the salivating Hellhounds who wanted to eat me for dinner?"

"Oh, they absolutely wanted to eat you, darling," he agreed. "But not in the way you're insinuating."

My nose scrunched. "Gross." Because I'd caught that connotation and no fucking thank you.

I gave up trying to free my leg and opted to throat-punch him instead.

Which resulted in him catching my wrist with a tsk and whirling me in his arms until my back met his chest. It knocked the air from my lungs but also released my knee. I drove my heel into his hefty boot, earning a hiss from my captor.

He muttered a spell under his breath, the words foreign to me.

Snakelike ropes of dark magic slithered around us, the bands suffocating and blinding my view of the campus grounds.

Shit!

I tried to fight him in earnest, to force him to release me, only to freeze as a blistering heat met my senses.

Hell.

Flames erupted around us, the sable rocks glowing with streaks of red and orange.

The Midnight Fae released me with a little shove. "I'll be inside waiting to see if you can make it across." He stepped in front of me with a cocky little grin. "Good luck, Camillia."

He flicked a coin at my feet, then disappeared into a shadow, leaving me in the middle of what appeared to be a lava land mine.

Ajax

"Now, was that really so difficult?" I asked as I shadowed into the other side of the paradigm walls.

Payan snarled, lunging toward me.

I hit him with a defensive spell that put the dog on his ass with a whine that had me rolling my eyes.

Six hundred and sixty-six captives, and Camillia De la Croix was the only one who'd required my intervention. All the others had been handed over directly by their relatives or kidnapped with ease from their sleep.

But not this little dark-blonde-haired Halfling pixie of a girl.

I'd sent three Hellhounds out for her, and they'd all come back in similar shape — with a blade to the balls. Two of them had also had daggers stuck in their chests.

All silver.

From what the Hellhounds said, the metal *burned*.

I'd spent nearly a decade in this realm, learning how to fight and blend with Hell Fae, and I'd never seen any of them suffer the way they had after being stabbed by this female.

Payan continued to whine on the ground, proving my point. I wanted to call him weak, but I'd sent him for a reason—he'd picked up over half of the other girls without a single issue.

Yet he'd lasted all of five minutes in Camillia's presence.

Fascinating.

It was like he'd taken one look at her breasts and forgotten his own fucking name. He'd lunged at her without any finesse, and she'd taken him down with a singular move to the family jewels.

While it hurt, that shouldn't have kept him on the ground for long. Except for the *burning*.

Since when does silver burn Hellhounds? I wondered for the tenth or eleventh time this week.

Well, at least it was done now. I'd successfully brought her to the entry point. If she proved worthy, the gates would allow her inside. If not, one of Az's minions would have the pleasure of cleaning up her corpse.

I checked my watch, then leaned against a burning thwomp tree just inside the gates. My left leg throbbed, reminding me of yesterday's sparring session. The girl's swift kick had aggravated it a bit, mainly because I'd nearly failed to block her mostly impressive move.

The bare limbs above me twisted in annoyance, the trunk bristling beneath my touch. It didn't appreciate me leaning against the bark, something the tree told me by stirring up a dance of embers and smoke along the leafless branches.

"Flame me," I drawled, not at all bothered by the thwomp's notorious penchant for lighting itself on fire. The Midnight Fae grounds were littered with them, so it only seemed fitting that Zen—the creator and mastermind of this paradigm—had added a few to her landscape.

9

She'd included the charcoal blades, gargoyles, stone architecture, and a sunless sky framing a solitary moon as well. A true gothic kingdom, painted forever in the darkness of the night.

Home, I thought, sighing.

But it was overrun with Hell Fae.

Now that the Quandary Bloods were allowed to live in the Midnight Fae Realm again, their former hiding place had been reformed into the prison around me.

With me as the Warden.

It was my job to keep the captives inside, not kidnap them. However, Camillia had proved to be a special case. Az and I had flipped for it—I'd lost, which meant I'd been sent to retrieve her after all my lieutenants had failed.

Pulling my wand from my cloak, I called up an enchantment that created a window of sorts for me to look through the walls of the paradigm. As I was in a somewhat alternate reality, I couldn't exactly see what was happening outside the gates without a little spell.

Just like all Camillia would be able to see from her current vantage point was rocks for miles and miles, with two blistering suns shining overhead.

This area of the Hell Fae Realm was uninhabitable for a reason.

Except for the area protected within the paradigm.

Life existed here just fine, thanks to the Midnight Fae magic keeping it all alive.

I spun the enchanted window to the place where I'd left Camillia and found her standing with her hands on her hips.

She didn't appear to be frightened at all, just annoyed.

That alone proved her to be a viable candidate for this unplanned trial. I hadn't subjected any of the others to this because all they did was scream and beg us to take them home. Those candidates would probably just collapse out there in the rocky terrain and wait until someone came to retrieve them.

But not Camillia.

Which was why I wouldn't be taking her directly to her new quarters like the others. She'd caused quite a headache, and this seemed to be a suitable punishment for her efforts.

Returning my wand to my inner pocket, I folded my arms and observed the girl through my magical portal as she bent to pick up my coin.

The air around her blurred with heat, and an enticing bead of sweat rolled down the arch of her neck. She wouldn't last long if she couldn't find a way inside, but this was the consequence for wasting my time.

Her lips pursed, her stormy gray eyes studying the object thoroughly. She blew out a breath, then flicked the item into the air to catch it, and lifted her gaze skyward to admire both suns. Or maybe she was trying to search for a teleportation portal in the sky. Either way, she appeared lost in her thoughts.

Her long dirty-blonde hair reminded me of burnt ash beneath the reddish-orange haze, her exposed skin already pinkening from the harsh elements. If she noticed, she didn't show it. Instead, she started looking around, her expression calculative.

A subtle breeze drew my gaze to the sky of the paradigm just as a stunning obsidian-feathered Phoenix blacked out the moon. The Hellhounds near me all took several steps back, not wanting to deal with the approaching being.

I didn't share their concern. "Show-off," I muttered as the majestic animal landed beside me. "You could use two legs like a normal fae."

Energy hummed beside me as Az engaged his ability to shift, his pale skin replacing the feathers. But his hair remained dark brown, the thick strands somewhat shorter than mine. And his chiseled jaw was decorated with inky fibers, his perpetual five o'clock shadow always in full effect no matter how many times he shaved.

"I'm anything but normal," he replied, his deep voice boasting his usual seriousness.

"Most Hell Fae could claim the same," I pointed out.

"Most Hell Fae are not me," he countered.

I lifted a shoulder. He wasn't wrong. Hell Fae were all abominations in their own right, coming from some mix of fae heritages. But Az, short for Azazel, was half Shifter Fae, his ancestry that of the rare Black Phoenix line. His father was a Paradox Fae, giving him quite a unique genetic makeup. The second half was also why Az usually carried around a sword, but having just shifted back into his human form, he was without clothes and his magical conduit.

Retrieving my wand again, I waved it over him with a muttered spell, gifting him with a pair of pants.

He glanced down as they appeared around his thick, muscular legs, then he cocked a brow at me. "You usually like me naked."

"Yes, but we're expecting company," I told him. "We don't want to frighten her with that monster between your legs."

His blazing eyes met mine. "Compliments outside of the bedroom? I'm flattered."

"You're welcome to display that flattery when we're done here."

"I just might do that." He flexed his hand before him, stirring an enchantment that was entirely his own. His sword appeared half a beat later, the purple magnetism swirling around the blade matching the violet embers of his irises.

The moment passed, and his focus shifted to the gates. "This is the girl?" he asked, studying the female in my magical window. "She's about to burn herself alive doing that. And Lucifer won't like losing a prospect."

I followed his gaze to find her kneeling beside a pool of black liquid, her curious expression reminding me of a cat. "She took down several Hellhounds, including Payan. I give her good odds on surviving."

Payan grunted, still aggravated by her assault. "She cheated with silver magic."

"It's not cheating if it works," Az replied, his attention still on the girl.

Payan growled before he hobbled off. He'd probably been hanging around expecting some sort of recompense for his injuries—he was lucky I didn't take him to Lucifer for being so inept.

With the two of us alone to watch the girl, Az cocked his head a little, the stance somewhat rivaling the black phoenix tattoo sprawled across his bare chest. It was all very birdlike, which made sense given his heritage. "Well, she's clever."

She turned over the coin I'd left for her before tossing it into the black liquid. The pit sucked the enchanted metal into its inky depths, then spat it back at her, detesting the wrongness of the magic.

My lips quirked. "Very clever," I agreed.

Camillia bent to retrieve the coin once more and flipped it between her fingers while evaluating the landscape.

She couldn't see us or the gate, the paradigm invisible unless appropriately approached. From her point of view, the surroundings would resemble a land of lava and fire and death. But if she passed through the rocks correctly, she'd see the obsidian arch, and then she'd find the gates.

Her gaze went right through us as she glanced toward our window and back again. Then she held up the coin and twirled it once more.

"Does she like the shiny quality of the metal?" Az wondered out loud. "Because if that's the case, she'll positively melt for my sword."

My lips quirked at the innuendo in his tone. I supposed that, as a Hell Fae, he could fight for her as a potential bride, if he so desired. He was old, powerful, and Lucifer's right-hand man. They were also already bonded, just not sexually.

Fortunately, Hell Fae could bond multiple times. Hence the whole purpose of this trial. The women who proved viable would be auctioned off to groups to be shared—a way for Lucifer to pacify the many males of his Hell Fae kingdom.

Of course, the key was *survival*.

Which, consequently, was why there weren't many women—the Hell Fae Source rarely accepted females into the inner circle.

Az stilled beside me as Camillia focused on the rocks, her expression determined.

Another flip of the metal, and one corner of her mouth lifted.

"Did you leave a magical trail on the coin?" Az guessed.

"Only a slight buzz to help nudge her in the right direction." Paradigms were alternate realities that couldn't be seen unless approached from the right angle and with an appropriate magical essence. Hence the need for the coin.

"Seems like more than a *buzz*," Az replied as Camillia

started forward with confident steps. "It's like you handed her a map key."

I didn't reply, because yeah, that was exactly what I'd done. I just hadn't expected her to figure it out so quickly. The coin's magic was tied to the paradigm's entrance, allowing the carrier to see the gates once they found the right arch to step through.

Which she seemed to have already located in record time.

Interesting.

Her files said she had a Hell Fae father of mixed origin and a human mother. They must have taught her how to sense magic for her to be able to navigate the lands so quickly.

The other candidates had all been taken directly to their new accommodations. But Camillia hadn't arrived willingly. So this seemed like a suitable form of castigation, except she navigated the path quickly, ruining my fun.

"Well, that was boring," I muttered as she spied the arch.

"But also intriguing," Az replied. "She's definitely unique compared to most of the others."

"Want to take bets on her survival?" I asked conversationally.

Az's violet gaze found mine. "Do these bets involve sexual favors?"

"Of course."

"Then yes." His serious tone implied he meant it. "We'll discuss it more in the ring later."

I sighed. "Again?" We'd just sparred the other night, and I was still recovering from his viciousness with the blade. My left leg still ached from his ruthless strike—an injury meant to taunt me as it stretched and pulled intimately at my flesh, reminding me of what had happened *after* we'd finished our fight.

Seriously, the damn fae had more than earned his title as the Commander, a term that translated to being Lucifer's lead warrior and enforcer. Everyone bowed to Az as if he were Lucifer himself.

Well, everyone except me.

Which was how Az and I had become friends and why he forced me to train with him. As he put it, I was one of the only fae with balls big enough to give him a proper fight.

Except I almost always lost.

"You like sparring," Az replied softly. His lips brushed my cheek before going to my ear to add, "And you like when I force you to submit, too."

I shivered, my window spell disappearing as Camillia found the gates.

"If you're expecting me to climb those slithering walls, then you're going to be waiting a while," she called from outside the stone exterior.

The snake-vines hissed at her in response, irritated by her presence, and several gargoyles took up arms by the gates themselves.

I sighed. "I suppose I should give her the grand tour now."

"I'd offer to help, but I don't want to."

"Of course you don't." Az didn't particularly enjoy socialization, preferring to communicate with his fists more than his mouth.

He pressed a kiss to my neck, then left me to handle the furious Halfling beauty outside the gates. I debated leaving her there to play with this paradigm's version of the LethaForest. Her punishment hadn't been all that fulfilling.

Although, she had been crafty, and that sort of behavior should be rewarded. At least a little.

I wavered, weighing the options.

A gargoyle grating out a command for her to step back made the decision for me.

It would truly upset Lucifer if a woman with her potential was killed by one of Zen's creations or the gargoyles she'd allowed to reside within this paradigm. He wouldn't be able to do anything to Zen, their agreement protecting her from his wrath. Not to mention her former Midnight Fae Queen title and her ties to the current royalty sitting on the Midnight Fae thrones.

But he could punish me.

And I very much preferred to avoid that.

"You think I'm afraid of a petite little stone creature with a sword the size of my hand?" She sounded both amused and annoyed, her voice carrying on the wind. "You're like a pissed-off little garden gnome."

The gargoyle growled in response, his little body sprinting forward with his sword raised. "That's enough, Sir Garmond," I said, using a whispered spell to force the gargoyle to remain still. "And it's really not wise to challenge them, Ms. De la Croix," I added as I moved into view. "Gargoyles are quite powerful for their size."

"So am I," she replied.

"Yes, it seems that you are," I agreed, snapping my fingers to call the gates to open. "But are you powerful enough to survive?"

She glared at me, her feisty energy causing my lips to curl. I hadn't met a woman like her in what felt like a very long time.

Most females submitted so easily.

However, not this one.

Hmm, she was definitely worth betting on with Az because she just might make it to the end.

She stepped through the entry, her expression darkening as she took in the castle-like buildings at my back.

I smiled. "Welcome to the Hell Fae Bride Trials, darling. I'm the Warden. Allow me to show you to your new cell."

CAMI

Having a Hell Fae for a father had prepared me for all sorts of bizarre situations.

This was not one of them.

"Hell Fae Bride Trials?" I snorted. "No, thanks."

The *Warden* ignored me, instead choosing to turn around with a "Follow me" command.

As I wasn't a dog, or at all interested in adhering to his order, I remained by the gates. He lifted his hand, presenting a wand to the air.

My brow furrowed in confusion, only to gasp as a bolt of purple fire left his magical conduit and lassoed me around the neck to tug me forward. *Like a leash.*

"Let go of me," I demanded, my fingers protesting the fiery strand as I tried to yank it away from my neck.

"I offered to let you walk on your own. You declined. This is the alternative choice." He turned to admire the magic sizzling against my throat. "And I daresay that collar looks very good on you, Camillia."

I growled in response.

He grinned. "Now, these are the entry grounds," he

said, gesturing to the dark landscape of leafless trees, black grass, and wandering wildlife. While it was a step up from the tunnels, chasms, and melted rock, I had a feeling I wasn't going to like this place all that much more than the previous location. "Just about everything in this courtyard will try to kill you, so I don't suggest visiting often."

As though to confirm that statement, one of the trees went up in flames, shooting smoke and embers several stories into the air.

That explains the bare branches, I thought, gaping at the giant black trunk.

"Burning thwomp," the Warden murmured. "'In case you were looking for a name." He tugged on the leash, dragging me down a cobblestone path rimmed by the shadowy landscape. "This whole paradigm was created by a Midnight Fae for Midnight Fae, hence the obvious influences."

He gave my makeshift collar a little tug when I started to bend and examine the reflective blades of grass. They appeared to be made of metal, and they moved as we walked.

"Did you miss the part where I said the courtyard is designed to kill you?" he drawled, yanking me to his side with another rope of magic around my middle. "Don't. Touch."

My jaw ticked. "Says the male wrapping me up in fiery ropes of Midnight Fae magic."

"To keep you alive."

I batted my eyes at him. "Oh, is that why you left me outside the gates? Was that just for me to work on my tan on my path to survival?"

He grinned. "You were looking a bit pale."

"Says the wannabe vampire," I returned.

His dark brow arched into his hairline. "Do you need

proof of my bite, sweetheart? Would that make me more vampiric in your eyes?"

I scoffed at that. "Not really in the market for a mate, but thanks anyway."

"Ah," he hummed, approval radiating in his expression. "Someone has studied fae kind."

"Someone didn't have a choice," I retorted, thinking of all the random literature my father had given me over the years. He might have been mostly absent during my upbringing, but when he had shown up, it had always been related to some sort of supernatural training.

"And what do you know about Midnight Fae?"

"That males dictate the mating bond through biting. A bit sexist, if you ask me," I added conversationally as I tried to unfasten the collar at my throat. The embers sizzled along my fingertips, eliciting a hiss from my lips. "Which explains your penchant for leashing me. I'm probably just some glorified pet to you, right? A female Halfling with a human mother. Just another exhibit for your *bride trials*."

His blue-black irises ran over me, his amusement seeming to bleed into a contemplative expression. "Definitely not a pet I want to keep," he finally said after a minute. The leash sizzled to ash. "Follow me like a good girl, and I'll leave your neck alone. Disobey me, and I'll teach you the meaning of the word *pet* by making you crawl."

My teeth ground together as my skin shivered in relief to be free from his spell.

Fucking wizard, I thought, glaring at the wand he kept in his hand. It served as a warning and a taunt all wrapped up in one obsidian stick. I could try to grab it, but from what I knew about Midnight Fae, they didn't require the magical conduit to access their dark source—it merely helped them control their power.

And yeah, that would probably make things worse, not better. Plus, I'd already underestimated him at our first encounter. I would bide my time and find his weakness, then I would strike.

Because I knew a few spells, too.

Spells my Hell Fae father had taught me that were meant for situations like this.

And I didn't need a wand to use them. Just a lot of energy, which I was running low on at present.

However, this Midnight Fae would underestimate me if I played along—another benefit that would give me a chance to reevaluate the situation and replenish my energy.

So I trailed behind him and surveyed my surroundings instead, being a "good girl," for now.

All I need is a portal.

My father had taught me how to use them as a kid, and he'd made me memorize, like, fifty different codes. One of them would work. He just hadn't taught me how to *create* one, which would have been really fucking helpful right now.

But if I could just locate—

A swarm of crows took off across the field, causing the Warden to grab me and pull me behind him as he created a shield of purple smoke magic. "Stop thinking about escaping," he snapped at me. "Those things are programmed to keep you here by any means necessary, and they've already killed three girls this week."

My eyes widened. "How?" I wondered, staring at their beaks.

It was then that I realized their feathers weren't the soft kind, but made of razor-sharp, rocky edges.

"Oh," I whispered, swallowing. "Right."

"The grounds are rigged with traps that will kill you just for plotting." He sounded winded as he whirled the power around us, crafting a protective layer of purple electricity that elicited a round of angry caws from the swarming crows.

"So you captured a bunch of fae just to kill them unceremoniously?" I couldn't help the note of incredulity in my tone. "Seems like you went through a lot of work to round up your cattle just to off them. Maybe you should just return me and save us both the trouble."

His lips curled into a cruel grin. "And what would be the fun in that?"

I glanced at the angry swarm of crows. "Fun indeed," I muttered. "Seems wasteful."

"Not wasteful. Just a factor of the game. And we have an overabundance of candidates. Six hundred and sixty-six, to be exact." He shrugged, but the sweat populating his brow suggested this show of power was taking a toll on him.

It made me wonder what those crows would be doing to me right now without his interference.

Would I survive them?

Would I survive *this*?

"Lucifer made sure there would be enough to go around. Deaths are an expectation," he continued. "The Hell Fae Source doesn't typically accept females, so don't pretend to believe you're special." The way he protected me right now from the angry crows seemed contrary to his words.

Or perhaps he did this for all the recruits.

"Six hundred and sixty-six, huh?" I mused, folding my arms. "Well, I think it's about to be six hundred and sixty-five." Because I would be leaving this place. "Sorry to ruin your very unoriginal number."

His gaze narrowed. "You don't want to test me, Camillia. And you certainly don't want to test them." He allowed a crow to come through his web of magic, the beak made of solid rock.

It went right for my eye.

I swatted at it, then cursed as the razor-tipped edge sliced across my palm.

Facing a swarm of these would be a terrible way to die.

His power wrapped around the bird like a noose, yanking it back to the swarm. "You have two minutes to get your urge to run under control, Camillia," he said through his teeth. "Otherwise, I'm leaving you to fend for yourself."

I sighed. "It's only natural to want to escape."

"Nothing about this world is natural," he returned.

"No shit," I muttered, trying to figure out how to turn off my brain. I'd been raised to analyze every potential exit point and search for weaknesses. Shutting that down would prove… difficult.

The crows picked up their speed before squawking out an earsplitting alarm.

I winced, my palms lifting to cover my ears only to find my wrists caught in the Warden's grip as he spun to face me. He dropped my hands in the next breath, then caught my chin between his fingers and forced me to meet his blazing irises.

The blue edges burned with promise, and not the good kind. "The sooner you accept that there is no changing the deal, the more likely you are to survive."

I blinked at him. "Deal?"

"Yes," he hissed. "The one your father made on behalf of your life. It's why you're here, as well as everyone else.

Because all these parents made deals at the costs of their daughters' souls. You want to talk about sexism? Chew on that for a minute, *pet*." He released me, his smokelike shield melting into the air and granting the crows entry.

However, all they did was beat their wings furiously around me before drifting back to the sky to black out the moon.

My heart stopped beating, not from the fright of almost being sliced up to death by their wings, but from the Warden's words. "I'm here because of a deal?" All my thoughts of escape had fled in favor of that single reveal. "*Fuck.*"

Both of his eyebrows lifted, then he huffed out a laugh. "Fuck indeed," he agreed, gesturing with his hand. "Shall we continue on our tour?"

"Of all the things that want to kill me?" I countered. "Sure, why not?"

At least he'd given my mind something else to focus on.

Because now I didn't just want to escape—I wanted to kill my parents, too.

The castle-like buildings loomed overhead, their obsidian stones writhing with snakes and crows that glinted in the moonlight. Tiny gargoyles littered the upper spires, resembling statues. Except one of them moved, confirming they were very real.

And creepy as fuck.

While I knew that we'd moved into a magically protected area of an otherwise inhospitable land—the Hell Fae Realm in all its glory—a heated breeze still found its way through the cobblestone sidewalks and charcoal-colored courtyards, sizzling my skin in a way that was starting to feel like a sunburn despite the midnight sky.

No one else seemed bothered by it.

The realm's inhabitants were more focused on the

Warden than on the environment, their gazes lowering in respect as we began to walk by them. Some of the beings even bowed.

Clearly, I'd been wrangled into submission by one of the more powerful members of this realm.

Not the best person to begin plotting an escape around.

As though to agree with my thought, the snakes writhed and hissed along the walls, the sound a stark warning to my senses.

Right. Not allowed to contemplate escape.

However, that didn't mean I couldn't find another way to leave—one I could do "legally."

Such as finding a way to break the deal my father had made with the proverbial devil.

"Do you have a copy of this deal somewhere?" I wondered out loud.

The Warden glanced at me, his gaze assessing. "I believe there's one waiting for you in your room. But I can assure you, there are no loopholes. Lucifer penned the documents himself."

Lucifer.

I'd never had the displeasure of meeting him, but my father had told me stories about the infamous Hell Fae King. Hell was a very real place, not somewhere for souls to live out their afterlives, but a prison for fae—the worst of the worst. Except Lucifer had made it his very own kingdom, one infamous for his twisted deals where only he came out on top.

"And this agreement trades me in exchange for…?"

The Warden shrugged. "I've not read your particular deal. It could be anything, really. Wealth. Power. Freedom."

"And are you here as part of a deal, too?"

He paused in front of a set of marble stairs, his cloak

billowing in a shadowy breeze that only seemed to touch him and not me. "It takes a naïve soul to deal with the proverbial devil." His gaze flicked over me before he added, "And I am not naïve."

"I'm not the one who agreed to a deal."

"No," he agreed. "Your father did."

"Then why are you here?" I asked him, curious. "You're not a Hell Fae."

His lips curled, but his smile wasn't kind. "And you're observant."

"You're avoiding the question."

"Because you haven't earned a response." He stepped forward until my breasts brushed his torso. "I helped you with the crows because Lucifer would be disappointed to lose yet another candidate to his alarm system. Don't mistake that as a kindness, because I am not kind."

"No, you're just the Warden."

"I am." He held my gaze for a long moment, then took a step back. "This way."

He started up the stairs with a flourish, his cloak billowing behind him on that shadowy breeze. It was like a perpetual dark cloud that followed his every step, all the way up to the top.

I followed, my heart in my throat.

What could my parents possibly have asked for at the price of my soul?

The Warden held open the door for me at the top of the stairs. "This is a communal area for food," he explained, leading me down a hall into a wide-open space filled with tables. A row of kitchens sat near the back, each of them occupied with several fae.

Male guards were also stationed throughout the room, their gazes all falling to the Warden as we entered.

Silence filled the space, all the seated females looking at

the Warden with a mixture of fear and awe. My brow furrowed at the clear reverence. Even the guards appeared respectful.

"We have all kinds of cuisine, including a human variety since you're not the only Halfling in attendance," the Warden said, ignoring them all. He spun on his heel with a click of his fingers. "Come along."

I nearly growled at the dismissive way he said it, but chose to obey because I wanted a copy of the deal he'd referenced—the one he'd claimed was in my room.

Cutting through the kitchens, we exited out onto the streets again.

He showed me a library next, mentioning something about figments and suggesting I avoid them. A few giggles followed that announcement, startling me, but by the time I turned around, no one was there and the Warden was halfway out of the room.

I practically ran after him and half listened as he pointed out the different dormitories and eventually the challenge rings that he claimed I'd become better acquainted with later. "They used to be academic buildings. We've repurposed the space."

"Was this some sort of university?"

"A Midnight Fae Academy for Quandary Bloods," he replied. "A place to hide them during the recent power struggles." He glanced at me. "Did you not read about that while researching the Midnight Fae?"

"No, I didn't."

"Hmm." He turned again, leading me back across the former academy grounds, pointing out more dangerous wildlife and plant life along the way. Another of those *burning thwomps* sat stationary beside another building, a swarm of fiery gnats kissing the dead branches. "And definitely stay away from those. They bite."

One flew into my face as though to tempt me into proving him wrong.

I didn't, instead choosing to follow him up yet another set of marble stairs. The gothic architecture around this place seemed very keen on stone and dark arches. There was even a spire of this building that reminded me a bit of a princess tower from a storybook. Apart from the dark shadows and inky aura, anyway.

So maybe a castle for a horror novel where the princess died would be more appropriate.

"Your quarters will be in this building. Curfew is at fifteen hundred hours. Which, I suppose, as an American, is your version of three in the afternoon, yes?"

"Three p.m. is my curfew?"

"Yes, and breakfast is at midnight."

"Midnight," I repeated.

"Did I stutter?" he deadpanned.

"No, just, *as an American*, I'm used to eating breakfast at eight or nine in the morning."

He smiled. "Well, your Americanisms do not apply here."

"Of course not," I drawled. "I doubt any of my preferences do."

"Now you're learning," he replied, sounding pleased. "However, we will be serving food from your realm. Not because you've earned it, of course, but because some of us actually prefer it. Any true favors will have to be earned."

I arched a brow. That sounded… ominous.

And sexual.

Alas, he didn't elaborate.

"So you'll eat breakfast at midnight, or you won't eat at all. Lunch is at three on the dot, and your dinner is served at seven." He glanced upward at the moon. "It's constant night in this paradigm, but there should be a clock in your room. I suggest guarding it and your time appropriately."

He opened the door to lead me inside.

I paused on the threshold, startled by the array of gargoyles lurking in the dimly lit foyer. Most of them didn't even come up to the middle of my shins, their tiny frames reminding me of stone garden gnomes. But their expressions were decidedly unfriendly.

"Warden," one of them welcomed in a gravelly tone.

"Sir Davis," the Warden returned with a nod. "Ms. De la Croix is here to be shown to her room."

A few of them grumbled in response.

"I see word of her proclivities has spread," the Warden said with a sigh. "I'll accompany you."

My eyebrows rose. "My proclivities?"

"For harming guards," he returned.

"You mean the fae who tried to kidnap me?"

"Yes, the *guards*," he reiterated.

"To be fair, none of them mentioned a deal or bride trials."

"To be fair, you never gave them a chance," he returned as one of the gargoyles took off in a flurry of stone wings, leading the way up an unending set of stairs.

I started to climb, wondering if I could see the top after a few more steps, but the stairway just kept going... and going... and... "Is there an end?"

"Yes. When we reach your room," the Warden informed me.

I frowned. "But the outside was only three or four stories tall."

"And you let your eyes tell you what to believe?" he asked, arching a brow. "How very human of you."

"I am a Halfling from the mortal world," I reminded him.

"Indeed you are," he agreed, continuing upward.

After at least a hundred stairs, the scenery began to change and revealed a platform that led to a single door.

"It's worth noting that these rooms are all enchanted to lock down at curfew, and that lockdown will happen with or without you inside the room."

Well, that was an ominous statement. "What happens if I'm outside the room when it locks down?"

He glanced at me, his blue-black irises flaring. "You don't want to know, Ms. De la Croix. I suggest you always be in your room by fifteen hundred hours."

The gargoyle sailed through the door half a beat later, causing my eyes to widen. "He just…"

"And there you go letting your eyes tell you lies again," the Warden drawled before following the gargoyle *through* the wooden door.

"Uh-huh." I'd witnessed a lot in my twenty-one years, but that was certainly fucking new. "Whatever." I wanted a copy of that deal, and if I had to walk through wood to get it, then so be it.

Energy pulsed around me as I entered, some sort of gate seeming to close at my back. I turned to study it, only it was the same door as the one from the hallway. I frowned. "Did it lock?"

"Yes. But all you have to do is touch it to unlock it again." The Warden walked over to demonstrate, his fingers running across the wood. "It's programmed to recognize you or someone with authority to open the door. It's a way to keep you safe once the trials begin." He looked up at the ceiling overhead and then back at me. "We anticipate that there will be literal backstabbing throughout the process. That's the other reason for the curfew. It'll help us know who has survived the day."

He took a step back and glanced around the small

living room before sauntering over to the kitchen, where the gargoyle stood waiting for something. "What do you fancy, Sir Davis?"

"Spritemead."

"Been talking to Queen Aflora, hmm?" The Warden pulled out his wand to magic the gargoyle a giant pint of beer-like substance. "Satisfied?"

"Yes," the small thing grated out before taking a deep swig. "Mighty satisfied, Master Ajax."

"Warden," he corrected.

"Yes, yes." He waved him off with a stone hand as he ambled back into the living area. He paused when he reached the door. "Rematch at sixteen hundred?"

"I already promised my afternoon to Az. But I'll happily win your stones tomorrow."

The gargoyle grunted. "Sixteen hundred tomorrow, then."

"Gambling's bad for you," the Warden warned.

"Only when I lose," Sir Davis replied.

Then he disappeared into a cloud of dust.

My lips parted. "Did he just… die?"

The Warden—*Ajax*—snorted. "No. Gargoyles often leave stone rubble in their wake." He opened the fridge, his lips pinching upon finding it empty. "Hmm."

He ran his fingers over the shelves, his lips moving with soundless words to create an array of foods. There were fresh fruits, vegetables, deli meats, and a variety of other items that made my mouth water with hunger.

"Consider it a consolation prize for being the most difficult captive to catch," he said, shutting the door once more. "You'll likely be everyone's number one target as a result. You can eat in your chambers instead of risking the cafeteria."

"What? Why?"

"Well, the whole point of the bride trials is to survive, and you've proved to be better at that than everyone else. Half the candidates just saw me giving you a private tour, too. Something I did not provide for any of them." His fingers fluttered over the kitchen nook table, causing a series of books and documents to appear. "Read. Learn. Study. The trials begin in three days. Then it's every woman for herself."

He started toward the door without another word.

"Wait, hold on," I called to him. "What about the deal? I want to see what my parents agreed to."

He paused and looked around. Then he disappeared down a short hallway to a bedroom at the end. I paused on the threshold to find him doing something to my blankets. "What are you—"

"Here," he said, turning to hand me a note as a silky purple comforter unfurled across the mattress. Two pillows appeared in his wake, followed by a flourish of magic from his wand toward the adjoining bathroom. "Don't share your comforts. The others are already jealous enough."

"What do you—"

"Goodbye, Ms. De la Croix," he interjected. "I'd say to enjoy your stay, but I know you won't. Not even with my *improvements.*"

Violet smoke filled the air in the next instant, his body vanishing into the cloud of it and leaving a lingering scent of pine needles behind.

I blinked at his disappearance, then the weight of the item in my hand captured my attention.

As did the name etched across the paper.

My name.

In my father's messy script.

CAMI

Son of a bitch.

My parents had sold me to the devil to absolve my father of all debts owed to the Hell Fae King. Not financial debts, but *soul* debts. The kind created as a result of my dad being a damn fae connected to the Hell Fae Source.

Lucifer provided power and protection for a price.

From what I understood, my father no longer wanted to pay that price.

So he gave me up instead.

"*Fuck*," I snapped, balling the contract in my hand.

The paper flattened itself in the next instant, some sort of dark magic restoring it to its true form. It must have been a fail-safe to keep fae from destroying their contracts.

I glared at my father's signature, then noted the date.

My birthday.

"Wow, well, that certainly beats the grenade cake, Dad," I said, tossing the paper onto the bed. "And all the other weaponized gifts you gave me over the years."

I wasn't really talking to him, because he couldn't hear

me here. *In Hell.* Where he'd subjected my soul to because of some fucking deal.

And now I was expected to compete in a series of bridal trials?

I walked back into the kitchen area to review the books the Warden had left on the table, my ire mounting by the second. Flipping through the top few, I noted that they were all about death and how to kill. *Studying material for my fate.*

"What the hell?" I demanded, shuffling through all the books and documents, searching for some explanation of the purpose of all this.

Bride trials was a pretty straightforward concept, but a bride to whom? Lucifer? Another Hell Fae? The Warden?

I paused, considering Ajax.

Then I shook my head. *No.* Just because he was pretty didn't mean I wanted to *marry* him. Besides, he was kind of a dick. Well, apart from the food thing, and whatever he'd done to my bed. And the tour hadn't been horrible.

Although, he was the reason for my current predicament.

So yeah, no to *the Warden.* He wasn't even a Hell Fae, but a Midnight Fae. And while biting during sex might be hot, I wasn't into the mating part of that equation.

"There has to be a way out of this," I muttered as I spread the documents out over the kitchen table. "Think, think, think."

I enjoyed legal issues, hence my political science undergraduate degree and pre-law status at the University of Florida.

Not that I would be going back there anytime soon.

Unless I found a loophole.

Ajax had claimed Lucifer's deals were ironclad with no

potential deviations. But the law could be very easily interpreted and manipulated by the right logical mind.

I went to the fridge to pour myself some juice—courtesy of *the Warden* and his magic wand—and settled at the table to begin reading.

The books kept me occupied for several hours, each of them detailing various aspects of Hell Fae life.

There were creatures—all of which were deadly.

Plants unlike anything that existed in the human world.

And a lot of rules.

I focused on the latter the most, searching for information about how Lucifer conducted his deals and finding nothing of use. It was all about the local society and how Hell Fae operated in general. Nothing about agreements or recruiting unwilling participants into bridal games. Just a few notes on acceptance of all creature forms —whatever the fuck *that* meant—and the importance of mutual respect.

The rules listed were quite dull in nature. However, apparently, there was a dress code for going outside. The curfews I already knew about were detailed as well.

I skimmed the rest, not finding anything truly useful.

Tapping my fingers on the table, I decided another avenue was required.

Hadn't there been a library?

Ajax hadn't shown me the interior, just the exterior, before continuing on our tour—a tour that he'd implied was uncommon for him to give a candidate.

Which made me wonder why he'd provided one for me.

Because I was the hardest to catch? Another "consolation" prize like he'd claimed the food and other comforts were?

It definitely wasn't because he liked me or wished to provide me with any favors.

A feeling that was absolutely fucking mutual.

The *whys* of the situation also didn't matter; only my survival did.

Hell Fae Rule #1: Don't Die.

My father had drilled that rule, along with several others, into my head as a child.

They were simple yet effective.

And I suspected I would be needing to recall several of those infamous Hell Fae rules now to survive my current predicament.

I glanced at the clock on the wall, noting that it was almost noon. The papers weren't providing me with any useful details. So maybe I could use the time to snoop around or find the library.

Maybe both.

I stood and started toward my room, muttering, "Dress code," under my breath.

Rules. Rules. And more rules.

Perhaps *that* was the result of my father's obsession as a child.

I plucked at the spaghetti strap top I'd worn to the party I'd been attending before rudely being yanked into Hell. The thin shirt was great for showing off cleavage, but not so much for blending in.

While I found the idea of a dress code ridiculous, I didn't want to risk being stopped and reprimanded before even reaching the library.

I opened my wardrobe.

Rows of outfits hung inside, paired with a small dresser filled with more shirts.

"Do I even want to know how they know my shirt and

pant sizes?" I wondered aloud. "And where are the underwear and bras?"

I checked every drawer, then went to the nightstands framing the bed.

Nothing.

"You've got to be fucking kidding me." I walked back into the other room to review the dress code section again.

And sure enough, there was a line in small print about undergarments not being permitted.

"Fuck that," I snapped, deciding to at least keep my bra on.

But the jeans and panties really did need to be swapped out, so I marched back into my room and traded them for the black pants.

"Of course the shirts are all white and thin." I was honestly surprised they weren't making us prance around in lingerie.

Rolling my eyes, I switched my tank top for the T-shirt.

At least it was a bland uniform. Maybe the proverbial target on my back wouldn't be as big if I looked like everyone else.

Hell Fae Rule #2: Don't Draw Attention.

A tingle of magic crawled up my back, making my brow furrow.

I frowned at the full-length mirror beside the wardrobe, twisting around to see what enchantment had just crawled across my skin.

Magical embroidery glimmered across my shoulder blades, the script not having been there when I'd selected my shirt.

Because I would have noticed *my name* written across the fabric.

Camillia De la Croix.

No wonder the Warden had said I would have a target on my back. The fucking shirt had my *name* on it.

Which meant everyone would know who I was. Cue the walking billboard that screamed I was a threat that should be dealt with accordingly—*in the midst of a deadly bride trial.*

"*Fuck.*"

Underneath my name were three black stars, also glittering from some unknown spell. *What the hell are they for?* There hadn't been any mention of *stars* in the rule book.

Tugging the shirt back over my head, I reviewed the fabric and growled as the black embroidery disappeared, leaving the shirt spotlessly white again. Pulling on a different one, I felt the same tingle of magic and sighed in frustration as my name and the three stars appeared again.

Great, my choices were to go out dressed as a target or break the rules.

Hell Fae Rule #3: Know Your Enemy Before Engaging.

Right, so if I wanted to survive, I needed to understand this place a hell of a lot better.

"Target-practice uniform it is," I grumbled, grabbing the boots I'd worn on the way here and pulling them on. If I did manage to find a weapon of some kind, I could use the boots to store them.

Besides, they were comfortable.

Unlike the weird slip-on shoes sitting in the closet. *They couldn't even give us socks?* I shook my head. *Whatever.*

As for the target on my back, I'd worry about it later.

Right now, I had bigger issues at hand.

Like finding a loophole in Lucifer's contract that would allow me to legally leave this place without being shredded apart by a bunch of crow-shaped blades.

Venturing into the bathroom, I found a full array of amenities that had likely been conjured by the Warden.

I traded out the puffy scrunchy that I'd worn to the party with a simple black band, securing it and giving myself a nod in the mirror before heading out.

Reaching my door, I ran my fingers over the wood and felt a soft *click* burst through the air. Drawing in a deep breath, I closed my eyes and ventured through the wood.

Emerging on the other side in one piece, I opened my eyes, only to glance at the long spiral of stairs.

Fuck.

I'd have to factor in a hundred steps into my schedule calculations for curfew.

Mentally ticking off the seconds, I jumped down the steps two at a time, reaching the bottom of the stairs after what seemed like ten stories. I couldn't remember how many there were going up, just that there had been a lot of steps.

Hopefully, I didn't run into any trouble that would wear me out, as these were going to be a bitch to climb again later.

Retracing my steps, I walked through the campus that, according to Ajax, was modeled after Midnight Fae Academy. The library wasn't hard to find—it was right in the center of the academy turned prison.

A few fellow candidates gave me curious glances, and I tried to keep to the shadows to hide my name. However, I took note of the few names I did see along my way to the library.

Sarah Williams.

Veronica Scottsdale.

Feyre of the House of Iron.

I raised my eyebrow at that last one. The first two had seemed like Halflings from my realm and not immediate threats, but the girl with silver hair pulled back into a neat ponytail exuded danger.

She was some sort of fae, based on the point of her ears, and I gave her a subtle nod as I slowed my pace. Her blazing obsidian irises marked her as something *other*.

She evaluated me for a moment, then returned the nod.

I didn't want to make enemies here. Even if we were all pitted against one another, we were still prisoners brought here against our will. Our parents had sold us out and left us to our fate.

Perhaps I could find a few candidates willing to work togeth—

I jolted as a blade cut the air inches from my face. My instincts fired, causing me to twist at an awkward angle to keep myself from being skewered alive.

It all happened in less than a second, my training barely keeping me alive. It was the whistle of metal against the wind that had tickled my ears, driving my reactions. All instinctual. And the result of my father's insistence that I learn how to protect myself.

Because he always knew I'd end up here? I wondered. Just the thought soured all my memories.

Not that I had many good ones of my parents.

They hadn't exactly been nurturing so much as frequently absent outside of certain activities—such as combat practice.

Feyre smirked. "Nice dodge, *De la Croix*. Maybe you'll be one of the survivors." She flipped her ponytail over her shoulder. "I'd recommend not judging others based on appearances alone," she added, then turned on her heel and waltzed back toward the dorms, her long legs quickly taking her through the moonlit fog.

Fuck. So much for allies.

Her words stuck with me, though. Had that been a

strange sort of peace offering? Or was everyone in this realm batshit crazy?

Catching my breath, I calmed my rapidly beating heart and spotted something glimmering against the wall.

Running my finger over the indent in the stone, I searched for the blade she'd just thrown and frowned when I only found a hint of lingering magic.

Right, we probably weren't allowed weapons, but whatever kind of fae Feyre was clearly provided her with an edge if she could conjure blades from thin air.

Midnight Fae?

Air Fae?

A mixture of both?

That would make her stupidly powerful—*an abomination*. Which meant I needed to watch my back.

CAMI

I ᴋᴇᴘᴛ an eye out for any and all potential threats on my way to the library.

Thankfully, only *Feyre of the House of Iron* appeared to be able to conjure knives out of thin air.

At least on my short trip across campus.

I paused just outside the library, taking in the magnificent stone walls and tinted windows. The gothic spirals decorating the corners were similar to those adorning the other castle-like buildings, yet each structure seemed to possess a distinct aura.

One I couldn't exactly define.

I also couldn't *see* it.

Yet…

It's as if magic forms the very walls, I mused, humming to myself. *Well, May as well find out what magic lurks inside the library.*

Shoving the double doors open, I stepped inside and craned my neck, impressed by the cathedral-style ceiling that seemed to stretch up into eternity.

The library was huge—much bigger than it appeared to be from the outside.

It was also completely empty. Wandering to the unoccupied reception desk, I coughed to announce my presence to anyone who might be lurking behind the shelves.

Silence.

"Hello?" I called, glancing around the large open space. The books spanned the walls with floating ladders, and the ceiling was at least ten stories over my head. "Is anyone here?"

"We're always here," a voice floated back to me with a giggle. "Always, always!"

"Yes, always here," another echoed. "No one visits anymore. The Quandary Bloods are gone, you see."

"Does she see, though?" a third female murmured.

"Perhaps not," the original hummed. "She's unique, yes?"

"Very."

"Original?"

"Like him, indeed."

"Indeed."

I frowned, trying to find the source of the voices and realizing that these must be the figments Ajax had mentioned. "You're invisible. Ghosts?"

A flutter of movement caught my senses. I whirled in a circle, trying to spot the phantoms, but only found the empty foyer.

"Ghosts?" one of them said, aghast. "How rude."

"Very rude."

"She's new."

"Virtuous, too."

"Yes! That's it, isn't it?" The singsong voice whirled around in the air, coupled by the flying of pages of nearby books. "What would you like from us, dear virtuous one?"

Virtuous certainly wasn't a term I would use to describe myself, but perhaps I was slightly more innocent in comparison to the Hell Fae. "I… I just want to know where your Hell Fae law books are."

"Law books?" the original voice repeated. "Regulations and legislation. How droll."

"Droll, yes," a deeper voice deadpanned. It was still feminine, but more guttural than the others.

"But she probably wants the book." A subtle gust of wind tickled my ponytail with the words.

"The one…?" a tinkling voice asked, trailing off.

"Yes, *the* one."

"Ah, yes, yes. Up we go!" the original voice chanted, a whirl of air sending more pages scattering and causing a few books to fall from the shelves. I watched in amazement as they were caught before hitting the ground and settled back onto the shelves, telling me there were numerous invisible beings floating around this massive library hall.

A tug to my ponytail had me taking two steps back, then a nudge to my side sent me toward a desk in the middle of the room, about twenty paces away from the main reception desk. "Down you sit," the deeper voice said. "And here you wait."

Silence followed.

I swallowed. "Uh…"

"Patience, virtuous one," one of them whispered, scattering goose bumps down my neck.

Then a book landed heavily in front of me, the leather binding worn and clearly well used.

I gazed at the large volume, tracing my fingers along the leather binding. It was worn but beautiful. Soft. There was something… ancient about it that demanded reverence. I was almost afraid to open it. It seemed too powerful, too old.

The figments had gone silent as though they held their breath.

Then I realized I was the one holding my breath, my fingers itching to open the book but an irrational fear at the back of my brain telling me that with my luck, it was a trap.

The Warden had warned me not to interact with the figments. If he truly valued my survival, no matter his motives, what would happen if I opened it? Why were the figments so focused on this book?

"What's she waiting for?" one complained.

"Yes. Too long."

"I hate suspense," another agreed.

A nudge at my elbow warned me that the figments were growing impatient, but something about this book called to me. I often listened to my instincts, and my instincts told me that learning more about this world was what would help me survive.

And sometimes gaining knowledge meant taking chances.

Biting my lip, I slipped my index finger under the worn cover and carefully flipped it open.

The front page was blank.

"What does it say?" one asked with excitement.

"Oh, please read it to us!" another exclaimed.

Hmm, maybe the figments were just bored and were hoping I'd read them a story, but this was the wrong book for that.

A blank page stared back at me, and I considered it as I ran my fingers over the soft paper, jolting when *power* slipped through my veins.

Words appeared, scrolling across the page as if written with wet ink.

"*Leges de Virtuouso Attingas Parvulorum,*" I whispered, recognizing the Latin context for Laws of the Old Ones. But… *Virtuouso.* That wasn't a word I recognized— certainly not Latin, anyway.

The figments whispered with excitement in a language I didn't understand. But I caught the awe in their tones. I looked around, wishing I could see them. "What? What is it?"

They quieted. One spoke with a nudge that was gentler this time. "Read, dear one. *Read.*"

"Leave her to it," one suggested.

"Yes, she must learn," another said.

The air rustled around me, and in the next moment, the weight in the air lifted, suggesting that I was truly alone now.

I frowned. If the figments didn't want me to read to them, then what had them so excited?

Shaking my head, I turned back to the book and lost myself in the pages. As I flipped through them, Latin-esque words scrolled across the paper, only to reform into English as I read. Unlike the title, the book seemed to be able to adapt to my native language.

It didn't make it any easier to read. The pages sprawled with laws and rules, customs and declarations that fascinated me. Absorbing the complex content, I almost forgot what information I was after.

The pages spoke about respect at first, and the division of power. I didn't quite understand everything, but the "Source of All" was mentioned the most, with sentences about division of access scrawled out beneath.

Then there were laws about sharing, laws about elderships, laws about formation of magic and the varying combinations of such. It was intriguing stuff, but not particularly useful for my situation.

Nothing about *deals*.

Then again, I was only about twenty pages in out of about three hundred. I began flipping through faster, trying to skim. But the more pages I turned, the more I realized that the right side of the book wasn't getting any thinner.

In fact… the book was creating more pages.

Right, magical *book*.

Just like everything else in this realm, nothing was what it seemed. My dorm room spanned upwards of a hundred steps, but from the outside, it had only appeared three or four stories tall.

Finally, I stopped, marveling at how thick the book had become. Glancing at the top right-hand corner, I saw that I was on page two thousand four hundred and seventy.

My lips curled downward.

"That's not possible," I whispered to myself.

"I would tend to agree." The deep voice came from right behind me, a warm presence wrapping around me in a cloak of reality.

I blinked, realizing he must have been standing there for quite some time for his heat to have seeped so deeply into my skin. "Uh…" I glanced over my shoulder, half expecting him to be an invisible figment, and gasped at the sight of a stunning male.

Holy Fae…

His blondish-brown hair fell in waves to his non-pointy ears. And he boasted a high-fashion look about him that models would kill for—the type of male who fit a suit perfectly and wore it with a regal flair that made others bow at his feet.

Yet it was his eyes that held me captive.

Because he possessed the most hypnotic multicolored eyes, framed by long, dark lashes.

Beautiful. Too beautiful. Almost distractingly so.

"Hello," he greeted, that single word containing an incredible amount of sensuality. This was the kind of man who killed women with his beauty, his features almost surreal, and distinctly inhuman. He was just too pretty to be real. His perfect cheekbones, square jaw, and piercing gaze made me want to weep at his feet and beg him to do wicked deeds to me.

Shit. I swallowed. "I, uh…"

"You were busy reading," he finished for me. "Yes. I've been watching."

I almost asked him to tell me how long he'd been watching, but I wasn't sure I wanted to know. "It's engrossing material."

"I have no doubt that's true," he agreed, canting his head to the side. "You're welcome to take it back to your room, Camillia. In fact, I strongly encourage it, as curfew passed by over an hour ago."

My lips parted. "Oh…" *Fuck.* I'd read the rule about that in my quarters, just as I'd heard it when Ajax had mentioned it. "Shit."

His mouth curled into a full grin, revealing impossibly perfect dimples on each cheek. "Want me to sneak you back in?" he offered. "I promise I'm quite skilled at it."

"I…" *Damn it.* My first night—*er, day?*—in this place and I'd already broken curfew. "The Warden said the doors all magically lock…" I trailed off. He'd also warned that I didn't want to know what happened if I stayed out past curfew.

Was this being one sent to punish offenders? He seemed far too amused by my predicament to be necessarily kind.

"As I said, I can sneak you back in."

"Why would you do that?"

He lifted a muscular shoulder, causing his white button-down shirt to shift across his broad chest. "Does it matter?"

"If you want me to trust you, then yeah, it matters."

"Oh, you shouldn't trust me, little angel," he murmured. "Not one bit."

"Right." I drew out the word, my lips pursing to the side. "Maybe I should just stay here until midnight, then."

"You could," he agreed. "But I wouldn't recommend it."

"The Warden didn't recommend staying out after curfew either."

He nodded, causing his blond-brown strands to tickle the edges of his perfectly carved face. "With good reason. Which I suppose is cause for you to allow me to sneak you back into your room. No trust required, just pure common sense." His multicolored eyes glanced over my shoulder to the book on the table. "Something I assume appeals to you, given your choice of reading material."

I chewed my lip again as I debated my options.

Hell Fae Rule #4: Don't Trust Anyone.

If I listened to my father's training, I wouldn't go anywhere with this sex on a stick, no matter how gorgeous he was.

Nothing in this place is what it seems, I reminded myself.

Which meant that I definitely shouldn't go with him.

A ferocious growling shuddered the shelves, making me jump to my feet, a chill skating down my spine.

That can't be a good sign.

The impossibly handsome fae chuckled, the sound emitting from deep in his throat. "Tick-tock, little angel. What'll it be?"

Ajax

"What the fuck was that?" Az demanded as he straightened into a standing position. "You never go down that easily."

"I've had a long day," I muttered, leaping back up to my bare feet on the mat.

"Really?" Az drawled, folding his arms over his bare chest. "Or do you just want me to put you on your back and get it over with?"

My eyes narrowed. "No."

"Then make me fucking work for it," he snapped.

"Fuck you."

"I intend to," he returned, his hands falling back to his sides. "We've only been at this for an hour, and all you've done is piss me off. You need to give me *more*."

I glanced at the shadow dial on the wall, which showed it was an hour after curfew. "Flame," I cursed, flexing my fingers. "Feels like a lot longer than an hour." Which said everything about my poor sparring performance. I usually enjoyed fighting with Az.

But not tonight.

Az rolled his shoulders, sending his phoenix tattoo stretching over his chest. A light sheen of sweat glistened over his abs, drawing my attention downward.

"Whatever it is, shrug it off, Ajax. I want a challenge, not a pathetic fuck."

"Asshole," I muttered.

"Pansy," he returned, making me crave my wand. He wouldn't be calling me a "pansy" then.

But that wasn't how we played this game.

Az began pacing, his black track pants hanging low on his hips, just like my own. He was ready, muscles flexing, wanting to spar. Hard. Fast. *Fiercely*.

Because if I earned it, we would fuck afterward. And that was exactly what we both desired.

But I couldn't focus. Oh, I wanted to lose myself to Az's violence, but I was distracted.

By her.

Every time I went to block one of Az's moves or became tangled up in his limbs, she flitted through my mind, demanding my attention.

The damn woman with an angelic face and pert tits had effectively taken over my thoughts, crowding out my drive to take on Az.

Making me *weak*.

What the hell had gotten into me? I'd upgraded her bedding. Stocked up her fridge. Even ensured her clothes were a little more resilient than they should be.

I'd fucking pampered her, treated her differently than the rest. Given her a damn tour of campus, too.

That went beyond some foolish bet with Az. It implied that I actually wanted her to *survive*.

And I had no idea why.

She meant nothing to me. She was *nothing* to me.

So why the fuck couldn't I shake this girl from my

thoughts? Because it'd taken me too damn long to pick her up? To capture her? Was it the chase that had me all bent out of shape?

"You're still distracted," Az accused.

I grunted, ignoring him, and went in for another hit to his ribs, only to end up on my back for the third time in five minutes.

Az landed on top of me, his elbows caging in my head. "I'm going to make you take me raw up your ass if you don't start giving me a fight."

Mother of all fire gnats. I could already feel him hardening against my thigh.

"What's it going to be?" he taunted. "More foreplay or a quick deed?"

"Get off of me," I snarled.

"Make me."

Fuck! I was torn between just letting him have me and flaming his ass with magic. The former would provide a reasonable diversion and perhaps give me an outlet for this pent-up energy Camillia had unleashed beneath my skin.

And the latter would seriously piss Az off—something I very much enjoyed doing.

Instead, I went with neither option and rolled him off me with a quick punch to his side and a flex of my hips. He went spinning with a laugh—the sound hungry to my ears—and jumped right back up to his feet at the same time I landed on the soles of mine.

Shoving the pretty Halfling from my head, I went after Az with the full force of my frustration, nailing him in the jaw with my fist before drawing my knee into his abdomen. He cursed, the grin disappearing from his features as he focused on the task of kicking my ass.

Or trying to, anyway.

This was why we sparred—I was the only one who

gave him a true challenge, and I reminded him of that while we danced around the training arena.

Az threw a punch and I blocked it, the bones in my forearms vibrating with the sheer power in his blow. I swept a foot behind his ankle, but he sidestepped me before I could knock him down.

"You can do better than that," Az drawled, grabbing me behind the neck and pulling me close enough that his teeth grazed my lower lip.

Fucking tease.

I grabbed his forearm, only for him to lock me in a hold and haul me over his body with ease.

Because yeah, a rare Black Phoenix was stronger than a Hellhound and a Minotaur put together—but much more attractive.

I turned to face Az, only to be met with a fist slamming against my jaw. A blow hit my chest next, and I went flying back, his violet irises turning to black with flashes of raw dark power.

"You're still holding back," he growled, his voice echoing with the power of his Phoenix. If I didn't snap out of it soon, he was going to do something he rarely did to me—bleed raw power through my veins. Not in an attempt to injure me, but in an attempt to empower me with his energy.

The unique talent came from his Phoenix side.

And the process fucking *hurt*.

I hissed out a breath as he took a step closer, tendrils of black magic searing flames across the ground, the edges of which threatened my bare feet.

"Az," I warned. If he continued down this path, I would have to call upon my own source of power, something I demonstrated now by allowing a small purple flame to dance around my forearm.

He canted his head to the side in a birdlike motion that betrayed what he really was, his power seeming to still. "There's something off tonight." He blinked a few times. "This is more than a distraction. It reminds me of—"

"I'm fine," I bit out.

"You've said that before," he murmured. "It was a lie."

"You're seriously going to bring that up right now?" He only did this when he really wanted to goad me. Which meant either he fancied a dance with my vicious side, or I really was fighting like shit.

He shrugged. "You were weak then. You're being weak now, too."

My eyebrows flew upward. "Are you kidding me?" How could he compare a little distraction to *that day*?

Fuck.

Magic crawled up my arms, my agitation mounting by the second.

"My Phoenix senses the darkness inside you, that lingering desire that leads to lethal thoughts." He narrowed his gaze. "Something has provoked it, as it wasn't there earlier today. What happened to encourage this change?"

Az never minced words. He also wasn't one for subtleties. He spoke his mind often and frequently, typically without regard to the emotional impact.

Something that didn't usually bother me.

But he didn't often bring up *that* event—the day I'd begged him to kill me.

Because of the nightmares.

Because of *Emelyn*.

The Elite Blood who should have been mine.

However, we'd never had a chance.

Because death had mated her first.

I shuddered, recalling the horrible moment as though it

were happening right in front of me. Right now. Right here.

Emelyn. Cold and alone. Marbleized on a stage for everyone to see. She couldn't move. But her eyes blazed furiously. All for a show to demonstrate that supporting abominations would not be tolerated.

I'd been held beneath an ancient Midnight Fae's power —*Constantine Nacht*—forced to watch Emelyn's execution while screaming inside.

Just after watching my parents suffer a similar fate.

I should have been strong enough. I should have *stopped* it.

Yet I hadn't been able to move. I hadn't even been able to cry.

I'd just stood there and watched her body shatter into a thousand pieces before a raving crowd of lunatic Midnight Fae, to join my parents' corpses below.

Dead. Gone.

My parents hadn't shattered. Their bodies were still there, serving as some macabre trophy for the madman leading the ceremony.

A madman who loathed abominations.

Abominations like Az. He was the product of two different types of fae—Paradox Fae and Phoenix Shifter Fae.

Constantine would have hunted him down and demanded his execution.

Which was why I'd seen it fitting to ask Az to end my life.

Yet he'd flamed me instead, filling me with renewed energy while telling me I wasn't ready for the other side yet.

I'd been enraged.

We'd truly fought that day.

Then he'd nurtured me back to life in his own way. Not tenderly, not kindly, but *violently*.

And we'd been friends ever since.

He stared at me now, his Phoenix darkening his irises from violet to black once more. "What has you perplexed?" he asked. "What concerns you?"

"You're not my therapist, Az."

"No, just a friend who wants to spar. But you're lost in your mind. Why?"

Because I can't save her, I nearly said, thinking of Emelyn. *Except…*

The thought hadn't been past tense. *Can't save her*, not *couldn't save her*.

My brow furrowed. *I can't save who? Camillia?*

Az drew a circle around me with his dangerous black fire, the flames hot against my senses.

I dispelled them with a wave of purple magic, killing the life within his enchantment by tainting it with death.

He smirked. "So it'll be that kind of battle, hmm?"

The phoenix on his chest moved, drawing my gaze.

Then his fist slammed into my jaw, sending me two paces backward.

"*Flames*," I hissed, furious with his distracting move.

I darted forward just as Az swung another fist laced with black flame. I caught it in my palm, wrenching him back so quickly that he didn't have time to react as he landed straight on his ass with me on top and straddling him.

Rage made my fists fly, punching him in the jaw, the mouth, his rock-hard chest. He'd picked at an open wound with his words, darkening my mood considerably.

And I took it out on him.

I took it *all* out on him.

My helplessness. My failure. My irritation over this new

development with Camillia and the odd sense of protectiveness I felt toward her.

I didn't know her.

I didn't owe her a damn thing.

And I certainly wasn't going to *save* her.

What the fuck is wrong with me? I wondered, losing my mind as I unleashed my fury on Az.

He only gave me a few seconds, though.

Then he flexed his hips, grabbed my wrist, and slammed me onto my back as he drowned me in his magic.

Pain licked across my entire body as the process began.

But all of the fight drained out of me in the next breath, my mind unraveling with a truth I didn't want to accept.

She reminds me of Emelyn.

That was why I couldn't stop thinking about her.

That regal attitude and those snarky replies took me back to a dangerous moment in time.

A time I didn't want to think about.

A time I refused to ponder.

A time I would not allow myself to succumb to ever again.

I lived in the present now. Not the past.

It will not consume me. I'm the Warden now. Not a weak Midnight Fae frozen beneath another's power, but a powerful being known for imprisoning Nightmare Fae beasts.

Az punched my jaw so hard my teeth cracked against one another. "*That's* more like it," he growled, retracting his dark magic to allow me to move. "Now fucking fight me."

With a roar, I rushed through the haze of black flame and knocked him off of me. He quickly rolled back and we tumbled together, both of us struggling to stay on top. His taunting laugh only made me more savage as he purposefully tapped into my fury—like he always did.

It was fine by me. I welcomed the opportunity to use Az, to release all my aggression, all my pent-up fury.

Emelyn is dead. And I couldn't do a fucking thing to bring her back. Which was why I needed to live in the present, not the fucking past.

Camillia De la Croix was not Emelyn Jyn.

Camillia could handle herself or die trying.

I didn't need to take on the burden of helping her. *Because I can't help anyone. Not even myself.*

A sense of hopelessness hit me in the chest, and Az took advantage of my weakness. He pinned me to the mat, his lips at the edge of my mouth as we both panted with exertion.

He licked a drop of sweat from my lip, grinding his hips against mine. His hardening arousal coaxed mine out to play as he dipped his mouth to graze his teeth along the shell of my ear. "I win. We fuck my way."

I growled in response, gripping his head between my hands and forcing his lips to mine. Our kiss was hungry and ferocious.

Bruising.

His tongue battled mine as we both fought for dominance, but he would win.

He always won.

However, I wouldn't go down without a fight.

I could taste my blood on his tongue, the intoxicating flavor calling to the Midnight Fae within me. *Bite*, my dark soul whispered. *Bite him.* I barely contained the urge, swallowing it down with a reminder of what it would do.

Midnight Fae *claimed*.

One bite and he would be tied to me for eternity.

Well, technically, it took *three* bites to do that, but even the first stage couldn't be broken. And he would have no choice in the acceptance. It was how Midnight Fae worked. At least for the males, anyway. Females couldn't claim. Only males. No idea why. And I wasn't in the mood to ponder it now, not with Az's dick rubbing against mine.

"Fuck," I growled, my fingers threading through his hair to tighten my hold on his scalp.

"Yes," he agreed, his palms going to the band of my track pants to tug them down.

This would be quick.

Rough.

Violent.

And just what I needed to forget all about—

A blaring alarm sliced through my thoughts, jolting up my spine.

Az flew up to his feet, his gaze instantly alert as I stared at the whirling flame a few feet away.

My gaze narrowed at what that enchanted fire meant. *A captive out after curfew.*

I'd created this spell shortly before the recruitment began, as the visual alert made it easier for me to track escapees. The flames would lead me right to the culprit.

Alas, the last three who'd attempted to escape were ripped apart in the charcoal blade courtyard, the hellish day creatures more than doing their jobs before I could reach them.

In fact, the flames dissipated almost as soon as they'd appeared.

But not this one.

Which meant someone had circumvented the initial round of beasts, thus coaxing all the creatures to come out to play and track their prey.

There was only one captive I'd met with the ability to test their limits.

Camillia De la Croix.

That damn pixie of a female was going to be the death of me. Not only had she cut into my duties for the day, but she'd also tugged on some hidden heartstring inside my chest.

And now, she was blocking me from a much-needed fuck.

"I'm going to shred her apart myself," I declared, slowly returning to my feet and fixing my pants.

"Who?" Az demanded.

"*Camillia,*" I growled.

His eyebrow lifted. "The little blonde thing?"

"Yes." I walked toward the flaming ball and morphed it into a map with my hands. "Show me where that delinquent little brat is now."

The sphere transformed into a tangible playground of buildings and paths, the various dots representing all my prisoners. When I pulled up Camillia's room, I found it empty. With a shake of my head, I began my search.

Once I found her, I would teach her a lesson she wouldn't soon forget.

And all those amenities I'd gifted her would burn into ash.

"Come out, come out, wherever you are," I hummed, scanning the grounds for her essence. "It's time for your first real lesson as a Hell Fae Captive."

CAMI

Uh, that can't be good, I thought, shivering as the growls reverberated off the bookshelves. I couldn't see the owner of that noise, and I really doubted I wanted to meet him.

"Um…"

"Ready for my help?" the handsome fae asked, his stance casual and completely unbothered by the snarling beast-like sounds echoing through the library. "Or shall I leave you to it?"

Shit. I'd handled plenty of Hellhounds and could certainly take care of myself, but I had no idea what kind of creature was making that awful sound.

I also had no idea what waited for me outside the library doors. Probably more creatures.

Or worse—razor-tipped crow wings.

I glared at the fae arching a brow at me. "Well, if I'm going to rely on you to help me, at least give me your name so I know who to curse later."

His lips spread into a tantalizing smile. "Melek."

"Well, *Melek.* Get us out of here. Preferably in one piece."

An arm corded in perfectly toned muscle looped around my waist, cinching me against his side like we were best friends. "Right this way, little angel."

I pulled away from him and grabbed the heavy leather-bound book from the table, clutching it to my chest.

He said I could take it, and the figments had all mysteriously disappeared, so they weren't around to tell me no.

I also wasn't done reading.

Melek merely cocked an eyebrow at me, then smiled as if he knew something I didn't.

"What?" I demanded. "Are there some sort of hellish library late fees I should know about?" I could only imagine how that might be handled.

Payment in blood.

Or perhaps in pain.

"No late fees," Melek assured me. "Not for that one," he added with a wink.

Whatever the fuck that meant.

We left the grand library, walking outside—*without touching*—just as a roar shattered the sound barrier. I ducked, tightening my grip on the book, and blinked up at the dark sky. "What the hell was that?"

Melek's lips curled into a sinful smile. "A Banshee, perhaps. Or a Siren. Honestly, I haven't the faintest idea. The dark-souled Nightmare Fae are all allowed to play after hours. Hence the purpose of curfew. Our dear Warden negotiated that deal. With the aid of our fierce Commander, of course."

I blinked at him as the ground began to shake. Between that and the residual effects from the shrieking roar, I wanted to take cover. *Now.* And the library clearly wasn't the place to do it.

So I needed to escape to the dorms.

I took off in the direction of the residences, my feet pounding against the sidewalks that lined the lethal-looking courtyards. However, the heavy book slowed me down. And the shaking ground beneath me didn't help matters.

I pitched forward as the rumbling intensified, rolling onto my back to protect the book before scrambling back to my feet.

"What *is* that?" I demanded breathlessly as Melek smoothly walked up beside me, completely unbothered by the earthquake unfolding around us. "What's coming?"

He simply shrugged.

Shrugged. This asshole had offered to assist me. *Doing a bang-up job of that*, I thought as I nearly fell again.

Apparently, I would have to find my own way.

Going by memory, I started walking again while scanning the night-clad academy turned prison for anything that might slink out to attack me.

The trembling ground had subsided, but an eerie silence had fallen in its wake. The way a forest grew quiet when a predator lurked nearby.

Hunting its prey.

I picked up my pace, occasionally glancing back at Melek, who continued his lazy stroll on those long legs, easily keeping up with me. An infuriating smirk seemed to be on permanent display, as if he found amusement in my mad dash to safety.

He's definitely not here to help, I decided.

Perhaps he just wanted to watch me die.

Sick fuck.

Gripping the book against my chest, I vowed not to let any of these assholes benefit from my suffering. If anyone was going to die here, it wasn't going to be me.

So all I had to do was make it to my room. Maybe the

angel-faced dick would give me the consolation prize of opening my door.

The dorm building had to be around here somewhere. It hadn't been that far from the library, and I remembered the direction I'd come from.

Yet nothing looked as it should.

The residences are definitely this way, I thought. *So where are they?*

A familiar building loomed to my right, the spires swirling with familiar magic, stirring a strange sense of déjà vu.

That's the library.

Am I going in circles?

Fuck this shit. I couldn't afford to lose my sense of direction when I knew *something* was out here stalking me.

"Where the hell is my dorm?" I demanded as Melek strolled up beside me and brushed his arm against mine. My skin flushed in response, his warmth a beacon that made me want to curl against him.

However, his expression made me want to punch him instead.

Rather than respond, he appeared to be holding back laughter.

Right. Definitely not *helping*, I thought sourly. *Well, then I'll just have to use the book.*

I blinked.

That was a strange deduction.

But it felt right.

Weird. But then an idea hit me square in the chest. *Breadcrumbs.*

Opening the book, I found a blank page waiting for me and ripped it from the spine.

Melek stiffened beside me. Then he sighed as though relieved when the book grew back another blank page.

Ignoring him and the magical book, I began to rip up small strips of paper and dropped them behind me as we walked, leaving a trail. It didn't take long for me to find the scraps of paper lying on the ground in front of me, confirming my suspicions—I was definitely going in circles.

Stopping in my tracks, I glared at Melek. "What are you even here for?" I snapped. "You just watched me walk in circles and didn't even bother correcting me."

"You figured it out."

"Asshole," I muttered and changed course, going in what I now knew was the *correct* direction.

Something in the air shifted. The hair on the back of my neck rose. Acting on instinct, I jumped out of the way, crashing to my knees, just as a massive beast leaped from the top of a building and landed with an earth-shattering thud. A large scorpion tail followed, plunging into the ground right where I had been standing milliseconds ago.

Scrambling back to my feet, I gaped in horror at the hellish creature. Black eyes from a human head stared at me as it bared its fangs, its furry ears pulling back as it growled.

The sound vibrated through my bones.

Its giant, golden lion body was nothing but thick slabs of muscle, deadly claws peeking out of its massive paws.

And the wings.

Fuck, they marked this thing as a creature of Hell with the leathery black quality. One flap nearly knocked me over again.

I didn't know what the hell this thing was, but I knew better than to challenge it to a fight.

Acid sizzled in the crater where the beast had struck. Its scorpion tail curled back up, its deadly barb dripping with venom.

Before I could come up with a plan, it lunged, jaws

snapping. It could have easily torn my arm off, but I leapt out of the way just in time, the rankness of its breath making me gag.

It roared in fury, sending my heart stuttering.

A paw swept past me, and I just managed to arch back.

It missed me by an inch.

And Melek just stood there, *watching*.

He was really going to let this thing eat me.

Ajax's words came back to me, chilling my blood. *No one survives being out past curfew.*

Now I understood why.

The scorpion tail jabbed again, but I didn't have time to do anything other than hold up the book in a pathetic attempt at defense. I flew back as it made contact, my ass sliding against the prickly black grass.

No, not grass.

Charcoal blades.

Hell really redefined the meaning of *park*.

I jumped back up. The tail hadn't left a scratch on me. Nor, thankfully, on the book. Apparently, it was a lot stronger than it looked.

I didn't have time to puzzle over why.

"The least you could do is give me a damned weapon!" I shouted at Melek as I dodged another paw swipe.

The monster's head whipped toward me, fangs on full display. I caught the rotting, stinking insides of its mouth before whacking him across the nose with the magical tome. The creature growled in response.

I gripped the book as if it held the answers to this conundrum. A ridiculous notion, yet it'd worked as a shield thus far.

"Come on," I said through clenched teeth, my gaze once again going to Melek—my lying savior. "Give me something!"

The book warmed under my touch in response, and magic rushed up my arms, going straight to my chest.

What the…?

Nothing spectacular happened, yet I'd felt the enchantment. Then the air revealed a strange sort of black aura around the beast.

If that was supposed to tell me the creature was bad, then that wasn't helpful at all.

"Melek!" I shrieked.

His lips twitched again. "I think that's enough for tonight. The lesson has been learned."

What fucking lesson? How to get mauled by a beast?

Melek lifted a hand to give a careless flick of his wrist as he murmured, *"Dimittee."*

The beast vanished.

The word seemed to float between us in the sudden silence that followed.

A torn page from the book floated down, drifting through the air with a word written across it. I frowned and squinted. *Dimittee.*

I blinked. *No. That can't be real. I'm just seeing it after hearing it out loud. Because Melek…*

My jaw tightened as I turned to gape at him. "You could do that this whole time and just stood there?"

"Yes."

I growled. "And you didn't *think* to do it a little earlier?"

"Do that again."

"What?" I snapped.

"That little growl. It was too adorable. Like a kitten."

I wanted to rip his throat out. Throttle him. Smash his head in with this massive book.

Instead, I bit back, "And you remind me of an ass."

His brows arched as he stalked toward me. "Do I?

Because I don't recall donkeys being handsome in your realm."

This fae really thought he was funny. I rolled my eyes and turned away to start walking, done with him. I just wanted to return to my dorm.

He caught up to me, his breath tickling my ear. "Perhaps I should take the lead this time?"

I whirled on him, scowling. "What? No way."

He shrugged. "Suit yourself. But your way hasn't led you home yet, little angel."

Frowning, I glanced back at the way I had gone.

And spotted more shredded pieces of paper rolling across the ground.

Fuck.

"Fine," I growled, eliciting a cocky smile from him.

He indicated which direction to start in with a flourish of his hands, drawing my gaze to the subtle tattoo peeking out from beneath his cuff along his wrist. It was there and gone too fast for me to detail it, but it left me wondering what he hid under his clothes.

Something I really did not need or want to think about right now.

So I shifted to a more important topic.

"What *was* that thing?" I asked as we passed the massive crater still oozing acid.

"A Manticore."

"And Hell Fae are really fine with giant Hellbeasts wandering around the grounds?"

"Indeed. Who do you think put them there?"

My jaw ticked. "So, they're Hell Fae creations?"

He considered me for a moment as we walked at his leisurely pace. "Hmm, well, rumors claim that Manticores —and others—are fae who broke their deals with Lucifer. Something I wouldn't recommend if you want to keep your pretty figure." His eyes roamed up and down my body.

I flushed at his full-on attention, but his words tore me away from admiring him right back. "That thing was once a fae?"

"Yes. Most transformed fae don't get to keep much of their original bodies." We paused at a crossroads and I stared at him, waiting for him to say which way we were supposed to go.

He leaned in, making my breath catch.

Why were all the fae in this place so damned beautiful?

I recalled the Warden's words.

"And you let your eyes tell you what to believe? How very human of you."

Closing my eyes, I tried to figure out what kind of fae Melek was.

Dangerous.

Untrustworthy.

My eyes flared open when I sensed his heat close to my skin. His lips were at my ear, sending shivers down my spine. "You would make a lovely Siren, as long as you don't mind scales and eating human flesh."

I shuddered.

He pulled away, his amusement palpable as I tried to figure out how to make my heart start again.

We arrived at the dorms without anything else attacking us. I still had the book clutched tight against my chest.

Inside, there was no staircase, and no gargoyles, just a single door where the stairs had once been. I frowned. "How do we..."

Melek approached the door and waved a hand over it. A *click* sounded and its surface turned murky.

"Ladies first," he said with a smile.

Perhaps it was a trap, but there was nowhere else to go, and whatever awaited me couldn't be worse than the creatures, so I stepped through.

My shoulders relaxed as I took in the living room and kitchen, the pile of books and documents just where I'd left them.

Magic hummed through my door as Melek stepped through a moment later.

"How did you do that?" I asked, both stunned and suspicious.

His gaze ran over me with a subtle flare of interest in his pupils. "Honestly, I'm much more interested in how you read that book." His focus locked on the book in my arms —the one I'd almost lost when fighting that Manticore outside.

"Ah, yes, that was tricky," I said softly, enjoying the flicker of curiosity in his expression. "I used my eyes."

The stunning male laughed out loud in response, his face turning into the epitome of beauty and grace and reminding me of a fallen angel more than a devilish fae. This man would never blend in around humans. He was just too *other*.

"Oh, I do like you," he mused, those striking multicolored eyes capturing mine. "And in the same token, I used my hand to open your door. Fancy that!"

I nearly growled in annoyance, but I also acknowledged that I deserved that retort. "Thank you for helping me get back safely." I couldn't say "unscathed" since he'd let that thing attack me outside.

"I assure you, the pleasure was all mine," he murmured with a wink. "Have a good rest, Camillia. Perhaps I'll see you again soon."

"Cami," I said without thinking.

He'd turned toward the door but paused at my word. "Cami?"

"It's… uh… my name."

"Cami," he repeated again as though tasting the name. "You prefer it to Camillia?"

"Yes." Camillia was my parents' favored name for me, and I really didn't want to think about them at the moment, considering they'd apparently made a deal with the devil that gave him control over my life.

"All right," Melek agreed. "I suggest you tuck yourself in, *Cami*. Ajax may drop by soon to check on your whereabouts." His eyes glittered with the words, then he stepped through the door rather than opening it. Similar to how I'd entered with the Warden earlier.

Frowning, I attempted to follow him but found the wood to be solid beneath my fingertips.

That must be the magic keeping me inside after curfew, I marveled, studying the frame and discovering that it appeared just like a normal door. Only without a handle of any kind.

So his opening it had been tied to whatever enchantment he'd woven that had allowed me to bypass the curfew spell and return.

"Hmm," I hummed, turning toward the living area and debating my options. Then the weight of Melek's parting comment settled across my shoulders.

"I suggest you tuck yourself in, Cami. Ajax may drop by soon to check on your whereabouts."

Because I'd been out after curfew and set off the creatures.

Shit.

I darted toward my room and hid the book beneath my mattress. There was definitely something special about it.

Both the figments and Melek had reacted far too strangely for this to be considered a normal text.

While Melek had seemed amused, I doubted the Warden would feel the same if I'd broken some sort of rule.

Again.

I paused to consider what I should wear to sleep in. Except footsteps coming from the other room gave me no time to ponder further.

I slipped into the bed to pretend to sleep.

But what if it isn't Ajax? I wondered. *Fuck, what if it is Ajax?*

I wasn't sure which option I preferred.

This whole thing could have been a trick of the imagination, a punishment meant to castigate me for being out after curfew.

How is this my life? I thought, exhausted and frustrated and overwhelmed. *What did I do to deserve this fate?*

"You can pretend to sleep all you want, but I can hear your heart thudding wildly in your chest." The deep voice carried through the room, slithering around me in a dark caress of sound. "I know you were out after curfew, little rebel."

"The question is, what will you do about it?" another voice asked, this one even deeper and holding a lethal edge that skated goose bumps down my arms and legs.

I refused to open my eyes.

Refused to move.

I barely even breathed.

"I'll keep an eye on her," Ajax replied softly, his minty scent taunting my nostrils as he stepped forward to run his fingers through my ponytail. "Don't abuse my hospitality, Camillia. You'll regret it."

"Hospitality?" I repeated, unable to stop myself.

But when I opened my eyes, he was gone.

As was his deep-voiced friend.

I blinked. *Did I just imagine all that?*

No. Impossible. I could still smell Ajax's minty aftershave lingering through the bedroom, along with a sharper, starkly masculine scent that had come from his friend.

A bottle of water suddenly appeared on my nightstand with a cupcake beside it. Fiery words appeared above it not a second later. *Congratulations on being the first captive to survive past curfew. I don't recommend tempting fate again. —The Warden*

I read the words twice before they fizzled into an ash-like confetti that melted into the cupcake.

"Fuck," I breathed, blinking at the display of magic. "Fuck. Fuck. *Fuck.*"

CAMI

I HADN'T SLEPT WELL, my mind running with the events of my first day—or night, or *whatever* it was—in this hellish paradigm.

Fortunately, my schedule for tonight only included meals—all of which I could access in my fully stocked fridge.

"Don't abuse my hospitality, Camillia. You'll regret it."

I suddenly understood what Ajax had meant, or rather, what he'd *implied*.

The food and the bedding were his versions of hospitality. As was the cupcake, which I eyed with interest now.

I'd already missed "midnight breakfast." Mostly because I hadn't wanted to leave my room and risk running into any of those monsters outside again.

I was too tired to face them in this state.

Maybe I should just eat the cupcake, I thought, my mouth watering in agreement. It smelled good.

Of course, it also might be poisoned.

But if that was the case, then all the food in this place was probably contaminated with something.

And I couldn't just not eat.

Besides, it really did look delicious.

Shrugging, I took a bite.

The fruity flavors were unexpected. As was the filling impact on my stomach after just a nibble.

I waited a few minutes.

Nothing happened, causing me to frown.

Maybe it's a weird sort of gift? I thought, puzzled. But that seemed strange, considering he'd all but threatened me not to go out after curfew, and then he'd essentially rewarded me for it.

With another shrug, I pulled the book out from beneath my mattress and started reviewing it while eating the cupcake.

More flavors followed.

All of them sweet and hitting me just right.

Except my lack of sleep was making it really hard to read and eat at the same time. I kept shaking my head in an effort to clear it, but my eyes continued to go cross-eyed as I reviewed the legal text. The words didn't seem to be auto-translating now, the vowels and nouns blurring together.

Ugh, I need more sleep, I realized, yawning. *I'll just take a quick nap and refocus in a few hours.*

I needed my strength for whatever was coming.

Hell Fae Rule #5: Be Prepared for Anything.

Couldn't do that on little to no sleep.

Closing my eyes, I curled up with the magical book against my chest. *Just a few minutes… that's all I need.*

———

DARKNESS.

Ice.

Desolation.

It stole over me, paralyzing me beneath a blanket of nothingness. I couldn't move. I could barely feel. But I could open my eyes.

Except I saw nothing.

Only a vapid sense of nonexistence.

What's happening? I thought, groggy from my lack of sleep. Or maybe this was a dream. Some sort of intense whirl of icy vapidness.

The cupcake, I realized belatedly. *Is it giving me strange dreams?*

Did this even qualify as a dream? Maybe it was more like a nightmare.

Of course.

This would be my punishment.

Shit.

Cursing my stupidity, I attempted to focus on my limbs.

Yet I couldn't see them.

Not in this sea of—

A sparkle of light blistered from above, drawing my focus upward, only for my eyes to slam shut in response. *What the fuck is that?* I thought, the light growing behind my eyelids.

I tried to peek below it, at the perpetual nothingness, but the glittering beam was moving at an insane rate, overcoming the darkness and blinding it all with brightness.

My broken world soon became consumed by the intense light.

Reaching up, I desperately tried to touch it, some foreign part of me recognizing it as an outlet that I craved. An outlet that I *needed*.

No... I whispered when it started to move away, releasing the darkness once more and leaving me alone again.

A stark sense of inadequacy touched my soul, telling me I wasn't worthy of that light, telling me I had to fight harder to reach it. To *earn* it.

What does that even mean? I marveled. *What is this place?*

A buzzing flickered in my head, causing me to want to grab it. *Ow.*

It grew louder, echoing all around me, jolting me into another reality.

The Hell Fae Realm.

My eyes flew open, the room around me making me dizzy and sending me tumbling to the floor. "Fuck!" I cursed as my head hit something hard.

A chuckle followed, causing my focus to shoot upward to the male standing over me.

Melek.

He bent to retrieve the object that had broken my fall —the book—then set it on a nearby chair before helping me up off the ground.

I wanted to snap something at him, something like *I don't need your help.* But I was too tongue-tied by my dream and his sudden appearance to speak just yet.

That residual energy continued to shiver across my skin, leaving goose bumps in its wake.

So cold.

Yet I'd craved the light. The heat. The blinding source of brightness.

Melek set me on the bed, his angelic face reminiscent of a different kind of dream. But he released me to take over the chair, the book sprawling in his lap.

"Nightmare?" His soft tones tickled my ears, making me blink. "I suppose that's appropriate, considering your situation." His eyes went to the book while he spoke, but a tray of food materialized on the nightstand beside me. "Perhaps a meal will help, hmm?"

I gaped at him. "What are you doing here?"

"Reading," he deadpanned, glancing up at me as he opened the book. "*With my eyes.*"

My lips threatened to twitch at the comment, and his mouth curled into a full-blown smile.

"There's my little angel," he mused, winking at me before returning his attention to the page he'd revealed. "Eat and I'll read."

Part of me wanted to say, *Excuse me?* The other part growled in temptation at the pizza waiting for me on the plate.

Grease.

Cheese.

Tomato sauce.

Goodness.

Yes. Please.

He'd even paired the meal with a beer. "If you're trying to seduce me, it's working," I informed him, shuffling to a more comfortable position on the bed in preparation of indulging in the feast beside me.

He arched a brow but didn't look at me as I pulled the plate into my lap. "There would be no need to try, angel."

I snorted, mostly to keep from reacting in any other way to his statement. Because I hadn't meant to say what I'd said, and I certainly didn't want to encourage his reply to my naïve statement. Rather than muddle it up more, I shoved the edge of the triangle piece into my mouth and groaned at the abundance of flavors. *Soooo good.*

Melek smirked like he could hear me, then flipped another page. "Ah, yes, here we are."

I licked grease off my fingers, watching him as his eyes danced across the words.

"*Quomodo tame a bestia,* which roughly translates to 'taming the beast.' A funny phrase, honestly. Speaking from experience, it's impossible to tame him. But I don't think that's the point of this passage, do you?"

I stared at him. "Uh, no?" I guessed, not having a clue where to begin with answering that or deciphering his phrase. Besides, he wasn't really listening to me anyway. He'd already started skimming the page again.

"Still, I might have to try it later. Or not. But you could, surely. All it takes is a phrase, according to this delightful reading material. *Somnum Dameonis.* Two words. Try them for me."

I finished swallowing a bite of my pizza—which was just as delicious as the first taste—and muttered the two words back at him.

He tsked. "With more force, Cami."

"*Somnum Dameonis,*" I said.

"Excellent." He shot me one of those alarmingly beautiful smiles, then dropped his gaze back to the book. "Ah, but you are missing something quite important. Hmm, however…" He trailed off as he patted down his pockets. "Ah, yes, this will do just fine." He held out his hand. "Don't waste time, Cami. Not anymore. Take it, please."

I wasn't sure what he meant by that, but I reached out to take the chain from his fingertips and jolted when his skin brushed mine. The contact didn't even last for half a breath, but I felt it all the way to my toes.

This being is powerful, I realized with a tremble. *Very powerful.*

I wasn't sure how I knew that or why it sent a chill through my insides, but my instincts flared with warning.

While my stomach heated at the thought of him touching me again.

An intoxicating conundrum that left me trembling in deep-seated confusion. Swallowing, I strove for a distraction, the pizza no longer holding my interest. So I cast my attention to the necklace in my hand, and the item hanging from the center.

"What do you think?" Melek asked softly, his voice reminding me of warm honey on an autumn day. *Succulent, addictive, natural.*

Focus, Cami, I told myself. *Ignore the godlike fae and his sensual presence, and* focus.

The diamond-like rock glistened in the low lighting of my room as I moved the pendant around to evaluate the edges. It was shaped like a star, but with an extra edge that protruded from the center.

"What is it?" I asked him.

"A conduit of sorts," he replied vaguely. "I would be careful what you say while wearing it."

I blinked at him. "What? Why would I wear it?"

"Because it's a gift and gifts are meant to be worn. I think you'll find it matches your initiation wardrobe quite nicely."

"Initiation wardrobe?" I repeated.

"For the opening ceremonies," he replied. "They're tomorrow, in case you were wondering."

"Tomorrow?" I searched for a clock to check the time and noted the afternoon hour signifying I was near curfew again. "I slept maybe six hours." If my math was right, anyway.

I did feel pretty rested, so that number of hours felt adequate, even if that was a bit indulgent. Given that I'd been up for over two days, though, it didn't surprise me. Between going to classes, partying with my friends, and then fighting to stay alive in Hell, it made sense that I would be exhausted.

"Try thirty-six hours," he corrected. "You must have had one of Ajax's infamous desserts."

My brow came down, then furrowed. "A *cupcake*."

"Ah." He smiled. "After your curfew snafu? Yes, that sounds like a trademark Ajax punishment—the loss of time to prepare. Good thing you have me in your corner, yes?"

My teeth ground together, my desire to throttle Ajax settling heavily in my gut. But I supposed it could have been worse; he could have given me back to that creature in the courtyard.

I shuddered at the thought, causing Melek's gaze to roam over me once more before flipping the page again. "Ah, now here's a fun bit of information. A powerful talisman—such as the one in your hand—can be used to protect from afar. How fascinating is that?"

"Are you saying this is a protection charm?"

His expression turned innocent. "Oh, darling angel, no. I'm not saying anything. I'm merely reading from the book. You really should study these chapters. They are *illuminating*."

The stone in my palm flickered with his word, catching the light at a weird angle. I frowned at it, trying to replicate the glimmer, and failing.

"Well, I must be going. There are preparations to make, but I'll stop by again tomorrow with more sustenance, should you desire it?" He phrased it as a question, but his expression was knowing.

"More pizza and beer?"

"If that is your desire."

"My desire is to leave," I tossed back.

His lips curled into a charming grin as he set the

book aside and stood. "Is it truly?" he asked softly, taking a step toward me and leaning down until his face was directly in front of mine. "I suppose we'll see in a few days, hmm?"

I took in a breath, his near proximity making me dizzy, and his scent washed through my senses. *Sinfully decadent. Dark. Masculine. Fresh air. A dream.* All those words ran through my head as I tried to describe his cologne. But it was... indefinable, and utterly addictive.

"Until tomorrow, angel," he whispered, his lips close enough to kiss.

But he stood upright in the next second, taking with him that intoxicating air of wickedness.

"Th-thanks," I stammered, feeling the need to say something.

"Oh, don't thank me, Cami. I assure you, my intentions are not at all what they seem." With that ominous statement, he winked and wandered out of my room just as the clock chimed the three o'clock hour.

Curfew.

Fuck.

Picking up the book he had left open, I scanned the pages, trying to look for the information he'd described.

But there was nothing there that mentioned talismans or spells. Only information about creation and light and power. Which, while interesting, wasn't what I was looking for at all.

So much for clarifying what Melek had been talking about.

Shaking my head and puzzling over the book, I closed its heavy cover, then shoved the last bite of pizza into my mouth.

Heading into the living room, I sat down and pulled out the documents Ajax had left me and flipped through them, searching for anything I could find about the opening ceremonies.

After scanning over what I should expect at the ceremonies tomorrow, my mind wandered, unable to focus.

My gaze landed on the talisman Melek had given me. It was a pretty little thing. Cupping it in my palm, I gently caressed the harsh edge with a finger.

There was something about it… something that called to me.

More magic, I thought with exasperation.

But with what I had to deal with tomorrow, I'd need it.

After another moment's hesitation, I slipped the chain around my neck. The talisman rested gently against my breastbone. Comforting.

I'd listen to my instincts even if I should have learned my lesson against accepting gifts.

I'd wear it, betting on Melek liking me more than the Warden did.

Because in this case, one more screwup could cost me my life.

CAMI

A DRESS APPEARED on my bed the next day, the fabric silky and black. Beside it was a note instructing me to wear it for the opening ceremonies.

Part of me wanted to rebel and burn the damn thing. But after reading several more chapters in the unending law book, I decided it was better to play by the rules. *For the time being, anyway.*

I still couldn't find the sections Melek had read to me. However, I had found some interesting parts about travel in the Hell Fae Realm. Portals were hidden in plain sight and activated with a few choice words. I'd memorized them in case I ever caught the signs of a nearby exit.

Of course, I still hadn't figured out what to do once inside one.

The pages had blurred when I'd reached that section, creating a new chapter all about edible items in the lands. When I'd tried to go back, the words had followed me, forcing me to read about various plant life and known animals in the Hell Fae Realm.

It was the strangest rule book I'd ever encountered.

And nowhere had it helped me understand the deal Lucifer had constructed with my parents.

Gritting my teeth, I pinned up my hair and hooked the necklace with the talisman around my neck. It'd become a part of me over the last twenty-four hours, the energy swarming around the enchanting stone an addictive sensation against my skin.

Slipping into the black dress, I grimaced at my reflection in the full-length mirror. *Wow, this thing doesn't leave much to the imagination…*

Magic hummed through it, curling the fabric around my body, leaving two long streaks that barely covered my nipples, rounding with cleavage on all sides, putting me on full display.

Two slits slipped up my thighs, hitting high on my hips, the hug of the fabric barely covering my ass.

And a graze of metal kept the dress around my neck, resulting in a low V down my back that revealed way too much skin. The finishing touch was a long silver chain running down my spine that felt far too much like a leash.

A knock sounded on my door.

The image of Ajax filled my vision, then flicked to Melek. Who would it be?

Who did I *want* it to be?

Smoothing my hands over my dress, I ignored the impulse to pull a giant sweater over my head and slid on the black heels instead. Then I went to the door to step through it—it was my only option without a proper handle.

No one stood on the other side.

At least not at eye level.

I dropped my gaze to the gargoyle below, his head barely reaching my knees.

"Oh." I hated the note of disappointment in my voice. Apparently, I had wanted to see Melek or Ajax after all.

Stupid Cami, I chastised myself.

The gargoyle's stone jaw grated as he said, "It's time." His wings shifted as he perused my appearance, paired with a gravelly sound that made my skin crawl. "Hmm, you're ready. Shall we, then?"

My brows lifted. "They sent a creature as tall as a cat to escort me to the ceremony?"

The gargoyle didn't seem fazed as he stared back at me with unreadable black eyes. Perhaps I'd been a bit rude in comparing him to a cat.

"A large cat, perhaps." He fluttered his wings again. "If you prefer to go alone…"

"No," I mumbled, tugging at the sides of my dress. The last time I'd tried to navigate the campus, I'd run myself in circles and faced a Manticore. "Any company that doesn't try to kill me would be nice."

"Stay on my good side, then."

Leaving my room behind, I walked alongside the gargoyle, who, despite his threats, didn't seem all that intimidating. However, every footfall reminded me a bit of an elephant. *Thunk. Thunk. Thunk.*

"What's your name?" I asked as we exited the building. The last one I'd encountered had been Sir Davis, if memory served me right. I was starting to be able to tell them apart based on their slight differences.

He glanced at me. "Sir Bachen."

"I'm Cami."

"I know." It was hard to tell past the gravel in his voice, but I thought I detected a hint of humor behind his tone.

We cut across the quad and made our way to an amphitheater on the other side of campus. Dozens of women flocked there with their own tiny stone escorts. It was almost like a high school prom, only the gowns left little to the imagination.

Totally not high school appropriate and more fitting for a brothel.

"I must leave you," Sir Bachen said with a small bow.

"Already?" I scanned the swarm of women and caught the alluring figure of Ajax lining them up. Seeing him made me stand a little straighter. "Sure you don't want to throw on a dress and take my place?"

Sir Bachen just stared at me like I'd grown another pair of arms—which, knowing Hell, shouldn't be surprising at all.

"I was joking. Forget it. See you around." Squaring my shoulders, I marched forward.

The air hummed with the chatter of thousands of Hell Fae and their captives. The male audience filled every seat in the amphitheater, seemingly eager for tonight's display.

I scrunched my nose in disgust. I knew better than to believe this was a "ceremony."

It was a parade.

A warm hand curled over my bare shoulder, and I twisted around to see Ajax steering me toward the line of women. "Don't touch me," I said, my voice low as I flinched away.

His hand moved to the low curve of my back, fitting perfectly against me, making my skin tingle.

I shouldn't respond to his touch this way. He'd brought me here. Tested me. Given me special treatment, only to screw me over with that cupcake punishment.

He didn't respond to my demand. Instead, he manhandled me to my place in line.

I scowled at him. "Are you hard of hearing?"

His jaw clenched. "Wait here until you're announced." He turned his back on me and started walking away.

I stepped out of line. Because clearly I possessed a death wish of some kind.

However, his antics had cost me thirty-six hours of precious time.

The least he could do was acknowledge that he'd fucked me over.

"Thanks for the cupcake, by the way. I really enjoyed my nap," I called after him.

Ajax paused midstep, then glanced back at me. "What the fuck are you talking about?"

"Your gift."

"I didn't leave you any gifts," he retorted. "Now get back in line before I put a collar on you like I did Item Twenty-Two up there." He gestured to a familiar female with a silver ponytail and blazing obsidian irises. She appeared ready to kill the Warden, but the sparks around her throat were preventing her from whatever she intended to do.

"So I'm an *item* now?" I guessed, arching a brow.

"You were always an item," he replied, spinning away from me. "Sixty-Six, in case you were wondering."

I frowned and noticed the number appearing over my head in smoke. It was there and gone in a flash, his spell seeming to have marked my spirit more than my corporeal form.

A deep male voice rang across the amphitheater, welcoming the spectators to the ceremony. He went on for a couple of minutes about how we were all selected candidates for the bride trials and that only the most suitable among us would survive. Then he called for Item Number One, and the line shifted a bit as the first candidate stumbled into the limelight.

Cheers and hollers erupted, making my stomach twist.

The line moved up as more numbers were called.

In front of me, girls fidgeted or stood proud. If these trials really were to the death, I should start sizing up my competition.

But I just couldn't entertain the idea of ending any of their lives. The more I thought about it, the more acid built in the back of my throat.

I'd been taught to kill, to survive, but not at the expense of other victims.

Plus, I didn't feel very capable of doling out badassery when I wobbled on a pair of heels.

I caught sight of Ajax standing by and watching, arms crossed over his broad chest.

His eyes landed on me.

And then the bastard smirked.

It was just like the asshole to be amused by my unease. I was a fucking badass and he knew it, but put me in a dress and heels, and I was a nervous wreck.

Landing my fist against that sturdy jaw would feel *so* good right now. Or using his body as a shield while I hid from the view of the crowd. Maybe I'd do both.

But in reality, I waited my turn like a good little captive, because I knew it wasn't my moment yet. The key to my survival rested in unraveling the deal my parents had struck.

Something that I had hoped the unending law book would help me with.

It hadn't yet. But I still had a lot to read.

The crowd roared again as the girl in front of me was called, leaving me alone.

And then I was next.

My heart thundered in my chest as my mind raced for a way out of this.

Perhaps I could negotiate a new deal. Or—

"Item Number Sixty-Six!" the deep voice boomed.

My gaze flashed up as I sucked in a breath.

Everything inside me screamed to run, but the thought of Ajax smirking at me hardened my resolve not to let anything faze me. I lifted my chin, straightened my spine, and walked into the bright light of the moon. It illuminated all the girls who were already in position on the field.

A Hellhound growled beside me as he led me to my spot, his teeth gnashing in obvious irritation. I risked a glance and recognized the Hellhound I'd stabbed with silver after he'd tried to abduct me.

Oops. "Glad you recovered," I told him, not really meaning it.

His lip curled into a snarl. "Don't worry, pet. I'll be repaying that favor *very* soon."

My stomach twisted at the thought, yet my disobedient mouth lifted into a smile. "Can't wait."

Yes, Cami. Taunt the already angry beast. That's intelligent.

Before he or I could even begin to react, a boom sounded from the stands, drawing our focus up to a platform set in the middle of the stadium.

I supposed the area could be considered the *box seats* of the arena, as it boasted a prime location at the center and jutted out in the front. But rather than being shrouded in glass like those in a typical sports auditorium would be, this area was lined in a shimmering light that parted slowly to reveal a set of thrones.

Gasps sounded down the lines of females as a shirtless male with chiseled features stepped forward. The armored plates on his calves and shoulders glistened menacingly in the moonlight. Yet his face was one of the most beautiful I'd ever seen.

Almost as alluring as Melek's features. Except this

male's bone structure and jawline were harsher in nature. Lethal, even.

Melek possessed softer qualities. Quite similar to—

Hold on… Is that…?

Holy shit. My lips parted. *Melek.*

He stood right beside the armored male.

His blondish-brown hair was styled messily in an artful sort of way, the strands dancing in the breeze against his ears as he surveyed the crowd with a slight twist of his full mouth. *A smile.* Because he was amused.

And as the hush of tittering responses met my ear, I understood why.

The females around me were losing their senses over the two gorgeous males on the platform, whispers of "King Lucifer" and "Prince Melek" warming the air around me.

You have got to be shitting me, I thought, my eyes narrowing up at the godly male who had made himself at home in my room just yesterday.

His striking multicolored irises met mine, his dimples flashing as his grin deepened.

Yeah, I just bet you find this entertaining, I wanted to say to him.

Indeed I do, he seemed to reply, the asshole winking.

My teeth clenched, my ire mounting. He'd been playing a game with me. Which, of course he was—he was a damn Hell Fae!

Lucifer's commanding voice yanked my attention away from the deceitful *prince* and directly to him—*the reason for my presence here.*

My ire was no less potent by the time the parade of females finished, which was fucking impressive, considering there were literally six hundred more of them after me in line.

If anything, I was even angrier.

Not necessarily at Melek, but at myself.

Because I damn well knew better. Yet I'd willingly allowed him to pull me into his twisted game.

Shit.

"Welcome," Lucifer greeted, his deep voice carrying throughout the massive space on an enchanted breeze. "Tell me, what did you think of the candidate preview parade?"

Candidate preview parade? Are you for fucking real right now?

Roars of approval bounded through the stands, the male fae stomping their feet in a parade of their own—one that reminded me of a stampede of elephants.

Animals, I seethed. *You're all fucking animals.*

Actually, no. That was an insult to all animal kind. These men were *monsters*. And they were all salivating for a taste of the female flesh on display below.

Shit.

I really regretted wearing this dress. Not that there'd been much of a choice.

Lucifer chuckled, and again the warm sound swished around me like a heated caress, his magic hypnotically charming. It matched his expression as well, his full lips curling into an enticing grin that rivaled the come-hither quality of his midnight-blue eyes. I shouldn't be able to discern that trait from this far back—he stood over a hundred yards away from me—and yet something about his stare radiated across time and space, allowing me a glimpse into the man himself.

I shook my head, trying to clear the daze from my thoughts. Because that wasn't possible. And yet I felt as though he were looking right at me from only a few feet away, his sharp cheekbones and neatly trimmed beard so close I could almost *taste* him.

What the hell is this voodoo? I marveled, swooning despite my obvious hate for this male.

Or maybe it wasn't so much him I hated, but rather, my parents.

Yes. They were the reason for this mess, the culprits who'd signed the agreement.

I didn't hate him at all. I barely even knew him. He was just the god among these fae who'd finalized the arrangement.

Your parents promised me your soul, I heard him whispering. *In exchange for their freedom. I merely work in terms of deals, not fate. Don't blame me for your parents' sins. That's on them alone.*

Yes, I agreed, swallowing thickly. *Yes, it's… hold on…*

I blinked and shook my head again. *Stop it.* I could feel his intoxicating presence inside me, morphing my thoughts, forcing me to *hear* him, just like I sensed him right before me, talking and drowning me in sensations that weren't my own.

No, I snapped, twisting away from his overwhelming presence. *No!*

But he held on to me with an ease I could feel more than see, and it tugged me deeper into a dangerous vortex of manipulation and false words.

I heard him welcoming all the brides, praising us for joining his trials—like we were here willingly—and outlining the coming festivities.

Words like *well-fed* and *pampered* bled into my mind, not through my ears but via some enchantment that I fought to free myself from.

This isn't real.

This isn't happening.

This is wrong!

But it slithered around me, heating my veins, settling my spirit, and making me feel like I *belonged* here.

Your parents signed the papers, sealing your fate. It's a simple business arrangement, with your soul as the collateral damage. I warned them what would happen. They chose your fate anyway. Hate them, not me.

Those words wove through the others that depicted my fate, saying something about a survival test. He told us to be prepared, to take the pampering of the next few days to ready ourselves for the eventual battle.

Only the worthy will endure, he concluded. *Then the real trials will begin.*

Growls and chants met those words, the male Hell Fae eager to move this along. To shred us apart. To *own* us.

There were very few female Hell Fae—a fact I somehow knew but couldn't determine where it'd come from. Perhaps the incantation swirling around me had something to do with it. That damn spell held me captive like some obedient pet tethered to a calming leash.

Stop it, I demanded, attempting to fight my way out of the addictive web.

Relax, it cooed in response. *This is your state of being now. Accept me. Accept us. Accept this world.*

Fuck you! I screamed at it, aware that I was partially losing my mind. Because I was arguing with a figment, some sort of invisible, intangible being that sounded a hell of a lot like the Hell Fae King seated on the throne before me.

Seated, I thought. *When did he sit?*

Oh, who the fuck cares!

My brow slickened with sweat as I continued to mentally battle this *thing* inside me, his speech worming through my brain to repaint my reality.

I could *see* him standing there, speaking, broadcasting the opening ceremonies, and telling us all to indulge and enjoy. His lips moved. His eyes smiled. He appeared almost angelic, beautiful, the epitome of *handsome*.

And yet I also saw him sitting there with a bored expression, his hand weaving a spell while Melek whispered something into his ear.

It was a dual reality that left me wondering what the hell I was truly experiencing.

Is he standing or sitting?

And how is he so loud in my head?

I screamed but my mouth didn't move.

Applause echoed around me, the hungry males excited for the next phase of the evening. *A meet and greet session to cast their votes on who they want to survive,* the Hell Fae King was saying. *Perhaps they'll give you items to help you along the way, hmm? I suggest you seduce them well, ladies. You'll need as much help as you can get.*

Melek's gaze my mine, a knowing flicker in the depths of his gaze. He was still seated by Lucifer, but he wore the same expression from where he'd stood minutes… seconds… whenever ago.

Then he gently stroked his throat.

Only, I felt that touch against *my* skin… and then the talisman against my neck.

Two words, he mouthed.

Somnum Dameonis, I thought, realizing what he wanted me to say.

Magic snapped around me, some part of me innately engaging the restraint around my mind and demolishing the spell to ash.

Oh! I hadn't meant to actually enact it, but it was too late.

One moment, I remained in that standing daze, allowing the Hell Fae King to play mental gymnastics with my mind.

And in the next, I was on my ass on the black sand ground of the auditorium, gaping up at the Hell Fae King.

Silence fell heavily around me. Even the males in the stands were quiet. But no one noticed me except *him*. The devil himself.

Because the others were all still *enchanted*.

What. The. Fuck.

My body shook with exertion, like I'd just run a marathon. But as I stared into a pair of midnight eyes, I realized it wasn't a marathon at all. I'd just broken from a majestic web of some kind.

And the irate gleam in his glowing irises told me that'd been the absolute wrong thing to do.

Because I'd just gained the attention of the devil himself.

While everyone else remained studiously quiet and hypnotized around me in the field.

"Warden," he said, his voice whisper-soft. "Inspect Number Sixty-Six."

"As you wish, my lord," Ajax replied, his hand grabbing my bicep and yanking me to my feet. "Good job, *cupcake*. You just earned yourself a night in one of my cells."

Ajax

"Not a smart move." I said to Camillia as I led her out of the arena.

"What was that?" she demanded, not at all contrite or concerned. "He had us all under some sort of enchantment. Like… like we were watching a movie that wasn't real."

Az snorted as he joined us. "Did she really just liken Lucifer's magic to a *movie*?"

"She did."

"Hope he didn't hear that," Az drawled.

"I sort of hope he did," I replied. "She could use a lesson on respect."

Az nodded, his thick hair shifting in a breeze that seemed to follow him everywhere. I suspected it had something to do with his Phoenix energy. "Indeed she could," he agreed. "Perhaps we could administer the initial course?"

"Or maybe you could talk to me rather than about me when I'm walking right here, between you," she interjected, her annoyance a spike to my senses.

Az glanced at her, a note of surprise touching his usually stern features. "You really do have a death wish, hmm?"

I grunted. "She certainly has something."

"Still right here," she reminded us, like I couldn't feel her skin burning beneath my palm.

Curling my fingers around the long silver chain down Cami's back, I tugged her out of the amphitheater.

She wanted to behave like an animal? Then that was how I would treat her.

Her adorable growl suggested she'd known the purpose of this chain. Good. She needed to learn her place here. Just as she needed a firm introduction to my role in these games.

I circled around to the back of the arena to the area I typically used to corral monsters into the portal. However, the open field had been partially repurposed for the trials. I hadn't expected to make use of this path so soon, but I should have known that Camillia De la Croix would be my first prisoner.

I muttered a spell to unlock the magical doorway, causing the air to swirl as it opened before us. The long, dark path of stairs appeared ominous and cold, something that gave me temporary pause, as I wanted Camillia to see her lingering fate.

She tugged against my pull. "You're not taking me down there."

"You're not in a position to make demands," I reminded her as I dragged her through the entryway. Az followed, bringing up the rear just in case she managed to free herself and bolt from me.

Or perhaps he just wanted to watch.

Az always did enjoy a good bout of voyeurism, not just with bedroom play but with torture, too.

The staircase technically bordered the edge of the paradigm, allowing magic to fluctuate between the stone walls. It changed the landscape and evenness of the steps, making them short and long and endless before giving them a twist into another set.

Camillia's calculating gaze didn't miss a thing, taking in the subtle changes as she navigated the stairs in her high heels.

"Sometimes it's a short trip of only a few steps to the bottom, and sometimes it can run for a mile," I mused. "Makes escape risky."

She said nothing, her focus on not losing her footing. I still held her chain. If she started to fall, I'd yank her back up.

But she'd probably bruise a little in the process.

Something told me it wouldn't impact her for long. She possessed a fighter's spirit, marking her as an ideal Hell Fae mate. *Does she even realize how much intrigue she's going to garner by being a rebel?*

She again reminded me of my past, of another woman who'd enjoyed *rebelling* against the powers that be.

She'd been killed for that rebellion.

That marked a distinct difference in their situations. Camillia wouldn't be killed; she'd likely be *rewarded* for her rebellion instead.

Torchlight flickered on the walls as we continued our descent, spiraling into the deep abyss, the paradigm's mood taking us the long route today.

I knew we hit the bottom when waves of heat stifled the air. An inky hallway materialized, causing Camillia to grip my arm like a lifeline as she stared head-on into the darkness. A part of me considered going in blind just to toy with her, but that would come later.

Using my wand, I whispered a spell and cast a blast of fire down the corridor to light the torches.

Camillia gasped, although I couldn't tell if she was impressed by my magic or if she'd realized where we were.

Because the light illuminated the cast-iron bars of rows of empty cages.

"Warden." She whispered the title as if it made sense now. Her bright eyes took me in as if for the first time.

I had expected to see fear.

Instead, I saw pity.

I don't care what this girl thinks.

She meant nothing to me.

To prove it, I cast an enchantment over myself and Az to protect us from the blistering heat and left Camillia to experience exactly what it meant to be in the belly of Hell.

Az met my eyes, knowing exactly what I'd done. He found it amusing. He also appeared a bit grateful since he was wearing a full black-on-black suit for tonight's ceremony. Just like me.

We continued onward, walking in silence, the only sound the crackling of the torches and our footsteps.

Camillia finally spoke again, her voice bouncing down the corridor. "How do you two stand the heat down here?" she asked, her pace slowing as sweat gathered across her exposed skin.

I yanked her forward.

"My magic protects us," I said curtly. "Not you."

"Very chivalrous," she drawled. "Just as you were with the cupcake."

I clenched my jaw. *What is with this girl and her bloody nonsense about a cupcake?* "Do you have an obsession with desserts?"

"Only the ones with spells laced through them."

Az and I shared a look. He mirrored my confusion. *What hell is she talking about?*

Probably some nonsense she intended to use as a distraction.

Whatever.

I let it go, focusing instead on the shimmering veil awaiting us at the end of the corridor. It had the appearance of a glistening waterfall but possessed a smokey quality.

We stepped through it and emerged in the Detention Dorms.

Otherwise known as my prison cells.

My playground.

Camillia flinched as she took in the various cages surrounding us. Originally, they'd been used for holding the tortured souls who'd broken their deals with Lucifer. They'd had a tendency for trying to escape Hell's realms after morphing into their new monstrous forms—Lucifer's favorite kind of punishment for naughty fae.

These iron bars had held them with ease.

At least until Az and I had found a better way to detain them within the paradigm. Now they were provided freedom every day during curfew hours, which served as a benefit for keeping the captives in line and allowing us to tame the monsters.

Of course, there were always the troublemakers, those who favored disobedience and death to their current forms. The first half of the dungeon was still reserved for them.

The second half was now designated for unruly candidates.

It seemed fitting that Camillia would be the first to visit.

A deep growl penetrated the area as a Minotaur glared at us from his cell. Camillia took a half step backward.

"Where's that defiant spirit now?" I asked, pulling her forward. "Did you leave it in the amphitheater?"

"Fuck you," she shot back, then yelped as the Centaur in the cell next to her made a guttural bull-like sound. She shuddered as she faced it, her face going white.

Smoke drifted from its nostrils, its tall, wickedly curved antlers promising a slow death to anyone caught in its path. It stomped one hoof as if it wanted to charge. Lucky for Camillia, there were magically reinforced bars between us and it. Red eyes glowed from an ever-present black shadow that perpetually lingered over a Centaur's humanoid face, this breed of Centaur having its magic derived from darkness and death.

It approached the bars, standing over a foot taller than me, and stared down at Camillia, its fingers curling around the iron.

"Perhaps the Hellbeast would like a roommate," Az drawled, causing Camillia to blanch.

The terror that crossed her face made Az's proposal tempting, but I had other plans for our little rebel. "Come on," I said, and Camillia eagerly followed now, sticking close to me. It was ironic, really, that she would seek comfort from *me*.

I slowed as we passed a Siren tank. One of the monsters lifted herself out of the water, blinking milky eyes at my captive.

Then the being opened her jaw lined with two rows of teeth and sang the most beautiful, haunting melody known to fae kind.

Camillia paused, taking in the deadly Hellbeast floating lazily in the water.

This breed of Siren looked truly terrifying, but their song could be difficult to resist.

"Ajax…" Az warned, but I held up a hand.

Let's see how strong-willed our candidate really is, I mused.

Camillia took a step toward the Siren, her gaze locked on the magnificent creature.

All Nightmare Fae were enchanting, their nickname of *Hellbeasts* well earned. It was hard not to respect them a little, their lethal grace rather admirable.

Of course, I was their Warden for a reason.

I knew how to see through their glamour. As did Az.

However, Camillia's eyes glazed over, and for a moment, I thought she really would try to climb into the tank to meet her doom.

But her hand reached for her necklace, and in the next instant, she shook herself, retreating backward.

She frowned as she studied the Siren again. "What a strange black aura," she murmured to herself.

I had no idea what she meant. I didn't see a black aura at all, but maybe the effects of the song were giving her hallucinations.

Az, on the other hand, crossed his arms at her subtle comment, his expression holding a note of interest.

The Siren quieted and reluctantly slipped back into the water, keening with disappointment as she extended long, gnashing teeth.

Camillia trembled once more, her grip tightening around her necklace.

"Well done," I said, hoping my admiration didn't show through my voice. "I didn't really feel like scooping out whatever was left of you from the tanks. They're a bitch to clean as it is."

Camillia fell into step next to me, her spine seeming to erect once more. "Poor you," she deadpanned. Then her gaze lingered on the other cages. "What is this place?"

"It's a taste of what you'll experience in the various trials," I replied. "Take notes, because it's all the help you'll get now that you blew your chances with the benefactors."

She likely could have seduced half the males in the amphitheater and scored more than one useful artifact with that outfit alone. My eyes wandered, taking in the way the fabric hugged her curves, cupping her ass in a way that made my hands ache to caress her.

But it was more than her alluring body that had drawn me to her. It was her fighting spirit.

Because she reminded me of someone from my past.

Which made Camillia a natural enemy to me, if nothing more than because of the emotions her presence seemed to evoke in me now.

That sense of doubt.

That need to *help*.

A desire that kept me up at night, one that frequently haunted my dreams of *her.* Of Emelyn.

I'd been helpless once. And it had cost me the lives of everyone I'd once cherished more than existence itself.

I would never allow myself to feel vulnerable in that way again.

I cared about Az, but he could protect himself. I didn't have to protect him. Just like the best friend from my childhood, Shade. He, too, could take care of himself. Thus allowing me to care about them both because they would never have reason to rely on me.

The same could not be said about Camillia. Fuck, she'd probably disappear within the week.

Her spirit might remind me of someone from the past. But she wasn't *her*. She could never be *her*.

This unhealthy correlation was just a result of their similar spirits.

As evidenced by Camillia's walk now—she'd gained some confidence after facing the Siren's charms. She strode along beside me with her head held high, her expression almost bloody regal.

Which, of course, just reminded me of *her* even more.

Because *she* had walked just like that. *Owning the Midnight Fae Academy halls. Wearing that regal smile. Making everyone, including me, bow in her wake.*

My chest ached with the memory, causing me to grit my teeth. *Enough. They're not the same. Stop thinking about it.*

We finally reached the second half of the prison. The cells still had iron bars, but the insides contained luxurious furniture and a welcoming interior.

No bed. Just a tattered rug in the center that no one would willingly want to sleep on.

Let's see if she figures this one out.

I pulled Camillia into a cell at the end. Sir Bachen lounged on a one-armed sofa, its leg broken from his weight. Gargoyles were tiny but made of stone, so they were fucking heavy.

I scowled at him. "You're paying for that."

He waved away my demand with a sound of gravelly annoyance.

Camillia stepped toward the other sofa. "I warn you, the couches aren't as comfortable as they look," Sir Bachen said, his voice grinding.

She paused, looking between me and Az.

My scowl deepened as I directed it at Sir Bachen. He wasn't supposed to be helping her.

She frowned, then surveyed the room again, taking in the fine velvet and puffy pillows before shifting down to the knotty, brown rug.

She marched over to it and sat in the center of the tattered mess, a triumphant look on her face, making me growl.

"Cheater," Az muttered.

"You didn't name any terms, bird," Sir Bachen retorted. "Don't blame me for using it to my advantage."

Az narrowed his gaze. "Consider it a new term—no helping recruits."

"You two bid on the success of this disciplinary test?" I looked between them. "Seriously? What were the stakes?"

Sir Bachen puffed out his chest. "Daggers."

I snorted, smirking at Az. "You should know better than to bet him something so valuable."

Az grunted, his expression turning to stone. "I'll get it back." He tossed a blade to the gargoyle without looking. "Don't fucking dent it."

"My precious," Sir Bachen cooed, stroking the metal before making a show of grinding it between his rocky fingers.

I sighed and shook my head as Az's gaze smoldered in fury.

No sense in repeating what I'd already said.

Too bad about the furniture, though. I'd been looking forward to seeing how captives reacted to it. And watching Camillia now, I could tell she sensed the sickly magic coating the surface of the designer furniture. It was similar to the compulsory magic used on the candidates in the amphitheater, only it weakened the mind even more, making the occupants more pliable and easier to manage.

Oh well. It probably wouldn't have worked on Camillia anyway. She seemed far too aware of her surroundings, hence her ability to break out of Lucifer's mind control earlier.

An impressive feat. One that would probably get her killed.

Pity.

"Ah, well, better get back to it, then," Sir Bachen said, hopping up with a little twirl of the blade. "I'd hoped

Typhos's sleeping spell would work on me. It didn't. Should have known. Haven't slept in, like, a decade, thanks to the heat." He scratched his shoulder as he spoke, his lips curling down in a grimace.

The gargoyles in the paradigm didn't seem bothered by the Barren Lands, but those who used the tunnels or ventured outside always complained about the sweltering heat and suffocating air.

Camillia seemed to be handling it all right, but beads of sweat were glistening along her brow, and one danced precariously close to her cleavage. I swallowed, the desire to lick her suddenly inspiring indecent ideas in my mind.

Definitely need Az later, I decided, shaking it off.

There was just something about this girl… something I couldn't seem to ignore. And that made her dangerous on so many levels. Because I couldn't afford to become attached to her—or anyone—ever again.

"Typhos?" Camillia repeated, frowning. "Sleeping spell?"

Fucking gargoyle.

"Lucifer's first name," Sir Bachen replied from the door before I could stop him. "He doesn't really use it, but I prefer it."

"Time to go, Bach," I interjected. "She's a captive, not a friend."

Sir Bachen grunted in response, his distaste evident. "Fine, fine," he muttered, waddling off through the door. "I have better places to be anyway."

Az snorted. "Take care of that blade. I'm getting it back."

"Sure, sure," Sir Bachen echoed as he stomped off down the hall, his stone wings dragging along behind him.

Turning back to Camillia, I found her with her arms crossed as she had the audacity to glare up at me. Instead of reprimanding her, I waited to see if she had anything else to say for herself or if she intended to continue talking about fucking desserts again.

Then she flipped me off and Az smiled.

Defiant little thing.

I opened my mouth to make a snide comment, but Az began to circle her position on the rug. Embers flickered in his gaze, something that happened when he was deep in thought and calling upon his magic.

Poor girl has no idea the mess she's waltzed herself into by not only pissing off Lucifer but also grabbing the attention of me and now Az.

He was amused by her; that much was clear. He studied her like he wanted to turn her into his own version of a *cupcake*—one he intended to devour thoroughly.

Leaning against the wall, I decided to let this play out, see where it went.

"There's something…" Az trailed off, his head cocking to the side. "Hmm, no, she didn't do that on her own."

I arched a brow. "What are you sensing?"

"Enchantment," he mused, his irises flaring with more of those gold flecks. I wondered if Camillia could sense his Phoenix side peeking out at her, or if she even knew how to recognize it.

Normally, I would say, *Probably not.* But given her propensity for doing exactly the opposite of typical expectation, she probably *did* notice it. Although, she did appear to be quite distracted by the handsome Commander at the moment. And her little show of defiance weakened with each passing second, until her crossed arms fell limply to her sides as though under some sort of spell.

Az possessed a lot of skills, his Shifter half gifting him the ability to seduce instinctually—an ability I very much enjoyed behind closed doors. He didn't appear to be using it on her now, but his natural prowess certainly had her caught in some kind of sensual web.

Az knelt in front of her and ran a finger over her bottom lip, then trailed it down her neck.

She didn't move, mesmerized by him as he lifted her talisman into his palm. He hummed.

I recognized the sound—it was one he used when he went down on me.

I cocked a brow, waiting.

Az finally spoke, his voice melodic. "Where did you receive this pretty necklace?"

My gaze dropped to the glittering talisman. I'd been so distracted by her breasts that I hadn't even properly noticed it.

But Az had.

Camillia blinked dreamily at him, her voice soft. "It was a gift."

Az smiled. "Hmm, very interesting. Unfortunately, gifts were not permitted before tonight's ceremony, so I'll be confiscating this item." His eyes lifted to mine. "Ajax?"

I nodded, agreeing to the unspoken question. He wanted to take the item to Lucifer.

Camillia pouted but didn't argue. She seemed to still be caught in the trance Az had weaved through her.

I walked behind her and crouched to remove the necklace. With Az directly in front of her, she was practically sandwiched between the two of us.

An image that I found I liked.

Her dress was made to be unwrapped like a gift, leaving her bare. I knew she wore nothing beneath, as undergarments were against the rules. And unless she conjured some in defiance—something that was absolutely possible, considering her propensity for breaking the rules —she'd be naked.

Mmm. I allowed the visual to taunt my mind, the image easily forming of me taking her from behind while she sucked off Az. A beautiful fantasy.

By the flash of interest in Az's gaze, I wasn't the only one thinking about it, either.

Too bad we couldn't follow through.

She was my prisoner, not our fuck toy.

Yet, some part of me whispered. A dark part that wanted to play.

But not here. Not like this.

Shoving the brewing fantasy out of my mind, I touched the back of her neck as my eyes trailed down the thin fabric of her dress.

Clenching my jaw, I unclasped the necklace.

"I'm surprised you were able to make a friend, let alone two, what with your lack of self-preservation instincts," I said, forcing my thoughts to behave as I stood. Befriending Sir Bachen was shocking enough, but this necklace proved he wasn't her only ally in this place.

Intriguing.

Camillia released a sarcastic sound from her throat. "*Friends.* Yeah. Sure. That's the dream, isn't it? Befriending captors and all that?"

Az stood. "Well, if we were your friends, we could help you."

"We could," I agreed.

"But we won't."

"We definitely won't."

"Well, that's good since the last *gift* you gave me put me out cold for nearly two days," Camillia retorted. "Not really interested in friendships like *that.*"

"What gift?" I asked her, confused.

"The cupcake."

And we were back on the dessert again. "I didn't give you a damn cupcake."

"Then why did the card with it have *Warden* on it?" she countered.

"First, I don't go around handing out baked goods. And second, I definitely don't leave calling cards behind."

She frowned at me. "Then who put the cupcake on my nightstand?"

"Maybe the same one who gave you this," Az drawled, gesturing to the necklace. Then he held out his palm for me, indicating he wanted the talisman. "I'll get some answers."

I dropped it into his palm, trusting him to see it through. He and Lucifer were bonded, something that marked Az as the better candidate to handle that conversation. Besides, I had a little hellfire kitten to play with in my dungeon now.

A hellfire kitten with an unhealthy obsession for *cupcakes*.

Az tucked the necklace into his pocket. "Enjoy playtime." He looked meaningfully at me, warning me with his eyes not to have too much fun without him.

Then he left the cell, locking Camillia and me inside.

Az

I need to show you something, I said, engaging my mental link with Typhos.

What is it? His mental voice sounded tired, probably from the show he'd just put on in the amphitheater. Or maybe his exhaustion stemmed from having to host these games for his men. He didn't want to hold these trials, but his need to satisfy his loyal subjects trumped his own desires.

Typhos was a notoriously fair leader, and he cared about the fae under his protection.

And they wanted brides.

So Typhos would give them brides.

Az? he prompted when I didn't immediately reply, his impatience evident.

A talisman, I told him.

From the girl? he guessed.

She was wearing it, yes. But it's the energy signature I think you're going to find interesting, I informed him.

I see, he replied after a beat. *I'm in my quarters.*

I'm heading that way already. Because I knew he would run

back there at his first chance of escape. The Hell Fae King might have run the opening ceremony, but he had no interest in attending the lavish affair afterward. He was only doing all this to appease his men, not himself.

Typhos Lucifer did not want a bride. He craved peace. And to achieve that, he needed to appease the men who all worshipped him like a god.

To become a Hell Fae, the source had to accept the abomination into the inner circle. And for whatever reason, the source rarely accepted women.

Which had created an abundance of male Hell Fae.

And very few female mates.

These trials would fix that—assuming Typhos's games properly prepared the recruits for the Hell Fae Source.

The woman I'd just left in Ajax's cell seemed like a suitable candidate. She had *warrior* written all over that feisty face of hers.

She was strong-willed. Utterly gorgeous.

Not that I would admit my interest to anyone.

Still, I'd probably enjoy a taste eventually. Likely together with Ajax. Having her between the two of us had been undeniably interesting, and there hadn't even been any real touching involved.

I suspected I knew what had Ajax so distracted now. Perhaps he wanted to keep her for himself. A notion that had me picturing her bent over with Ajax taking her from behind.

That'd be a hot view.

Of course, Number Sixty-Six had cheated. And that was a problem.

Ignorance was no excuse. Someone had given her a talisman boasting a very specific type of enchantment, magic capable of being crafted by only a handful of fae.

Someone powerful.

And he hadn't even tried to hide his energy signature.

Which meant he wanted to be discovered.

Little trickster, I mused, shaking my head. *Always playing games.*

All I had to do now was prove my hunch.

Or let Typhos handle it for me.

I entered his rooms without knocking—a perk of being bonded to the Hell Fae King. Not only did he know I was on my way to him already, but he would also sense my presence. And he'd welcome it, even if he wasn't expecting me.

I found him lounging on an ivory and gold chaise, holding a glass of blood-red wine. He was like a lion, all relaxed and majestic with his long, dark hair sprawled out around him like a mane.

As soon as he saw me, he beckoned me forward with a hand.

"Don't," he said. "You know how I hate hovering."

"I was only admiring, my liege," I said with a smirk, approaching him. He also hated suck-ups, making my words pointed and irritating. I'd never desired him in that way, our bond a bit different from the sensual one he maintained with Melek.

Typhos's midnight orbs lifted to the ceiling above, his agitation palpable as I joined him on the chaise.

He arched a dark brow. "The talisman?"

I fished it from my pocket and handed it over, watching as he fingered the chain with a heaved sigh. "Yes, I see why you thought I would find this interesting," he rumbled. "I recognize the signature."

"And the girl?" I pushed. "Shall we punish her?"

"No," Typhos said, tilting the talisman so it glinted in the warm light. "She used what she was given. An intelligent move, but one that will unfortunately not be repeated in the next round. She must prove herself on her own, not through the overly generous gifts from others."

"Isn't that the whole point of the affair in the arena? To gain favors?" I drawled.

"Hmm, yes, but not ones of this magnitude," Typhos replied. "The others have been provided a stern allowance and rules as to how they can help their pets. This talisman certainly doesn't qualify." He pocketed the item with a smile. "But don't worry. I'll have a private word with the benefactor myself to ensure this doesn't happen again."

I stood, imagining exactly how that conversation would go down—with Melek dropping to his knees.

Reaching over, I plucked Typhos's wine glass from his grip and tipped it to my lips. He watched me expose my throat as I downed its contents before I handed it back.

"I suppose I must return to the festivities," I said. "Resume my role as Commander."

"Indeed," Typhos purred, turning the empty glass in his hand. "Thank you for the talisman."

I nodded and left him, heading for the amphitheater. However, I wouldn't be seducing or flirting tonight. With Ajax busy taming a wildcat in his dungeon, I needed to make sure none of the men were too overzealous with the competition over the female brides.

And knowing Hell Fae, competition would result in bloodshed and death.

My kind of party.

Typhos

"Oh, Melek," I called as I entered our bedroom.

"My liege," he murmured, sauntering into view wearing a towel low on his hips. "Are you joining me in my bath? Because I would very much enjoy the company."

My lips twitched at his seductive play. He knew I would find out about the talisman, just as I knew he would play innocent about giving it to the girl. His energy signature was all over the diamond pendant, making it obvious who had given it to her.

He wouldn't express regret for it.

Nor would I make him apologize.

We had our games, and it seemed my devious mate intended to make this one of them.

His multicolored eyes smoldered with wicked promises and duplicitous deeds. Nothing that would hurt me. Just things that would entice me to punish him in sensual ways.

"What did you think of our welcoming ceremony?" I asked conversationally, my gaze running over the defined lines of his muscular form.

He was exquisitely beautiful in a way that almost hurt my soul. And he knew it, too.

"Very telling," he replied in a melodic tone. "Although, I'm disappointed that we didn't stay to watch them all interact. I would have enjoyed observing the seduction games between the Hell Fae and their potential mates."

"Hmm, that's exactly why we left." Well, that and I had no interest in the festivities that followed my opening ceremony.

The girls weren't mine to court or to fuck. Nor did I have any interest in learning more about them. They were here to appease my men, not me. Which was why I'd left a few generals behind to supervise the interactions. They'd keep the girls and my men in line. And my Commander would ensure that everything ran smoothly as well.

Meanwhile, I'd handle my errant mate.

I moved toward Melek with purpose, my palm wrapping around the back of his neck to pull him into a kiss. His lips were soft beneath mine, yielding, and yet deviously curled at the same time.

Mmm, Melek adored pushing boundaries, and he'd done exactly that when he'd given the captive that talisman.

"I think you would have been bored within minutes," I whispered against his mouth. "Which is why you're already mostly naked and trying to entice me to fuck you in the shower."

"Is that what I'm doing?" he asked just as softly.

"You're playing."

"Am I?"

"You are," I promised, my mouth gliding across his cheek to his ear. "Check my pocket."

"Which one?"

"You know which one," I replied, nibbling his

earlobe. He'd be able to sense the charm's energy because it was riddled with his signature as the item's creator.

His palm skimmed my groin, the touch knowing and purposeful. "I'd much rather…" He trailed off as he drew the zipper of my dress pants down, his fingers tracking along the seam to find me bare beneath the fabric of my slacks.

"You can't distract me," I warned him.

"I think I can," he countered, grazing my skin on his way back up to unfasten my belt.

I grinned, allowing him to tease. It would make pushing him to his knees so much more fun in a few minutes. "Why did you give her the talisman?" I asked him softly.

"What talisman?" he asked, his tone so angelically innocent that I almost couldn't detect his fall from grace. My Virtuous Prince still possessed all the powers of his birthright, hence the charm he'd created for the bride candidate.

"Why her?" I pressed as he finished removing my belt.

"She's pretty," he murmured. "And feisty, too. Did you know she actually presented somewhat of a challenge for your Warden to capture?"

I considered the question and recalled all the reports Ajax had provided during the recruitment phase of our project. "She's the one he had to go after himself."

"Yes."

"I see." I supposed that did make her somewhat unique since all the others were caught successfully on one visit. I pulled my lips away from his ear, curious to read his expression. "What makes her different?"

Melek's gaze glittered as he popped open the button on my pants. "I have no idea."

"Liar," I accused, the word leaving my mouth on a sensual taunt more than a harsh tone.

"Not entirely a lie," he promised, pushing the fabric from my hips and gently down my thighs. "I have yet to discover exactly what makes her unique. But I want her."

"Do you?" I cocked my head to the side, causing my long hair to fall like a dark curtain around my face.

"I do." He went to his knees to finish removing the fabric from my legs. He also pulled off my shoes and socks in the process, giving him a false glow of servitude from my angle above him.

"As a bride or a pet?" I wondered aloud.

"Oh, definitely a pet." He leaned forward to place a kiss on the crown of my cock, my shaft swelling both at the sight of him on his knees and the sensuality of his movements.

His tongue darted out to lick the underside of my head, making me growl low in my throat.

"I think she would be very pretty between us, my lord," he hummed before standing once more. Then he opened his hand to reveal the charm he'd taken from my pocket while disrobing me. "Which is why I'd very much like her to survive."

I caught his wrist, bringing his hand up to my mouth to sharply nibble his palm. "You know how I feel about cheating, little prince."

His irises smoldered in response, his own arousal tenting the towel around his hips. "You said gifts were allowed."

"After the opening ceremony."

He shook his head. "No, my lord. You said gifts were allowed *during* the opening ceremony. And so I gave her one to wear *during* the ceremony."

With anyone else, I would have been irritated by his clever maneuvering around my rules.

But Melek wasn't anyone else.

Melek was *mine*.

"Then I suppose I will need to be clearer going forward," I murmured, releasing his wrist to grab the back of his neck again. "No more gifts."

He arched a brow. "No gifts at all?" He pouted a little, his full bottom lip a delectable distraction that called to my baser instincts. "That hardly seems fair, my lord. She's already at a disadvantage now that you've put her in Ajax's prison. Surely I should be allowed to show favor in some way. There is nothing in the rules that says I'm not allowed to court a captive."

"I wasn't aware you desired a bride." And I wasn't sure how I felt about it. While I was bonded to both Melek and Azazel, Melek was my only lover. Just as I was his only lover. "Have you grown tired of our arrangement?" It wasn't a question voiced from jealousy so much as curiosity. We'd been together for thousands of years. Perhaps he yearned for change, even if temporary.

"Our arrangement will keep me satisfied for eternity," he vowed, his expression turning uncharacteristically serious. "You will always be my king, Ty. I love you with every breath."

"And I love you," I replied, pressing my forehead to his. "Which is why I would give you anything you crave, including the captive."

I would drag her up here right now if it meant satisfying my mate. But I knew he didn't work like that. He would prefer a game. One she would either pass or fail, and only then would he decide how to proceed with her. The fact that he wanted to play with her, however, spoke volumes about her potential. Because Melek hadn't shown interest in anyone in thousands of years.

Anyone other than me, anyway.

"I'm interested," he confided softly. "But I don't know how I want to proceed with her yet, only that I would prefer she remain alive."

"I see." I lessened my hold on his neck and lifted my forehead from his. "Then I won't take away her right to gifts, but they should be within reason, Melek. She needs to be able to prove herself."

"And didn't she?" he countered. "That talisman is only a gift of minor power. Her ability to use it to break through your mind control tonight showcases a rare talent, one the diamond simply amplified. Nothing more. Nothing less."

I took the charm from him and studied it, determining that he was right. Except for one minor detail. "To use this would require knowledge of ancient spells."

His lips curled. "I have no idea where she would learn such things."

"Oh, I think I have a good idea of who might have given her a nudge," I drawled, narrowing my gaze at him.

He blinked innocent eyes at me. "I would never do that."

"You absolutely would do that." But I wasn't going to press it. If he'd chosen a pet he wanted to toy with, I'd allow it within reason. "No more physical gifts." It was purposefully worded. Because we both knew words could be just as powerful, if not more powerful, than items.

"No more physical gifts," he repeated.

"From now through the Nightmare Fae Trials," I clarified, knowing he'd find some way around my words if I wasn't specific.

"All right," he agreed. "Unless it's food."

My eyebrows lifted. "You're negotiating with me? Over a captive?"

"I like her," he replied, his palm circling around the base of my cock to give me a firm stroke. "And I'm willing to deal, Ty. In her favor."

Fuck, those were intoxicating words to hear from his tongue, and the twinkle in his gaze told me he knew it, too.

Devious prince, I thought, moaning inside as he gave me another languid caress with his hot palm.

"No physical gifts other than sustenance," he reiterated as his opposite hand came up to begin unbuttoning my dress shirt. "Through the Nightmare Fae Trials."

"In return for?" I prompted, his breath hot on my sternum as his tongue traced his fingers down the center of my torso.

The fabric fell from my shoulders seconds later, his movements quick and skilled and so fucking perfect. I threaded my fingers through his long hair, wrapping his thick strands into a fist as he trailed kisses down my body. He went to his knees again, his wicked mouth nibbling my hip bone while he gazed up at me with dark intent in his expression. "Name your price, my lord."

Dealing with Melek was always a risk. He knew exactly how to play my body, to draw out my desires and needs, and frequently navigated me into a position where he could easily win what he wanted from me at the lowest price imaginable.

But this was why I considered him mine.

I liked that he played these games. I loved that he knew how to draw out the best bargain with just a few licks and bites. And I fucking adored the way he looked up at me now, his body in a position of worship and his features filled with licentious purpose.

He loved deals just as much as I did. Particularly, deals

that ended with him in this position with my hard cock only inches from his mouth.

"Suck me off," I demanded. "Then I'm taking your ass."

His irises glittered. "For how many nights?"

Now it was my turn to smile because that question was proof of how well he knew me. "Seven."

"Consider it a deal, my lord," he replied, his lips moving to my crown. "Our bargain begins now."

CAMI

I RELAXED ON THE GROUND, my legs limp and my arms loose at my sides.

Focus, I told myself. *Inhale. Exhale.*

The scents in the air reminded me of a barn, only tinted with a sulfuric undertone that made me want to gag. These cages had clearly been used to hold more of those creatures from the other side. But they'd been revamped to include some elegant furnishings and the ratty rug beneath me.

After the gargoyle's subtle warning, I knew better than to touch the fancy couch or footstools. I could almost taste the scent of magic surrounding them, too. But I wasn't sure if that was real or just my imagination.

The hours passing me by in this cell were beginning to mess with my head.

Ajax had left shortly after his hypnotic buddy had disappeared. The sexy, dark-haired fae had remained nameless during our interaction, yet I'd fallen deeply into his swirling violet gaze, my mind melting beneath a wave of need unlike any I'd ever experienced. Then he'd snapped me out of it with a sharp yank of the chain from my neck.

I touched my throat, recalling his touch there and the way it had made me feel.

Dangerous, I decided. *That male is* very *dangerous.*

I couldn't tell what kind of fae he was either. Some sort of mix, which I supposed made him a Hell Fae. But I'd sensed an animal within him, perhaps because of the predatory way he'd watched me with those eerily beautiful eyes.

Stop thinking about him, I commanded, trying to focus again on my breathing.

I needed to sleep or rest. Otherwise, I wouldn't be able to fight whatever came next.

However, the stomping of shoes nearby told me my time for rejuvenating myself was done. Without a window, I couldn't say what time it was or if a full afternoon of rest had even passed.

It could have been ten minutes since Ajax had left, or a few hours, or a day, and I really wouldn't know. Not with how time seemed to shift around down here.

Although, my stomach wasn't too heavily complaining, so that implied I hadn't been down here for too long yet.

Metal dragging over concrete sounded, drawing my attention to the shimmering doorway. Ajax hadn't locked me in here the traditional way with an iron door. No. He'd woven some sort of sickly web over the exit as though to dare me to try to flee.

"I'm disappointed," he admitted as he sat on the stool. "I half expected you to at least try to undo my compulsory enchantment."

"Why?" I drawled. "So you could punish me more severely?"

His lips curled. "Exactly."

I rolled my eyes and returned my focus to the charred ceiling above me. They'd redone the cage to boast fake opulence, but they'd forgotten the burn marks over my head. Perhaps they'd been in a hurry to redecorate. Or maybe that was supposed to serve as a clue that nothing down here was what it seemed.

"You're not even going to ask how long you're set to stay down here? Or about the party you're missing upstairs?"

"I find it best not to waste time on questions I won't receive informative answers to," I replied dryly. "Waste of time and breath and all that."

"A fair assessment," he agreed, the chair shifting again and drawing my gaze to where he'd propped his feet up on the web of magic functioning as a door. "That doesn't make it right, though."

I met his flickering blue irises. "You want to talk about the party?"

"No, I definitely don't," he replied. "But I'm going to anyway."

I studied him. "Why?"

"Because it serves as a punishment," he drawled.

"Oh?" That stirred my interest. "You're being punished, too?"

His lips twitched. "Certainly feels like it."

"Doesn't it?" I countered sweetly, giving him my best smile.

His gaze slid down to the neckline of my gown, reminding me that I was wearing a rather revealing dress on the floor. But I didn't bother to shield myself from him. That would display discomfort, which could be translated as a weakness. And I knew better than to appear weak in front of these beings, especially one as powerful as this Midnight Fae.

"Hmm," he hummed, removing his feet from the web and wiping away the magic with a casual flick of his wrist.

I swallowed as he stepped into my cage, the air between us shifting as I realized the very big advantage he had over me.

This was his prison.

I was his captive.

And he had all the control in this situation.

But he doesn't have my dignity, I thought, my teeth clenching.

He pulled his wand from his cloak and muttered a spell I didn't catch, unweaving whatever enchantment he'd cast over the couch, and wandered over to sit down. Then he patted the cushion beside him. "I promise not to bite."

"Famous last words from a vampire," I retorted.

Now he truly smiled. "I can't tell if you have a death wish or if you just don't comprehend your current situation."

I sat up at that, crossed my legs beneath my gown, and faced him. "I'm a captive in a dungeon being guarded by a Midnight Fae who apparently works for Lucifer, the Hell Fae King. And I'm here to fight for my life. If I survive, I'll be rewarded with a Hell Fae mate, or several mates, if I understood the literature correctly, all because my parents —or more accurately, my *father*—made a deal with the literal devil." I arched a brow at him. "Does that answer your inquiry?"

"I didn't ask a question."

"No, I suppose you didn't."

"But yes, it tells me you're entirely competent, which means you have a death wish." His eyes narrowed. "I'd like to know why you court death."

"Having a backbone doesn't mean I want to die," I

retorted. "I'm not a simpering idiot who takes my fate lying down."

He glanced pointedly at the floor and arched a brow. "No?"

"Resting isn't the same as accepting my fate," I informed him dryly. "I will find a way out of this."

That seemed to intrigue him. "How?"

"I don't know yet," I admitted. "Maybe I'll create my own deal with Lucifer."

His eyes lit up at the prospect, and he released a surprised laugh before shaking his head. "You certainly have a high opinion of yourself, Camillia De la Croix. I'll give you that."

"Cami," I corrected him, tired of hearing my full name on his tongue. It sounded too... *intimate*... and I wanted that intimacy to go away. "And it isn't about having a high opinion of myself. It's about being unwilling to accept this situation. They are entirely two separate scenarios, but I wouldn't expect someone like you to understand."

"Someone like me?"

"A blind follower," I replied, waving a hand at him. "I mean, that's why you're here, right? You agree with all this bullshit?"

"Why I'm here is none of your business."

I shrugged, unbothered. "Your reasoning means nothing to me. Your actions say everything I need to know. You're a minion with a desire for power. And you're enjoying wielding it over me now."

"What power am I wielding over you?" he countered. "I've literally left your door open, and I've removed the enchantment from your furniture, yet you choose to remain on the ground."

"Because it's all a power play." And if he thought I didn't see that, then he severely underestimated my intelligence. "You want me to feel indebted to you for releasing the enchantments around my cell, just to put them back in place later to reaffirm my place as a prisoner. It's a boring game, and I'm not interested in playing. So find another captive to fuck with because I'm not your girl. And I *will* find a way out of here. Just wait."

He studied me for a long moment, the lines of his jaw tightening with a severity that chilled the air. "You know nothing about me, Camillia."

"And I would argue that you know nothing about me," I told him, holding his gaze. "You can underestimate me all you want, but I will survive this. And I will not become a bride. I choose my fate, and no one will ever take that away from me."

I uttered the words with a conviction I felt to my very soul. It was key to my survival, imperative to my continued existence, because without it, I'd crumble. And I refused to bow. I refused to submit. I refused to play this fucked-up game.

The blue rim around his pupils smoldered with an emotion I couldn't define. Anger? Sadness? Some mixture of both? I couldn't say, but I sensed the fury vibrating off of him. However, it didn't seem to be directed toward me.

Silence fell between us as he battled with some sort of decision. I could see it playing out through his hypnotic irises, some kind of haunting revelation that he appeared to be chasing through his mind.

Power radiated from him, his Midnight Fae heritage strong and lethal.

There were several types of Midnight Fae, all of them possessing links to different forms of magic. I didn't know much about their respective classifications, but I caught the purple tint circling the tip of his wand. He'd stuck it back into his cloak pocket, just not all the way, and an incantation appeared to be curling around the top of it.

If he noticed, he didn't show it.

Instead, he pegged me with a severe look. "Sometimes we have no control over our fate."

"I refuse to believe that."

He smiled, but it wasn't an expression of joy. "Then you're sadly naïve." He stood, his palms brushing over his thighs as he stepped toward me.

I looked up, maintaining eye contact, determined not to show an ounce of fear.

"What you're missing upstairs is an opportunity to network with the Hell Fae men and garner favor," he murmured. "And by 'favor,' I mean *gifts*. Items to help you survive. Food. Clothing. Water. Because you're about to be dropped into your first trial. A trial in an inhospitable landscape designed to kill you."

He paused to let that sink in.

But I didn't react.

Because being in a new land meant I would be venturing through a portal or some other form of magic. And that magic might provide freedom.

I really need that book to tell me more about portals, I thought. *Too bad it's in my room, not in this cell.*

"Each Hell Fae is allowed to give a candidate of his preference up to three offerings to aid in the captive's journey," Ajax continued, making me wonder what this *journey* would entail. "Without any aid, you will die, Camillia. And unfortunately, you're missing your one and only chance to network upstairs. So not only are you entering the first trial malnourished—because the other females are all being fed as we speak—but you are also entering it without any aid whatsoever."

A chill skated down my spine at how resolutely he spoke, as though my fate had already been decided.

"If there's anything I've learned in life, it's that destiny has a plan for us all. And only the naïve believe there's an alternative." His gaze met mine, an acute sadness lurking in his depths. "I know this because I once tried to alter fate, and the path my alteration created was something far worse. So I sincerely hope you don't make the same mistakes I did. Because even if you do somehow manage to survive, your choices will haunt you for the rest of your life."

With that, he stepped out of my cell and shut the door, locking it with finality, and disappeared down the hall.

I shivered, his words settling like stones in my belly.

It was like he'd walked out of the cage with all my confidence in his hands, leaving me in a puddle of insecurity on the floor.

No food. No water. No help.

And a trial set in inhospitable lands.

Survival was a must. But how could I manage it when all the odds were already stacked against me?

MELEK

I STUDIED Cami through the bars, noting her uncomfortable position on the ground, and frowned. The magic had been removed from the furniture surrounding her, yet she'd chosen the ratty rug.

Hmm.

I couldn't make her a bed—that would be breaking Ty's rules—but I could give her a spell that would allow her to do it herself. Her unique bloodline would allow her to use the ancient tongue. Maybe.

I really wasn't sure. The talisman had amplified her spirit, granting her abilities she probably didn't know she possessed. Without it, I wasn't sure she could access her true soul.

Assuming I was right about her heritage, anyway.

It could all be a clever ruse, one meant to ensnare Ty, and if that was the case, I would kill the girl without a second thought.

But until I determined the truth, I would keep her safe.

With a wave of my hand, I unlatched the door to step inside.

She immediately stirred, her instincts flaring to life in response to my abundance of energy. While I cloaked my essence, some part of her recognized the power within me.

And *that* was what intrigued me most.

Well, and her ability to read *the book.*

I leaned against the wall, waiting for her to wake up, and smiled when her pretty gray eyes landed on me.

"*You,*" she hissed, a low growl in her voice that entertained me immensely. Although, I didn't quite understand the vehemence radiating from her. "I don't want anything to do with you."

My eyebrows lifted. "Well, that is certainly not the reception I had anticipated," I murmured, canting my head. "Can I ask what I've done to earn such a reaction?"

"You're the Hell Fae Prince!" she accused.

Hmm, not quite. But that was a conversation for another day.

"I wasn't aware that my title mattered," I admitted, frowning.

"Of course it fucking matters!"

I tilted my head, taking in her unexplained rage. "Nevertheless, I'm here to continue where we left off." Whispering ancient words, I cast a summoning spell, and the giant law book fell into my hands.

Her eyes flared with shock as I grinned, settling myself onto the couch and cracking the book open.

"Knowledge is technically a gift, but it's not tangible, yes?" I asked, glancing up from the book to meet her confused gaze. "Yes. My thoughts exactly."

"I didn't say anything."

"Then your silence is compliance," I replied softly, flipping a page and pretending to read the contents. It was all for show, of course.

The spells I wished to teach her weren't the words

scrawling across these pages as the book chose what it wanted to display with no real order at all.

Right now it was showing me a summary of ancient events involving the Virtuous Source. I ignored the historical text and focused on what Cami actually needed to know.

"Ah, yes. Here it is," I lied.

I began to recite a passage from memory out loud, giving her the incantations required to create natural shade and another enchantment that would cool her body in the sweltering heat.

"I do hope you're paying attention, Cami," I mused without looking at her. "This is riveting information." And truly, it was, because I'd flipped to a page within the text that talked about the creation of the Hell Fae Source.

How fascinating that you're choosing to show me this now, I thought at the charmed book, curious.

The book wasn't a standard manual with a table of contents. Instead, it showed authorized readers—meaning those with a link to the magical pages—information pertinent to an existing situation. Which was why Cami's ability to see and understand the words had fascinated me so intensely.

This treasured item belonged to Ty. It was spelled to react to his energy signature, and his energy signature alone. I could only read it because I was his mate. Az would also be able to read it.

And, apparently, Cami could as well.

Hence, my intrigue.

I glanced up to find her glaring at me. "Do you not approve of the spells?" I asked conversationally.

"Did you give me the cupcake and say it was from the Warden?"

My lips curled at her direct change in subject. "Why would you think that?"

"Because he didn't seem to know what I was talking about."

"Ah," I hummed. "Well." I shrugged. "It doesn't matter much now, does it?"

"Your charm is the reason I'm in this cell."

"Hmm, no," I said thoughtfully. "You using my charm is why you're in this cell. That was your decision to make, not mine."

Her expression told me she did not like that answer. "Why are you here?"

I studied her, questioning her ability to hear. "I'm providing you with the *gift* of knowledge. So I do hope you've been listening."

She muttered two spells back at me, causing the air to tingle a little with magic. "I'm listening," she added. "Just not sure I should trust anything you say."

"And yet, you can probably sense the correctness of my words now, yes?" I asked her, noting the sweat along her brow and her visible sigh. "Feeling a bit cooler, hmm?"

She opened her mouth like she wanted to say something, but paused before any voice could escape, and instead furrowed her brow.

"Yes, I can see that you do." I flipped the page, noting the continued history lesson about Ty creating the Hell Fae Source from his Virtuous heritage, and skimmed the page while saying unrelated words out loud about other spells regarding atmospheric items.

Technically, the limit was three gifts per captive.

But that only applied to tangible gifts, such as food—which Ty had said I could give. He'd never said anything about knowledge.

So I spent the next hour pretending to read while I

gave her all the magical tools she would need to survive her opening game.

"Ah, and this section is about creation," I said, partially telling the truth since it was still showing me notes about the Hell Fae Source. But instead, I told her the enchantments that could turn rocks into edible items and lava into drinkable water. Then I hummed a few additional items about morphing sand or other items into weapons.

By the time I finished, she was watching me seriously, her gaze telling me she'd not only heard every word but had also committed them to memory.

Smart little angel, I thought, pleased.

"What kind of fae are you?" she demanded after a beat of silence. "Because you're not a Hell Fae."

"I'm not?" I asked innocently.

"No. You're too… too… *ethereal*."

Hmm, an apt definition. "Well, once upon a time, we were all ethereal. So I suppose that makes sense, doesn't it?"

"That doesn't answer my question."

"No, I suppose not," I admitted, pushing up off the couch. "Alas, our time is quickly coming to an end, and I still have another… non-gift… to give you."

"More spells?"

"Not quite," I murmured. "Stand, please. I would prefer not to kneel." I only did that for Ty.

She swallowed, appearing uncertain.

"I'm not going to hurt you," I promised.

"Like your cupcake didn't hurt me?" she countered.

"Did it hurt you, or did it ensure you restored all your energy reserves in a peaceful manner?"

Her eyes narrowed. "I prefer to sleep willingly, not by force."

"Duly noted," I drawled. "Stand, please. I won't ask

again." And if she refused, then I would be forced to leave without offering her the kiss of my protection.

Ty would not be happy with my decision to do this, but it was the only way to guarantee she survived the opening games. It also served as a way for me to test a theory.

Once our souls brushed, I'd know for certain if she was what I suspected her to be. And if I proved myself right—which I strongly expected to happen—it would be best to keep her as close as possible. What better way to do that than to engage in a first-level bond?

She wins by accepting my protection.

I win by having access to her spirit, and through it, her intentions.

Ty would call it a reckless decision and punish me for it.

But I considered it pragmatic.

And I'd enjoy his brand of retribution, too.

Wins all around, in my opinion.

"Cami?" I prompted, arching a brow. I'd said I wouldn't repeat myself, and I'd meant it.

She chewed her lip, a gesture that I found adorable, before she finally decided to comply with my request by gracefully rising to her feet.

"Very good," I said, taking a moment to admire her form in this scrap of a dress.

Stunning was an understatement.

Clearing my throat, I refocused on her beautiful face. "I would like to give you a vow of protection. Will you allow it?"

Her eyes narrowed. "Why?"

"I think the purpose of the gift is implied by its name."

"No. *Why* would you protect me?"

I let a slow smile stretch across my face. "Because you're down here and the other candidates are up there, receiving their own gifts and vows of protection." Well, not the latter. But she didn't need to know that.

"What do you want from me in exchange?" she asked warily.

Clever indeed. She was already learning her way around Hell, and she'd only been here a few days.

"A kiss." I extended a hand. "Just on the cheek will do."

She still didn't seem convinced.

"I don't think you understand what it is I'm offering," I said softly. "This vow will allow you to call on me whenever you need aid. Trust me, in the Nightmare Fae Trials, you'll need my help."

"You've just armed me with spells to survive," she countered.

I slipped my fingers through hers, tugging her closer to me. She didn't pull away. "What do you have to lose by allowing me to protect you?"

"My dignity?"

I smiled. "I assure you that your dignity will very much remain intact."

I could tell she didn't quite believe me, but she wasn't resisting, either.

This would only work if she had a heritage that rivaled my own, something I had suspected the moment it'd become clear that she could read Ty's book.

Something Ty would very much expect me to tell him.

But we had a game to play, and I had two more gifts I could still bestow on this little treasure, as knowledge only counted as one.

A kiss of protection couldn't be considered a gift. A promise, yes, but not a physical gift. I was well within my bounds.

Drawing her closer, she held her breath as I whispered the vow in the ancient tongue. "*Nadeehar Laki*

Nafsi." Then I grazed my lips across the high arch of her cheekbone.

She shivered as magic ignited between us, the opening of the spell preparing to link our souls.

Similar to a Midnight Fae's bite, this would be a permanent bond, with the main difference being that it required mutual agreement.

"You'll have to repeat—" I began, only to go rigid in surprise when she reiterated my words with exact precision, her lips sealing the vow as she pressed them against my cheek.

The fires that stirred in my belly demanded that we do that again, except with tongue and skin. Just not yet. Not until she fully understood.

I shivered as the bond snapped into place, stirring a sharp inhale from deep within as her soul blossomed with mine, proving everything I'd already suspected to be true.

She's of ancient blood, I marveled. *I knew I felt that magic lurking in her soul, and now we're linked. Which means her spirit is mine to explore.*

Of course, that also meant my soul belonged to her as well. Something that might prove problematic later. But we would cross that bridge should it ever arrive.

This would allow me to keep a better eye on her, both to protect her and to ensure protection of Ty.

Because if Cami betrayed me—or if I found out she intended to hurt Ty in any way—I'd kill her. It would hurt a little to do it since we were bonded now, but I would accept the pain as my due for establishing an unworthy connection.

Ty wouldn't be happy, and he'd be able to feel this change in me immediately.

But it couldn't be undone now.

The options were to either ensure she survived or kill

her. And I wasn't going to let him do the latter without just cause.

I always acted instinctively. This was no different.

My soul had told me this was right, so I'd reacted.

Ty would understand. And if he didn't, I would drown him in my logic until he agreed.

Or make him a deal he couldn't refuse.

Just the thought had my lips curling in excitement. *Yes. A deal is the way to my mate's heart.*

I released Cami and she curled into herself, blinking hard as her eyes flashed with the golden echo of my soul. "What... *was* that?"

Instead of answering, I brushed another kiss against her cheek. "Good night, little angel."

I backed away, leaving Cami standing on her dirty rug.

"Oh, and remember that creation spell I taught you. Consider using it to indulge in another cupcake. You deserve it." I winked and locked the cell door behind me.

Then I walked out of eyesight.

And engaged my wings.

TYPHOS

My eyes flew open, the power pulsing through my heart ancient and overwhelming.

Melek.

I sat up to find our bed empty, the silky black sheets twisting against my hips.

What have you done? I demanded, instantly initiating my link to him.

Shh, he hushed. *I'll be back to explain soon.*

Those were not comforting words, not when I could *feel* his bond inside me pulsing with a new soul link. *Tell me you didn't bond that female.*

You said no tangible gifts, he returned softly. *This is hardly tangible, my lord.*

Melek, I growled, rolling out of the bed to find my pants. My fucking mate was always impulsive. But to mate a captive? *I thought you wanted a pet, not a bride.*

He didn't reply.

Something that only infuriated me more.

I'm going to make you fucking bleed, I threatened.

I know. He sounded almost excited by the prospect.

Fucking masochist. I ran my fingers through my hair, the edges flirting with my shoulders. This… this wasn't just unexpected; it was *unprecedented*.

Virtuous bonds were for life, even at the Spiritual Vow level.

The ancient incantation served as a binding contract, displaying the promise of intention. Initial power exchange would occur—which was probably what had woken me up. It wouldn't be overwhelming or even all that noticeable to the candidate, but I'd felt the disturbance to the source.

Because Melek was mated to me.

His soul was mine.

Just as mine was his.

And he'd tainted that bond with this new link.

Would he continue into the Blood Vow level? And later initiate the third and final Mate Vow level?

Ty? Az whispered into my mind. *Everything all right?*

No, I snapped, heading toward the kitchen off the seating room. I needed a fucking drink.

Are you in your quarters? Az asked.

Yes.

I'm on my way.

I didn't reply, instead opting to pour myself the strongest liquor I could find in the cabinet.

Maybe Az could help me beat some sense into Melek.

Not that it mattered now. The devious little prince had already sealed his fate.

By taking a fucking captive as a mate.

How could you tie your soul to her? I demanded, reigniting my mental link to Melek as I took several swallows of the burning liquid. *You don't even know the girl!*

I know enough, he replied cryptically. *Perhaps you should consider this from a different angle, my lord. Ask yourself* how *I was able to mate her.* The door to our suite opened on the tail end of his statement, his power announcing his presence before he drifted into our living area.

Not walked.

But *drifted*.

Because he was in an ethereal state.

"That's not going to save you," I told him, my eyes narrowed.

"I didn't use my wings to hide." He turned corporeal again. "It was faster to fly than to walk. And you need to calm down."

There were very few fae who could provoke me to violence.

Melek was one of them.

Especially when he engaged in dangerous games that endangered his life. "Your spirit is tied to hers," I hissed, the alcohol doing absolutely nothing to cool me down. "What if she dies tomorrow?"

"Then I'll be in a lot of pain." He shrugged. "And I suspect you won't be very willing to heal me, which is fine. But again, I suggest you consider *how* I was able to bond her."

"Bond who?" Az asked as he materialized in the middle of our suite, having opted to also fly up here via his Phoenix energy. Both males possessed wings of a sort. My shoulder blades tingled with the memory of my own, my feathers long gone.

Sizzled to ashes. Burned. Destroyed. Fallen.

But that pain didn't compare to what I felt now.

A pain I allowed Melek to feel. A pain I shoved at him through the link. A pain underlined by fear of what this could do to him.

"Ty," Melek said with a sigh. "It's fine."

"It's not fucking fine." I threw my empty glass at the

wall, not at all satisfied by the shattering noise it left behind.

"What the hell happened?" Az demanded, black energy pulsating around him as though ready to kill whoever posed a threat.

If only it were that simple. Not even a Paradox Fae could go back in time to fix this. Virtuous bonds surpassed everything in existence for a bloody reason.

"Melek took a new mate," I explained, barely able to grate out the words. Because never in my wildest imagination would I have expected this from him. "One he claimed to only want as a pet."

"A very powerful and useful pet," he clarified. "Because I was able to link my soul to hers." His multicolored eyes held a note of severity that demanded my focus. "Think beyond the rage, my love. Consider why and *how* I could do that."

I ran a hand over my face, my desire to bend him over the bed and fuck him into submission riding me hard.

Not just because I wanted to punish him, but because I wanted to reclaim him. *Mine. Melek is mine.* And I didn't want to share him in this way.

No. It wasn't even that.

Sharing had never really been an issue between us, more of a lack of interest in others.

It was his soul I worried about. His soul that would fracture if something happened to the girl. Which made me want to pluck her out of that cell and put her in a glass cage for the rest of her existence, just to keep Melek's spirit safe from potential injury.

"Ty." He stepped toward me, and I took a step backward, conflicted.

"When I bonded Az, we spoke about it," I told him. "You *agreed* to it."

And it wasn't a sexual bonding so much as a familial one.

I didn't necessarily see Az as a brother, but rather, as a friend I needed to protect. He was too powerful, his energy threatening to consume him. Linking him to me provided him with an outlet for some of that all-consuming power.

But I'd spoken to Melek about it before engaging in the bonds.

Fuck, he'd even been there for each level.

"You just linked your soul with this captive without any regard for me. For *us*."

Melek's irises flared to life with raw power. "Everything I do is for *you*, Typhos. *Everything*." He went ethereal again. "I understand you're upset. When you've overcome this tantrum, let me know. And we'll talk."

He engaged his power and winked out of existence, eliciting a flurry of curses from my lips.

He dared be mad at *me*? He was the one who had acted recklessly, putting himself at risk. A risk I refused to accept. A risk that made my heart hurt just thinking about what it might do to him.

I gaped at the space he'd just occupied. *Melek.*

No answer.

Not even a whisper of a sound.

Because he'd blocked me from his mind.

Another growl built in my chest, the source pulsing in my veins. I grabbed onto a random chair in the lounge and closed my eyes, trying futilely to calm my rapidly beating heart.

"Use me," Az said softly. "I can take it."

"No," I gritted out.

I would not shove this angry energy into him, not when he needed me to ground him. I'd been his anchor for over a millennium.

Admittedly, it'd become harder as my own powers continued to grow, but I could handle it. I could handle *this*. I just had to breathe and shove it back down. Feed it back into the source. Let it swirl and burn.

I swallowed, my muscles tensing as flames threatened to engulf me.

Contain it, I told myself. *Just gently spin it back into the web.*

My teeth clenched as I focused on weaving the abundance of hot energy back into the Hell Fae Source. It gave me the distraction I needed, calming my racing heart and allowing me to breathe.

Melek took a mate.

A female.

Via Virtuous means.

That shouldn't be possible.

"Consider how I was able to bond her."

His words whispered through my mind, my ire weakening in favor of the puzzle unfolding inside my head. I slowly opened my eyes, the room coming back into focus.

Az was no longer standing near me.

He sat in a lounge chair, drinking his own crystal tumbler of auburn liquid. Some sort of hellsprite, I imagined.

The glass I'd shattered was nowhere to be seen, suggesting he'd cleaned it up.

"You didn't have to do that," I said, my voice gruff.

His lips curled, his Phoenix staring back at me through his darkened irises. "It's not the worst of your messes I've cleaned up."

I grunted and walked over to fix myself yet another drink.

Then I took the chair opposite him.

We drank in silence for several long minutes before he asked, "Was it Camillia De la Croix?"

"Is that her name?" I hadn't even bothered to gather that information from Melek. "The girl with the necklace? Candidate Sixty-Six?"

He dipped his chin. "Camillia De la Croix." He took another sip, then set his glass to the side. "She's quite spirited. Ajax seems rather taken with her, too."

My eyebrows lifted. "What is with this female? Does she have a magic pussy?"

Az smirked. "I'm not sure, but if you'd like someone to take it for a trial run, I volunteer."

"Fuck. You, too?" I blew out my breath and drew my fingers through my hair. This female had earned the attention of both my mates and my Warden. That couldn't be a coincidence. I put my drink on the table beside me and held out my palm. "*Vita. Ven ad me.*"

Az said nothing, aware of what I wanted.

It took a few minutes—longer than expected—but my book finally appeared, the familiar leather putting me instantly at ease. "Show me everything about Camillia De la Croix," I commanded.

The pages flew open to reveal the contract between me and her father, a Hell Fae I barely knew. "Pierre De la Croix, mated to a human, desired freedom from the soul payments he owed for my continued protection."

All fae under my rule gave back to the Hell Fae Source via soul payments—simply energy exchanges that tied them to me and the source, allowing the underworld to flourish with renewed energy.

"Find him for me," I said, looking up at Az. "I think we need to have a discussion about his *charming* daughter." Because I didn't trust her in the slightest.

Melek hadn't been drawn to anyone other than me for thousands of years, yet this woman had seduced him into a bond within days.

No. Something was very wrong here.

Az nodded. "Would you like him brought here to the paradigm?"

"Here," I said.

"Understood." He picked up his glass to finish the contents, then wandered over to put the glass in the sink. "I'll likely be gone for tomorrow's trial."

"I'll supervise the proceedings," I told him. It would give me an excuse to observe this little captive who had captivated my men.

Az dipped his chin again. "Speak soon." He phased once more, his dark energy a kiss to my senses.

Thank you, I whispered into his mind.

No gratitude needed, he replied. *I'll return as soon as I find him.*

I almost thanked him again but hummed back in agreement instead.

Then I refocused on the item sprawled out in my lap. "Vita," I murmured, using my name for the book. "What else can you tell me about Camillia De la Croix?" The contract was useful, but I wanted her full file.

Except the book flipped to a page that had nothing to do with the candidate.

I frowned at it. "Why are you showing me this?" Of all the texts documenting my history, it selected these details? "I don't want to walk down memory lane, Vita. I want to know more about the girl."

The pages bristled, magic whispering in the air as Vita denied my request. I flipped the paper in protest, but it only revealed the same event.

The day of my Fall.

The day everyone had turned their backs on me, including Melek.

Only, Melek hadn't actually betrayed me. He'd pretended to play along to *save* me.

My mate. My beautiful prince. My love.

I'd been so broken, so *lost* without him. Then he'd appeared in a flurry of blinding light, livid that I'd doubted him and his love.

"Everything I do is for you, Typhos. Everything."

He'd spoken those words to me that day.

Just as he'd done today.

Fuck.

I ran my hand over my face.

"So you're on his side, hmm?" I asked Vita, shaking my head. "Of course you're on his side." The book had always favored him. Oh, the text belonged to me. But he'd somehow won over the intangible entity that controlled the pages.

I relaxed into the chair on an exhale that caused the pages to fly once more, depicting the events of the Hell Fae Source creation.

"I already know all this," I told the book. "I was there."

A flurry of names scrawled across the page, all ones I never wanted to see or think about again. But I read each one, committing my hatred for them to memory.

The fae who had forced my Fall.

The ones who had betrayed me.

The *female* who had initiated it all.

I narrowed my gaze. *Vivaxia.*

Melek had pretended to choose her over me, breaking my soul and my heart on the same day the others had cast me out of the heavens.

But he'd played her.

He'd *killed* her.

For me.

That had been the source of the blinding light,

followed by his pain over finding me shattered on the ground. *Wingless. Broken. Destroyed. And enraged.*

So. Fucking. Enraged.

I'd pulled the power into me, absorbing it, morphing it, *re-creating* it.

And all of fae kind had changed.

I flipped through several pages outlining the impact and the shifting of the faedoms, the creations, the aftermath, the insanity and splicing of power that had followed.

Then I sighed and closed the book. This wasn't about Camillia. This was about Melek.

"You're telling me to trust him," I surmised, aware of tonight's lesson. The book was reminding me of our sacrifices and everything Melek had done for me.

I'd lost my faith in him once, and we'd both almost died as a result.

Vita was telling me not to make that mistake again now.

I had no idea why he'd chosen to mate this girl, but Melek never did anything without a reason.

However, if I found out she'd tricked him in some way, I would put her in a magically induced coma to keep her alive, and lock her in a fucking box.

Just to protect his soul and heart.

No one harmed those I considered to be mine.

I love you, little prince, I whispered to Melek. *I'm sorry.*

He didn't reply.

Because he still had me locked out of his mind.

He'd let me back in once he realized I'd "overcome my tantrum." Until then, he'd give me space.

And I'd grant him the same in kind.

"You may go," I told Vita.

The book disappeared in a blink, returning to a place

that made it feel safe—which was typically in a library somewhere. It often ventured through the realms to hide in plain sight. If someone else found it, the pages would reveal nonsense. Only I could truly read it.

Well, Melek and Az could technically read it, too. Since they were bonded to me. But Vita was mine. My history. My deals. My magic. And she protected me just as much as she protected herself.

Sighing, I cleaned up the drinks in the sink, then went back to bed to wait for my devious prince.

Ajax

I GLARED up at the ceiling, unable to sleep.

"I choose my fate, and no one will ever take that away from me."

Camillia's words played through my thoughts on repeat, her conviction one I felt to my very soul. She truly believed that she was in control of this situation, that she could find a way out.

I both pitied her and envied her. Pitied because I knew her odds of success weren't favorable, if they even existed at all. Envied because I used to feel the same way. I used to believe in controlling my own destiny, too.

Just like Emelyn.

She'd been betrothed to a Midnight Fae Prince.

Yet she'd chosen me over him. She had refused to conform to society's expectations of her. Which had led to her death sentence.

Not because she'd desired me.

But because she'd defied the Elders in her beliefs that Quandary Bloods shouldn't be rounded up and killed at random.

A rebel until the end.

Just like Camillia, I thought, sighing. *Fucking Camillia.*

I couldn't shove the woman from my mind. She was giving me a damn headache and holding my dreams hostage.

"Flames," I muttered, sitting up and rubbing my eyes.

Az had never returned after the party, probably because his other duties had held him back.

Maybe I'd go find him now and try sparring again. Because I really needed to hit something. *Or fuck someone*, I mused darkly as I rolled out of bed to find some appropriate fighting clothes.

I'd chosen to sleep in my forest cabin rather than in my dungeon quarters tonight, mostly to get away from Camillia. Yet she'd followed me here like some dark phantom I couldn't de-spell.

A portal allowed me to venture between the two residences with ease, so I spent most nights here and relied on my spell alarms to let me know if anyone acted out in their cells.

Things were usually quiet with the magic holding everyone captive.

But I wouldn't put it past Camillia to test those limits, just like she'd done her first night here.

Maybe I should have stayed underground.

However, I preferred this home on the edge of the paradigm. It allowed me to visit Zen—the creator of this little kingdom—as I wished. She reminded me a bit of home with her mixed Fortune Fae and Midnight Fae heritage. She also happened to be my oldest friend's grandmother. So she sort of felt like family, but without all the emotional strings.

That didn't stop her from trying to mother me from time to time.

Hence the fresh batch of cookies on my table.

I stole one with a whispered "Thank you" on my way out the door. She wouldn't be able to hear the words, but she likely had *seen* them.

Her powers sort of freaked me out.

Just like Shade's, her grandson.

I really needed to call him soon just to check in. Ever since mating the Midnight Fae Queen, Aflora, he'd been a bit busy. What with becoming a dad and all. His little hellion of a daughter had him wrapped around her tricky little fingers. An adorable sight, yet it left me feeling uncomfortable.

Because it was the life I'd once craved.

A life I would never have.

Still, I owed him a visit. If anything, just to amuse myself by watching his creation wreak havoc everywhere she went. As the daughter of his and Aflora's bloodlines, she was immensely powerful and difficult to control.

The perfect little abomination.

Even Lucifer had liked her when he'd met her, and Lucifer did not enjoy children. At all.

I nibbled on my cookie as I walked through the forest, deciding to take the long way back to the campus part of the paradigm.

Zen had originally created this place to protect the Quandary Bloods—a Midnight Fae bloodline that had been hunted and killed by Constantine Nacht for being "too powerful." They were Midnight Fae who could reroute power to the source, which meant they could easily unseat him from his position as king. He'd called them abominations, saying they needed to be exterminated. And enough Midnight Fae had agreed to lead to mass genocide.

But Zen, being part Fortune Fae, had foreseen the chaos.

And she had struck a deal with the Hell Fae King.

One that had allowed her to create a paradigm—a magical world invisible to those who weren't invited to see it—within his Hell Fae Realm.

In return, she'd agreed to let him use it as needed when the time came.

That time was now.

The Quandary Bloods had been allowed to rejoin the Midnight Fae Realm, thanks to Queen Aflora and her mates, and Lucifer was finally ready for his bride trials.

Zen likely knew that had been his goal all along, which explained her lack of a reaction to the events occurring within her paradigm. But I knew deep down she disapproved.

Just as she disapproved of my helping Lucifer.

Yet she never voiced that disapproval out loud. Instead, she spoke in riddles. Similar to Shade. It was no wonder the two were related.

I peeked up at the starry night through the bare tree branches as I moved. It wasn't technically real so much as an alternate reality. But it *felt* real. And it truly did remind me of the Midnight Fae Academy grounds.

I didn't possess the power required to build a paradigm.

It was intricate and needed an abundance of energy from the source. Because it functioned as a world within a world.

Maybe one day I would grow enough to be able to harness that sort of ability, but I doubted it.

My Death Blood soul flourished with deadly energy, not life energy.

The campus gates came into view after about fifteen minutes of walking. Az's home lurked on the outskirts closer to this paradigm's version of a LethaForest.

Because of course he chose to live near the trees littered with lethal creatures who adored killing.

He wasn't quite inside the burning thwomp line, just close enough to feel the heat when their branches exploded in fire.

It probably reminded him of his Black Phoenix side.

I walked along the wall of hissing snake-vines, my wand tucked casually into my pocket. I'd chosen just a pair of black pants and a matching T-shirt. No cloak. So the snake-vines could see the tip of my wand, which was the cause of their agitated reaction.

"You know I'll only use it if you try to bite me," I told them conversationally. "Calm down."

"Maybe it's a bite they desire," a voice said from the sky as Melek floated down on a pair of magnificent white wings.

I arched a brow, surprised to see him in his angelic form. I wasn't sure what type of fae he was, but I knew it wasn't a Hell Fae. Something uniquely other. An abomination that Lucifer had saved long ago.

"Out for an evening flight?" I asked, taking in the sight of his pristine plumes. They made him appear even more innocent than usual, for obvious reasons.

But I knew it was all a lie.

There was nothing "innocent" about Melek.

His expression gave nothing away, as per usual. "An evening flight requires more than a mile-high sky, so no, not really."

"Maybe Zen can extend it for you."

He lifted a shoulder. "Zenaida has other concerns. I can also shift to another realm to explore."

"And is that what you're on your way to do?"

He considered for a moment. "No. I think I'll stay for now. Especially with Az having left to run an errand."

My lips curled down. "Az left?"

"Ty needed a favor." He didn't elaborate. Which meant he didn't want me to know what favor Ty had requested of Az.

And Az wouldn't tell me either.

Az and I might fight and fuck, but we weren't bonded. Not like him and Lucifer. It left me firmly on the outside of their little trio, something I preferred, as I didn't want to tie myself to anyone. Knowing Az would pick Lucifer over me also helped me put our relationship in perspective and keep my distance.

"I see." I tucked my hands into my pockets and glanced up at the moon again, the orb always in the sky here, day or night. "I was hoping to spar. But I guess that'll have to wait."

Because I wasn't about to try fighting with Melek.

Not only was he way too powerful, but he was also mated to the literal king of Hell. Only someone with a death wish would touch the famous Hell Fae Prince.

"Maybe the little rebel in your dungeon will spar with you?" he suggested, his multicolored irises twinkling beneath the moonlight. "Of course, she may be too sore for it, what with having to sleep on a ratty rug and all."

I narrowed my gaze. "Have you been wandering my dungeon?"

He grinned. "Have I?" He shrugged, not bothering to confirm or deny it. But that was answer enough—he'd been playing in the cells.

"Did you do something to Camillia?" I demanded. Because it would be just like Melek to cast some sort of spell to fuck with her in some way. He didn't view the candidates as potential brides so much as pets to amuse him, and Camillia would absolutely be an ideal prospect for his amusement.

"You're asking all the wrong questions, Warden." He cocked his head, his wings disappearing as he turned corporeal once more. "But your concern for her is intriguing. Has this *Camillia*, as you call her, caught your fancy?"

"I'm not interested in claiming a bride," I countered. "That's why I'm the Warden."

"But that's not what I asked at all, is it?" His lips curled into a breathtaking grin, one that belied the sinister energy beneath his skin. This male thrived on tricks and games, something I'd learned early on in our acquaintance when he'd let a series of Nightmare Fae loose from their cells just to see how I would catch them.

So yeah, he knew all about my dungeon.

Which meant he'd very likely been down to see Camillia.

Fuck.

I should have slept down there—if anything, just to ensure she remained untouched.

With a growl, I started in the opposite direction of Az's home, heading toward the portal in the LethaForest that I could use to wander down into my dungeon.

"Is it customary for Midnight Fae to leave without a proper goodbye?" Melek mused as he fell into step beside me. "Or are we going on an adventure together?"

"I'm going down to my cells to make sure Camillia is still alive."

"Because you care for her?" he asked.

"Because she's my charge and under my protection for the moment."

"Only for the moment?" he pressed.

"Why do you care?" I demanded, whirling on him. "What do you really want to know, Melek?"

"Oh, that list would keep us here for months." His eyes ran

over me in an assessing manner, like he was just seeing me for the first time. Considering the fact that we rarely spoke, maybe this was the first time he'd ever truly noticed my presence. He had this enigmatic air about him that made him hard to read.

Whenever we'd interacted in the past, it'd been some sort of test—like him releasing the Nightmare Fae—but this interaction felt different somehow. More serious.

At least until he asked, "How do you feel about rope?"

My brow furrowed. "Rope?" *What the fuck?*

"Hmm." He canted his head again. "As I thought." He lifted a shoulder. "Maybe I'll teach you someday. Cami can be our test subject."

"What are you talking about?"

"Rope," he replied, giving me a look like that was an obvious response. "Are you listening to me at all, Warden?"

"You're not making any sense."

"I'm making perfect sense," he countered. "You're just not *hearing* me." He sounded almost aggravated by that fact, like I should understand these riddles of his and know exactly what game he intended for us to play next.

Shaking my head, I resumed my journey toward the cells, convinced he was fucking with me just to delay the inevitable.

Which meant he had done something to Camillia.

Something I wasn't going to like.

"She'd better be alive," I muttered at him.

"Who?"

"*Camillia.*"

"Your desired bride?"

I bristled. "I already told you that I don't want a bride."

"Ah, but I think you want her." He kept pace beside me with ease, his hands tucked behind him as we moved along the burning thwomp tree line toward the portal. "Pretty little angel, isn't she?"

Those words just proved even more that he'd visited her. "You really can't leave things alone, can you?"

"I'm sure I don't know what you mean."

"Right," I drawled, pulling my wand out to open the portal. "She'd better be unharmed, Melek." Because it would be my ass on the line if she wasn't.

"Perhaps you shouldn't have left her unguarded," he offered as he trailed behind me through the shimmering dungeon entrance. This one took me straight into my quarters, not down the long stairs.

Melek glanced around with interest, his fingers running over my bed.

"Stop," I told him. "Go back to your evening flight."

"I would, but this intrigues me more than my own thoughts. And I'm in need of a mental distraction." He gestured toward my bedroom door. "After you, Warden."

My jaw tightened in irritation.

Melek was one of the few beings in this paradigm that I couldn't command. Which meant he was coming with me whether I wanted him to or not.

Fucking Hell Fae Prince.

Ignoring him, I pushed out into the hallway and immediately cloaked myself in a heat protection spell. I did not share the enchantment with Melek. Although, he appeared to be fine even though he wore gray dress pants and a cream-colored button-down shirt—one of his preferred outfits.

I couldn't feel his magic but assumed he'd done something to guard himself against the warmth.

Cami would absolutely be feeling that heat now.

And I hadn't even left her with water.

I'd also left her unguarded because I'd wanted to escape her.

Yeah, I'm a dick, I decided, irritated with myself not just for my actions but also for *caring* about said actions.

I couldn't afford to feel anything for this girl.

Yet I couldn't fight the relief I felt at finding her unharmed in her cell.

Well, *mostly* unharmed.

She was drenched in sweat, the fabric of her dress clinging to her skin as she attempted to sleep on the rug. My heart panged at the sight of her trembling, not from cold but from something inside her mind. *A nightmare.*

Gritting my teeth, I glanced at Melek. However, he no longer stood beside me.

I whirled around to find a lone white feather on the dusty floor, his presence a gentle lingering energy in the stifling air.

What game are you playing? I wondered, sighing.

Camillia released a soft little moan, distracting me from the Hell Fae Prince. It wasn't a moan of pleasure but one of anguish.

Sighing, I flicked my fingers toward her and swathed her in a cooling blanket of ethereal energy.

That technically qualified as a gift despite the fact that she couldn't see it. But she could feel it. Which meant I only had two more to give.

Fuck it. I didn't want a bride. So what did it matter if I gave the gifts to Camillia? At least then she would stand some sort of chance tomorrow. And if she died, well, I'd at least tried.

That would relieve me of any and all guilt.

Water and food, I decided. *That's all I'm giving her.*

I turned away from her cell to go find something suitable.

CAMI

REALITY MELTED into a vision I didn't understand.

Part of me recognized that I'd fallen asleep. Yet I felt very much awake.

Hot.

Burning.

Fire.

But there were no flames, just an abundance of light.

I'm dreaming, I told myself. *I'm… I'm definitely dreaming.*

Except, this felt so real. There were fae shouting at each other. Feathers falling from the sky. A flaring star beckoning me to step closer. Seducing my soul. Telling me to move… move… *move…*

I blinked, not understanding. However, my legs shifted, my feet whispering across the ground as I crept closer to that alluring brightness. *Touch me. Take me. Keep me.*

The words were a chant in my head, but my voice wasn't the one urging me to act. It was deep. Foreign. Unlike anything I'd ever heard.

And then it shouted at an approaching mass of darkness.

Lucifer.

Black wings spanned along his back, stretching out to the sky and darkening my view. He was furious. Yelling. Threatening the voice with a sharp blade of magic.

I stumbled backward, uncertain of what was happening, terrified of what this all meant.

Take it! the voice roared. *Take what's ours!*

My head swayed back and forth, my feet continuing to carry me away. And then I was running into the stark coolness of the night, away from the brightness and the sun and into the land of the unknown.

Ice drizzled down my spine, chilling me to the bone, but I couldn't stop sprinting. I had to escape. I had to run. I had to *hide*.

I dove inside a frozen sphere of darkness, curled into a ball, and willed myself to wake up.

"Cami?"

I blinked, startled by the closeness of that voice.

Ajax.

I jolted my head up from my knees to find him standing at the cell door with a tray in his hands. I frowned, momentarily frazzled by my surroundings. *I… I'm… I'm awake?*

But I hadn't even felt myself stir. One minute, I was in the darkness, and now… *I'm back in my cell.*

What just happened?

"Cami?" he repeated, his use of my nickname befuddling me even more.

Ajax calls me Camillia. Did that mean I was still asleep?

The tray in his hands suggested this could be a dream. His last words to me were essentially, *You're going to die.* So why would he bring me food?

I swallowed, my throat scratchy as though I'd just spent hours screaming. Then another chill swept over me, eliciting goose bumps along my arms and legs. Yet my dress was soaked through, the fabric clinging to my skin. It felt like I'd just jumped out of a lake into an air-conditioned room.

My teeth chattered.

Ajax frowned, entering.

His magic was tangible, his presence warm and oddly appreciated.

What's happening to me?

I tried to recall what had happened before I fell asleep. Melek had visited and asked me to whisper those strange words. I'd felt something snap into place inside me, a strange flicker of comfort and protection underlined in his essence.

An essence I still felt thriving through every inch of my being.

What did he do to me? I wondered, shuddering at the foreign presence consuming my being.

Ajax said my name again as he settled onto the floor beside me, his appearance bewildering me even more. *Why is he here?*

But as he set the food down beside me, I no longer cared. My mouth was watering, my stomach aching with the need to devour everything on the plate.

I grabbed the sandwich, stuffing it into my mouth and swallowing several bites before another thought hit me. *This could be poisoned or bespelled.*

That realization was quickly followed by, *I don't even care.*

Because I was *starving.*

I had no idea how long I'd been out, but clearly, it'd been a while.

A bottle of water appeared in my peripheral vision, and I grabbed it without thinking. I was just an animal reacting to the nourishment, something that seemed to sober Ajax significantly because he didn't comment at all. He just watched me eat and drink with a look of concern in his features.

This is definitely a dream, I decided. Because the Warden *never* looked at me like that. *Better enjoy it while it lasts.*

I finished off the plate, then accepted the second bottle of water he passed me, before I finally started to wonder if this was real again. Because dreams weren't usually this long or this coherent.

Ajax shuffled beside me, drawing his knees up to his chest and wrapping his strong forearms around them.

It was then that I realized he hadn't just fed me, but he'd also sat with me on the floor.

"Is this real?" I asked him dumbly.

"Yeah, Cami. It's real," he murmured softly.

I narrowed my gaze. "If this was a dream, you'd still say that."

He considered me for a moment and nodded. "True. But I promise you're awake." He hesitated, running his fingers around the cuff of his T-shirt. I wasn't used to seeing a nervous tic on the Warden, but something was clearly bothering him. His entire demeanor had changed, and in the next breath, he admitted why. "You remind me of someone," he said softly. "Someone I couldn't save."

His words from his last visit returned to me, the ones about how sometimes we couldn't choose our paths or our destinies. Sometimes they just ended badly.

Was this admission related to his previous speech?

The haunted look in his eyes told me it was.

He cleared his throat and shook his head. "I shouldn't be helping you, Cami," he admitted almost hoarsely. "But I can't seem to stop myself." He sounded kind of mad about it but palmed the back of his neck and blew his frustration out with a sigh. "They're going to drop you near a lava pit. It may look like a border crossing. Don't fall for it."

I blinked in surprise. "Okay…"

What had brought on this change? Was it another ploy to make me fail so he could punish me again?

Although, it was the *prince* who'd sent that cupcake, not the Warden.

Now that I thought about it, Ajax had always been straight with me. Even if he'd been a blunt asshole, he'd always told me the truth, and he *had* provided the amenities for me that first night.

And now more sustenance.

And from what I could tell, he hadn't woven a spell over the furniture again, unless he'd concealed it somehow.

Which would explain why he was sitting on the ground with me.

He continued, oblivious to the war I was waging internally on whether or not I should trust him.

"The first trial will last for several hours with no help from the outside," he went on, making my eyes go wide. "You'll be on your own in the Barren Lands. Maybe even the Nightmare Fae realms. It depends on your choices along the way."

Several hours in Hell's realms. No safety from the paradigm. No help.

Except, that wasn't true. I'd received help in the form of spells from Melek, and now guidance from Ajax. I leaned in, listening intently.

"There are deadly creatures you'll want to be on the lookout for. Remember the cells in the first half of the prison?"

I nodded. "How could I forget?" A toothy Siren had tried to seduce me to crawl into the tank with her.

He didn't smile, his expression remaining solemn.

"Right. But those beings were locked in cages. It's very different when you come face-to-face with them. Especially the Centaurs." The blue rim of his irises thinned as the darkness bled outward from the center. "They hunt in packs."

A moment of silence passed as I internalized this new piece of information. "Shit."

"Yeah. Then there's the Manticore…"

"Oh, I've already fought one of those," I said, although I didn't look forward to facing another.

He frowned. "Right. When you were out wandering *past curfew*."

"Hmm."

"You can't afford to test the rules like that outside of the paradigm," he pressed. "Listen carefully to what I have to say and you *might* survive."

I sealed my lips shut, ready to absorb every piece of information he was willing to share.

Because for whatever reason, Ajax wanted to help me.

Because I remind him of someone.

Someone he couldn't save.

Which meant he had tried and failed. Not an encouraging track record, but I didn't have much choice in the matter.

Ajax was providing me with much-needed details that might help me with this insane trial.

"Stay away from any tunnels that smell like sulfur. Minotaurs guard them, and if you're lost inside them, they'll find you. Their sense of direction is impeccable, and they never lose their way. They'll know exactly how to trap you."

"No tunnels. Got it."

He readjusted his position on the floor, crossing his long legs. My gaze threatened to fall, but I snapped them back up to his face. Because I was *not* about to be distracted by the way his white shirt clung to his body. Or the way his black track pants defined his thick, muscular thighs.

Focus, Cami, I told myself. *Your life depends on it.*

"The creature you should be extra wary of," he continued, "is the Naga. Their true forms are snakelike, with female heads and chests. But they can camouflage themselves with magic to look like Hell Fae or someone you might trust. If you see someone who doesn't belong, or seems suspicious, or perhaps too good to be true, then *don't* approach them until you're sure of their identity."

I swallowed, thinking of Melek's vow of protection. What if I called on him and ran to the open arms of a Naga, thinking he had come to help me?

I made a mental note not to trust *anything* out in the Barren Lands. Or Nightmare Fae kingdoms. Or wherever the fuck I was going.

Hell Fae Rule #4: Don't Trust Anyone.

I could only trust myself.

"You may also come across Banshees and Harpies. They'll act intimidating, but they won't harm you as long as you leave them alone. They're both scavengers and can be found among the dead." He gave me a serious look as he added, "Of which there will be many by the end of the week."

"How exciting," I deadpanned with a shiver, then wrapped my arms around myself. I suddenly found myself leaning toward Ajax, craving the warmth from his body.

How was I actually *cold* down here?

Focus.

"Where did all these creatures come from?" I asked instead of doing something stupid, like curling up against Ajax's side. "Did Lucifer create them?" Melek had already told me one answer, and I was curious if it was the truth.

Ajax shook his head. "No. At least, I don't think so. The Hellbeasts, otherwise known as Nightmare Fae, were once other types of fae. Specifically, fae who reneged on a deal with Lucifer. These forms are their punishment, which makes them dangerous and angry and oftentimes lethal."

Double-crossing Lucifer probably led to a fate worse than death. *Noted.*

Ajax rubbed his hands together. He was agitated, which meant he wasn't supposed to be helping me.

I shuddered to think who would punish the Warden.

"Next, it won't be easy, but there is sparse nutrition available in the Barren Lands if you know where to look. Fire plants, namely, although they're rare. They're red and resemble fire—hence the name *fire plants*—but their stems are edible. Just don't eat the leaves. Those will kill you."

My jaw ticked.

Melek's spell that could conjure food from objects sounded like a better option, but magic had its limits, so I took a mental note of the edible plant. Although, I would have to be pretty fucking starved to eat something that resembled fire and had poisonous leaves.

"Only the stems," I reiterated when I realized he was waiting for confirmation. "Understood."

He narrowed his eyes. "For water, there's a cactus-like plant—it's obsidian and spiny. If you break into it, you'll find a few droplets. But avoid the thorns, because—"

"Let me guess," I interrupted. "They'll kill me."

"They're coated with deadly toxins, yes."

Great.

Everything in the Barren Lands was fatal.

Literal Hell.

Survival sounded impossible. But at least now I was more prepared than before.

Between Melek's and Ajax's crash courses on how to survive the upcoming trial, I had a chance.

Curling my fingers, I vowed to make my chance count.

Assuming they're telling me the truth and not trying to kill me faster, I thought irritably. The last time I'd trusted one of them, I'd ended up in a cell.

Of course, Melek had said it was my fault for using his knowledge. Would he do that again if I tried one of the spells he'd taught me?

I would reserve his spells and his *vow of protection* as a last resort. Ajax had given me enough to survive without Melek's help.

Assuming all went according to plan.

Because that had worked out for me so far.

I'm so dead.

"You should try to get some more sleep," Ajax said, pulling out his wand. He murmured an incantation in a language I didn't understand, causing the items to disappear. Then three bottles of water appeared in their place. "I can't give you new clothes, as I'm only allowed three gifts, which I've used now between the cooling spell, sustenance, and knowledge."

"Cooling spell?" I repeated, frowning. "Is that why I'm so chilled?"

He nodded, then used his wand to create a stack of blankets. "We'll just say this is part of the cell accommodations." He stood then and returned his wand to his pocket. "I'll be back in about six hours to take you to the trial. Try to sleep, Cami. You're going to need it."

With that, he slipped out of the cell.

And shut the door.

I had a feeling I would be needing a lot more than just *sleep*. But he was right. That would be a good start.

Because who knew when I'd have another chance to rest again?

Hell Fae Rule #5: Be Prepared for Anything.

That included resting, hydrating, and fueling myself in preparation for the fight to come.

I picked up one of the blankets he'd left behind, marveling at how soft it felt against my fingertips. Then I made myself a better bed with it.

Curled up.

And allowed Ajax's minty fragrance to swirl around me in a comfortable blanket of warm masculinity. A hint of pine lurked in the air as well, his magic seeming to have a unique scent from his usual aftershave.

Together they created a strange sort of protective shield that lulled me to sleep.

No nightmares waited for me this time.

Just calming darkness.

And blissful silence.

TYPHOS

Melek never returned last night, leaving me more agitated than usual.

An emotion I had to ignore because I had a field of six hundred and sixty-six candidates to address.

I didn't enjoy ceremonies on a good day. And today certainly did not qualify as "good" by any stretch of the imagination.

About the only positive aspect of today was the fact that I would be losing at least fifty candidates, thus beginning the process of narrowing the numbers. If I was lucky, it'd be closer to a hundred souls dismissed from the Hell Fae part of these games.

The rest would go on to my royal lieutenants for their own set of trials.

Every layer of this competition had been strictly outlined and expertly planned for several hundreds of years. I'd factored in every possible twist and turn, created thousands of safeguards, and ensured each series of choices had an appropriate path.

Those who failed would be lost forever. However, that was the risk.

Not everyone would be a perfect fit.

And many would prove themselves unworthy or biased toward our kind. Appearances could be deceiving, a lesson many of the females would learn today.

Those who did not would die.

Because while I couldn't guarantee all six hundred and sixty-six candidates would meet our requirements, I could guarantee that only those suitable for mating would survive.

That was the purpose of these trials—to ensure the brides went to their appropriate kingdoms. And to remove those who shouldn't be here at all.

Deals with parents were only half the battle.

This was the true test. The games I'd spent far too many centuries perfecting.

My fae were worth it. They deserved their brides.

And in the end, these women would be grateful, too. Otherwise, several of them would have gone through life without finding their true mates, their souls forever searching for an abomination hiding behind my gates.

Melek had jokingly called me a matchmaker.

I wasn't a matchmaker at all. Just a king looking after his subjects.

The Hell Fae Source rarely accepted females, making mating difficult among my fae. While many of them had formed clans together, there was still a strong desire for women.

Specifically, *fae* women.

Because my men needed partners who could endure their touch, and humans tended to be too fragile for a Hell Fae mating. Halflings were fine. And there were mortals who could withstand it, but they were very rare.

And mating any of them right now required my Hell Fae to leave the underworld, something several of them could not actually do.

Especially the Nightmare Fae.

If these games went well, we'd do another in maybe six hundred years or so, just to keep it fresh and interesting.

If the games didn't work, then I'd be forced to find another recruitment method.

Sighing, I stepped down from my podium to begin the candidate inspection. Several of them had been given gifts, all of which required my evaluation.

I couldn't have another incident like yesterday with the talisman.

Fortunately, all the gifts seemed to be in order—food, clothing, and a few defensive items. The heat shield talisman I'd approved could be found on a number of the females as well.

As for weapons, only the regulated items were allowed. They were all bespelled to only lethally injure the dark souls. That way, the light souls would remain unharmed. Any permanent damage to the true Nightmare Fae would severely piss off my royal lieutenants—hence all the safeguards I'd put in place. They weren't there to keep the brides safe, but to protect the Nightmare Fae under my care.

Except for a select few whom I wouldn't mind losing.

But that was another story entirely about lost souls who could never be forgiven. They deserved their fates.

I continued down the line of females, several of whom boldly made eye contact with me. A few even gave me inviting looks. I returned their grins because many of these females would become my future subjects. It would serve me well to win them over now rather than later.

Of course, the spirited ones were the females most likely to make it to the final rounds.

Females like Item Sixty-Six. *Camillia De la Croix*. I stopped right in front of her, my gaze searching her for any tangible gifts.

She still wore her dress from last night, the fabric barely covering her tits. And the scent coming off her suggested she hadn't been given an opportunity to shower either. Which was unfortunate because it gifted me a rather potent introduction to her feminine perfume, one that reminded me of blossoming roses beneath the sun.

A hint of decadence underlined the fragrance. *Melek*. I inhaled deeply, both aroused and irritated by this development.

I supposed I could see the physical appeal, but other than that, I felt no draw toward her.

At least until her stormy gray irises met mine. *Challenge. Spirit. Defiance.*

An intoxicating blend.

Yes, perhaps I could see the allure after all. But I didn't want to fucking mate her. If anything, I wanted to put her in a glass cage and guarantee her safety so that she couldn't hurt Melek.

I narrowed my gaze, tempted to ask her about their mating.

But then I recalled the book and what it had reminded me last night. *Trust.*

I had to trust that my devious prince knew what he was doing here.

So rather than speak to her, I glanced at Ajax. "Anything worth noting?"

He shook his head. "She slept on the rug. I gave her food and water."

I arched a brow, intrigued by that last bit, as they functioned as gifts. "Oh?"

My Warden lifted a shoulder. "She was under my care. I take that seriously."

My eyebrow winged even higher. "Did you feed Clarence as well?" I wondered aloud, referring to the Centaur currently in his custody. He'd given my Warden quite the chase through Hell recently.

"Clarence isn't scheduled for today's trial. So no, I did not."

"But if he was?" I pressed.

"I still wouldn't feed that fucker."

I smiled. "Good. He doesn't deserve food." As for Camillia De la Croix, well, that remained to be seen. I glanced at her once more, noting that hint of defiance still lurking in her gaze. Perhaps she would make it through this trial after all.

A good thing.

Because the last thing I desired was for Melek to feel true pain.

I dismissed Ajax and the girl with a nod before finishing my rounds.

All the while, I pondered the female that had ensnared the attention of my mate and my Warden. Ajax didn't provide luxuries for any of the Nightmare Fae in his custody. So why Camillia? Because she was a potential bride? Because he actually wanted her to survive? Did he fancy her, too?

I would have to check in with him sometime after today's trial, just to see how he reacted.

Ajax was a newer addition to my realm, his life experiences marking him as an ideal candidate to serve me as Warden. Az had also taken to him almost immediately, something that had factored into my decision. And Ajax maintained connections to the current Midnight Fae royal court. All of those items together pointed to the Midnight Fae Death Blood being a valuable asset.

And he had yet to fail me.

Nor had he ever actually requested a deal or anything from me at all, other than permission to reside within Zenaida's paradigm. I'd agreed and requested he assist Az.

He'd risen in my ranks from there, earning his title as Warden.

I actually rather liked the Midnight Fae rebel.

Hopefully, that opinion never changed.

As for the girl, well, I'd see how she fared and go from there.

I made my way back up to the platform in the center of the field, the archway glittering with power. Several of my royal lieutenants stood around the magical arch of obsidian stone, their gazes giving nothing away. They were all in their humanoid forms, too. Something they'd done to placate the females in the field.

Not all Nightmare Fae could shift, though.

So only those with the ability to do so had been invited for today's opening game.

As soon as the candidates disappeared, the others would venture out to observe the trial. Some were even participating today.

But most had sent delegates from their home kingdoms to test the candidates.

Just as I'd added a few dangerous beings of my own to see if anyone noticed the difference between them.

My goal was to show everyone that looks could be deceiving.

Those who learned the lesson would succeed.

Those who didn't would die.

I raised my hands to capture the focus of all the

females in the field. Not that I really needed to move, as they were all watching me anyway.

No, I realized. *No, they're not watching me.*

I glanced to my left to see whom they were really watching and found my prince casually walking toward me. Relief stroked my heart, lessening some of my inner agitation.

Melek, I whispered, thankful to feel his mind opening to me once more.

My love, he replied, gifting me with a smile that had several of the women in the field sighing. I ignored them all, my focus on the angelic being strolling across the platform. *Open the portal and begin your game.*

He spoke before I could grab him, helping me focus on our audience. Something I quietly thanked him for, as I'd been about to devour him in front of all six-hundred-plus women, and that would have set a very different tone for today's festivities.

Melek paused beside me, his arm brushing mine as he redirected his smile to the women in the field.

I followed suit and cleared my throat. "Today marks a historic occasion, one where the hopes for the future of the Hell Fae rest in your feminine hands. Your sacrifices will be counted, and you will be awarded a star for every achievement. A star that you may keep, or a star that you may place at the feet of your future mate, should you deem him worthy."

My words stirred a curious murmur through the crowd, coming from both the candidates and my subjects.

Melek hid his smirk well, but I felt his amusement.

The stars were metaphorical, of course, not tangible. However, the power that the Hell Fae Source would award the females who proved themselves worthy would be equal to their actions and their achievements.

While the candidates didn't have a choice in their mates, I would allow them a choice when it came to their power. Which meant they could either choose to share their increased abilities and energy with their intended mates, or they could keep the Hell Fae Source's gifts for themselves.

A true mate-bond would be rewarded, and so I would encourage my subjects to woo their potential mates just as much as these females were instructed to woo their benefactors.

It was a dance that both sides would play, with a potential of high rewards for each.

"Today's trial will not be easy," I continued. This trial would actually be one of the more difficult, an intentional tactic to thin the herd. "I advise you to follow the rules."

A few inquisitive glances had me indulging myself in a grin.

I swept my arms out and released my power. Heat surged through me as I opened the gates of the Hell Fae Source. It burned brighter every day, its power threatening to flourish and purge all the realms with its eternal fury.

Fortunately, I knew how to control it, as it was just as much a part of me as I was a part of it.

I tamped down the stream of power like a faucet, ebbing the flow so that it thrummed through the ground and lit the brilliant arch that I used as a conduit.

Those inquisitive stares implored me to finish my statement.

I curled my fingers into fists as I sent the power from the arch blistering through the six hundred and sixty-six females anxiously awaiting their trial.

"There are no rules," I told them.

Then I opened my hands, releasing the taut power as

an individual portal opened beneath every female I had targeted.

They gasped a last gulp of air, my magic too quick to even allow them to scream, as they fell through the ground on their journey to begin the test of their spirits.

I heaved a sigh of relief as the ground swallowed them up. It was a sigh that echoed through the field as my royal lieutenants in attendance engaged their own portals to move to their next posts—either to a viewing area or to the trial itself.

But my attention went to my Virtuous Prince, the world around me disappearing for the moment as I calmed the energy around me and focused entirely on Melek.

"I'm sorry," I said, grabbing him by the back of the neck and not caring who heard me. This male meant everything to me, and anyone who didn't know that was fucking blind. "Forgive me?"

"Always, my king." He gave me a sweet little smile, then pressed his lips to my jaw. "Are we heading to the club?"

"We are," I confirmed, using my grip on his nape to pull him closer. "But first…" I captured his mouth in a savage kiss meant to *claim*. And he welcomed it with a soft swipe of his tongue.

Mine, I told him. *You can bond her all you want, but you're still mine.*

Yes, he agreed.

But I heard the whisper in his mind, the curiosity about what it would be like for him to claim her, to make her *ours*.

I tasted the notion and allowed it to flourish a little, just at the back of my mind. *I'll go through that portal right now and bring her back for you,* I told him. *Just say the words.*

I want to test her first, he whispered back to me. *She needs to earn it.*

She could die, I warned him.

181

It's a risk I'm willing to take. He palmed my cheek, his tongue still dueling with mine. *I'll endure the pain of the loss if she fails.*

I started to shake my head, but his teeth caught my bottom lip, holding me in place.

It's my burden, Ty. Let me carry it. The sternness in his mental tone told me he wouldn't be allowing me to argue. Which meant I had to see this through. To *trust* him, just like the book had advised.

All right, Melek, I whispered. *We'll play this game.*

I wrapped my opposite arm around him and engaged my ability to phase through the realms.

Hold on to me, I told him.

Always. His arms encircled my neck. *Let's go watch our future.*

I wasn't sure what he meant by that but suspected it was a code word for his Camillia, the female he'd chosen for us.

Future or not, I did want to observe her.

If anything, just to see if I could determine any negative intentions.

Or perhaps she'd prove herself worthy.

Doubtful. No one was worthy of Melek. But I'd follow his lead on this. I'd play his game. And I'd see where it led us.

Thank you, he murmured, obviously hearing my acquiescence.

I would do anything for you, I vowed. *Anything, Melek.*

Likewise, my king. Likewise.

CAMI

There was no warning.

No indication of what was coming.

Just a burst of power that jolted through my system, sending me through the ground with the words *"There are no rules"* chasing after me.

Everything *burned*.

Hot. White. Flames.

Engulfing me from head to toe, reminding me of my nightmares.

The world turned upside down, whirling me around in rapid circles as I traveled through some sort of portal. My ears rang with the whooshing sound, the reverberation reminiscent of a speed train.

Fuck.

I closed my eyes, my stomach rioting at the foreign sensation.

Only for my feet to hit the ground half a beat later.

Gasping in the dry air, I ran my palm along my throat. All that water Ajax had given me no longer mattered. I could barely breathe, let alone swallow.

Intense heat bled into my body from all directions, threatening to suffocate me.

Focus, Cami, I thought, attempting to calm my stuttering heart. *Breathe. And focus.*

I tried and failed to swallow, the air resembling that of a stifling desert.

But after several seconds, my lungs finally pulled in enough oxygen to help soothe my thundering heart.

I flexed my fingers, counting to five, and slowly reopened my eyes.

I had to squint, my sight having been accustomed to living in the dark for the last however many days. It took several minutes and a lot of blinking for me to finally *see.*

The reason for my blindness hung overhead in the form of two suns, casting flame-like ripples through the air.

I curled my toes against the burn from below, my thin heels providing a poor barrier against the infernal crust of this realm.

The suns warmed my skin, but my feet felt singed, causing my focus to shift down to the source of the intense heat. *Lava pools.*

They were scattered throughout the charred landscape, making my lips part.

Melek's spells whispered through my mind, reminding me that I knew how to shield myself with a few murmured words.

But Lucifer's intense gaze followed, his prolonged interest in me earlier making me wary about using any of the details Melek or Ajax had shared with me.

I was clearly on a watch list of some kind.

Which didn't bode well for me.

I could handle the worst of the heat for now without using magic. I just had to stay away from the lava pools and I'd be good.

Taking in a deep breath, I forced my lungs to adapt to the dry air. It took a few more minutes, but eventually my body figured out how to acclimate. My muscles still ached, my legs reminding me a bit of stiff boulders, but I wasn't overly hot.

Actually, I felt quite cool.

Why? Had Ajax's spell remained with me? Would that be considered cheating? Would I end up in trouble again like I had because of Melek's necklace?

My throat tried to swallow again, the dryness resembling sandpaper.

Or maybe it was my dream? I wondered, recalling the icy plane I'd escaped to after running from the intense light.

I rubbed my chest, recalling the bizarre sensation. *Incredibly bright heat followed by icy cold.*

My insides clenched in confusion, that odd feeling returning as though I'd conjured it.

Fire and ice.

One resembled darkness and sin—the life I lived now.

While the other made me think of my previous world, all light and innocent.

Except, no, that wasn't quite right. Nothing about my past was light or innocent.

I shook my head, dizzy from the weird thoughts. *I'm losing my mind.*

Maybe because of the heat. Or perhaps it was just my way of giving the nightmare meaning. Because I swore my bones were soaking up the warmth to dispel the cold even now.

However, it was probably just Ajax's spell still playing with my body temperature.

And my mind reacting to the fall through the portal.

Regardless, I needed to focus. All this debating was a waste of time. I should be paying attention to my surroundings and the other candidates. I suspected that many of them were as much of a danger to me as the landscape or the monsters, based on my experience with the knife-creating candidate—Feyre of the House of Iron.

Fortunately, I didn't see her anywhere near me.

But she was obviously here somewhere.

Because we were all here—all six hundred and sixty-six of us. A realization that had my gaze narrowing and a hint of fire flickering to life in my veins.

I knew the score. I knew why we were here. But something about seeing everyone sprawled out on this dangerous landscape drove the point home.

And it infuriated me.

We were all here because of some bogus deals.

Bullshit.

I'd lost sight of finding a way out and had played into Lucifer's hands instead. He'd been right in front of me. Why hadn't I tried to deal with him?

Because I'd been a bit lost in his dark stare.

And a little terrified of the power swirling around him.

But damn it, I should have said something.

This was so much different than being lined up in pretty dresses and marching into an amphitheater for entertainment. We'd just entered some sort of death match here. A field... many of us would not survive.

I could see that realization etched into the expressions of others, their grim features likely matching my own.

This isn't going to end well.

While there should have been a sense of camaraderie between us, I knew that wasn't how this would work. We all wanted to live.

And a desire to make it to the end could make even the gentlest person cruel.

I didn't see any friendly looks from those closest to me.

Many of them gave me a raised brow because I was still wearing my dress from last night's ceremony.

The other girls, however, wore more appropriate gear.

Most of them were in the white T-shirt and black pants uniform, but not all of them. A select few wore stronger leathers, likely a donation from a Hell Fae benefactor, like Ajax had mentioned.

Their loose-fitting clothing and the obvious weapons beneath made me envious. I spotted daggers, bows and arrows, and even a few pistols.

Then there were those who had backpacks and supplies.

I also noticed quite a few talismans that glowed with blue power. After a moment's perusal, I suspected they were some kind of heat wards based on the lack of flushed skin or sweat-drenched curls. My skin burned, and my hair was already sticking to my forehead. The strange sense of coolness lingering around me had either been superficial or was simply keeping me from burning.

I, of course, had no such kind of talisman, or anything else that would help me survive in this wasteland.

Well, I had *knowledge*, but I would be careful how I used it. If I used it at all.

A voice boomed across the landscape, startling me into a crouch.

"Welcome to the trials, bride candidates."

The voice was Lucifer's, although I suspected this was a magical projection, like the one from the arena when he'd given his speech.

"Your first trial is to find your way across the border. Your progress will be monitored, so please remember the rules."

I snorted. I remembered his *rules*.

There are no rules.

How cliché.

The suns flared in a spectacular display of Lucifer's power. He seemed to be able to stretch his claws across realms with a mere thought.

The sheer amount of power he held at his fingertips made my breath catch.

"Venture onward and prove yourselves to the Hell Fae Source."

His words sent a path illuminating across the stretch of cracked red land. The road wound between lava pools, dipping around a structure in the middle. I had to squint against the light to make it out.

"It's bottles of water," one girl excitedly announced, a pair of binoculars in her hand. She also boasted a backpack and a sweater wrapped around her waist, which I definitely found odd.

"*Ouch*," she snapped when a girl jabbed her in the ribs.

"Don't be such a blabbermouth, Jade," the other hissed at her. "I'm not going to ally with you if you're going to be this dumb, no matter how many suitor gifts you have to share!"

I arched my eyebrow at the pair. It didn't surprise me that the girls were making alliances, but I certainly hadn't managed to make any friends so far.

Well, except for Melek and Ajax and the little gargoyle. But they didn't really count.

Jade pouted as the other girl snatched away the binoculars. "Sorry, Beatrix."

Noticing I was watching, Beatrix glowered at me and grabbed Jade by the arm, hauling her out of my range of hearing.

Jade stumbled after her, the oversized backpack clearly bulging with supplies and goodies.

I could see why Jade had so many gifts. She was

gorgeous with her blonde curls that bounced behind her. She turned and blinked at me apologetically with striking blue eyes, her pretty look completed with flushed, pink cheeks.

Seemingly satisfied they were far enough away from the others, Beatrix let go of Jade and peered through the binoculars.

Jade screamed *innocence* when she folded her hands and looked at her feet. She'd impressed a Hell Fae, but likely for all the wrong reasons.

These bastards probably wanted to corrupt anything beautiful and sweet.

A part of me felt compelled to protect her. I had no doubt the other girls would take advantage of someone not trained for this, but a rumble across the landscape kept me rooted to the ground.

Hell Fae Rule #6: Only Look Out for Yourself—No One Else.

My father had certainly practiced that rule. He'd traded away my soul for his own benefit.

This was his realm, where his rules made sense, and unlike Jade, my father had had his fucked-up way of looking out for me by teaching me how to survive in this place.

And survive I would.

If only to claw my way out of here and find him and my complicit mother, just to show them how *grateful* I was.

Still crouched, I watched as the girls hesitantly ventured down the path.

It seemed too obvious a route, so I decided to wait it out.

Jade and her ally started whispering to one another, but my father had taught me a spell that could amplify my hearing. Most of the spells he'd made sure I'd learned were physical in nature, boosting my strength and my senses.

I was part Hell Fae, even if I hadn't been accepted by the source, so I'd still learned a few tricks of my own. Tricks that Melek technically hadn't taught me. Which meant they should be safe to use.

I wasn't sure if I was supposed to be able to utilize magic without actually having a source to draw from, but based on my need for sleep and nourishment after using magic, I probably took the cost out of myself. I'd never thought much about it, as I rarely ever used it.

However, thanks to Ajax, I was well fed. And besides some unsettling dreams, I'd had more than enough sleep to feel rejuvenated and prepared for the tasks ahead. A little spell wouldn't cost too much of my reserves, and right now, I required information.

Focusing my power inward, I whispered the enchantment, engaging my ability to hear across the long distance.

Beatrix's voice floated back to me on the heated breeze.

"There's more than just water. Look, there are multiple pedestals with different items. I see weapons, food, and that one over there has some sort of packs. I bet there's something good in those." The girl poked Jade again. "Your suitor said he'd rip my arms off if I stole any of your gifts, but he didn't say anything against sharing. Give me your talisman and I'll make a run for the water supply point, and you watch my back, okay?"

When Jade fingered the talisman, the other girl sighed.

"Look, I'll give it back, but if I'm going to run all that way through the lava pits, I need your talisman. I'm not going to make it before the other girls if I pass out from heatstroke. Unless you want to run off the path and face gods know what? Be my guest."

Jade frowned but silently handed over the talisman.

Her curls visibly wilted as moisture beaded across her brow, but she didn't complain.

I hoped her ally would hold up her end of the deal.

And if she didn't, I hoped the girl's Hell Fae suitor made good on his threat. I hated anyone who took advantage of weaker souls.

Following Jade's gaze, I spotted the specks in the distance that were the supply points. However, they appeared to be pretty far off of the illuminated path that led to a shift in the landscape.

Something didn't feel right.

Ajax's warning lingered in the back of my mind.

"It may look like a border crossing. Don't fall for it."

He hadn't mentioned anything about the supply points, though. It seemed odd to me that the Hell Fae would make such a big deal about earning gifts from suitors if there would just be all these supplies up for grabs.

Unless… it isn't what it seems.

The moment the thought crossed my mind, the first supply point placed in the center of the path wavered and misted into ash, revealing a shadow that certainly didn't belong in the blistering heat.

A monstrous form took shape through the fog.

Muscular chest.

Legs of a horse.

Horns of a bull.

I gulped. It was a spitting image of the creature from the dungeon.

Except this time, there were no barriers between us. Just a lot of land.

The creature's red eyes opened, and the girls screamed.

"Centaurs!" a feminine voice shouted over the horizon as the other supply points transformed into groups of monsters.

They stayed still as if waiting for something.

Then a gunshot sounded, cracking through the air, sending the Centaurs into action.

They charged.

Scratching my nails against the cracked landscape, I watched the scene unfold, waiting for my moment to make a break for it, although I didn't want to leave my position without having a destination in mind.

Did I trust the illuminated path?

Did I try one of the supply points for a weapon and hope that not all of them were mirages?

Or did I turn around and go back the way we'd come? A glance over my shoulder revealed more of the cracked red landscape with no evidence of escape or supplies.

None of my options seemed very good. I didn't have enough information to make a decision.

Still, I couldn't just sit here and wait to be picked off by Centaurs.

Fortunately, the girls appeared ready for a fight, their training evident. So maybe our parents had cared about us a bit after all, helping to prepare us in their own ways for this fate.

Or maybe it had to do with pride. I imagined it looked good to have a daughter who proved herself to the Hell Fae Source. At least to some of fae kind.

Knowing my father, he'd try to take all the credit for my success.

Asshole.

A beast-like snort from behind me made my heart skip a beat and reminded me that I still had a decision to make.

Coiling every muscle in my body, I slowly twisted to see what had made that sound.

Two red eyes stared at me through a veil of darkness lingering around its face, obscuring the Centaur's features and making it seem even more mysterious and terrifying than it already was.

A hoof from his lower body pawed at the ground, daring me to run.

"Easy, big guy," I said in the most soothing voice I could manage as I gently backed away. I kept my front to him, treating the being like I would a wild dog.

Don't run.

Don't show fear.

My heart pounded in my chest and my vision wavered. Not from heat, but from adrenaline.

My father had never prepared me to face creatures like this. Sure, I'd come across a few ambitious Hellhounds, but they weren't *scary* in any sense of the word. I actually found them entertaining.

Hellbeasts, on the other hand, were downright horrifying.

The Centaur's red eyes homed in on me and locked me in its sights, seemingly waiting for me to make my move.

It occurred to me that the Centaurs hadn't attacked until the gunshot. Maybe they only charged if provoked.

As I backed up, my shoe caught a loose stone, and I yelped as I fell straight on my ass.

Fuck.

I was better than this, but I hadn't trained to run around in fucking heels on red rocks framing lava pits.

The Centaur reared on its hind legs at the sudden movement. It came at me with its antlers, and I twisted to the side. Pain streaked across my cheek as it grazed me, but I managed to tumble out of the way.

A weapon would be useful right about now!

It came at me again, and this time I dove toward it, taking a risk as I slammed my fist where I thought it might have balls—at the place where the human form merged with a horse's chest.

A deep-throated chuckle sounded.

Okay, that's not where its dick is, then, apparently.

When it reared again, I rolled and gained some distance, this time gauging my enemy.

A strange aura took shape around the beast. I'd seen something similar before around the Sirens, but I wasn't sure what it meant.

Maybe I was losing it.

Or maybe this was another key to the puzzle, and my ticket to survival during these insane trials.

Inky darkness bled into the air around the Centaur, stirring a strange sense of sizzling ice-cold magic that didn't blend well with the Hell Fae Realm's heat. The fur along the creature's haunches stood on end, and it bellowed a roar that rumbled through my bones as I forced myself to stand again.

Then the obsidian mist shifted to reveal an entire row of the creatures with blinking red eyes, making my heart drop.

I'd forgotten a key bit of information from Ajax's lesson.

Centaurs hunt in packs.

"Shit," I cursed as the monsters charged.

I did the only thing I could do—I ran.

Ajax

"For fuck's sake," I muttered, shaking my head at the screen before me. "I warned you."

But did Camillia listen?

No. Of course not.

She just fucking stood there while the Centaur eyed her like a piece of meat, waiting for his buddies to join him.

"I'm very unimpressed with you right now, Camillia." She couldn't hear me, of course. But that didn't stop me from speaking the words out loud anyway.

I grabbed my glass of blood wine and finished it in one swallow.

Then I shoved away from my leather couch to grab a refill from the bar.

I wasn't even supposed to be watching the Hell Fae Trials. Hence the reason I was in my dungeon quarters and not at Lucifer's infamous underworld nightclub. He'd asked me to remain here for the day, just in case he needed to call upon me to go chase down some of the disobedient Nightmare Fae.

Which explained why I'd returned to find the trials playing on my screen.

I hadn't expected to have access to them since I wasn't technically a Hell Fae, nor did I want a bride. However, I'd used the remote to move the screen around until I found Camillia.

Because I had no self-control and I'd wanted to see how she was faring.

Not well, apparently, I thought, growling.

Although, that wasn't entirely true. She hadn't fallen for the supply mirages. And she'd paused to evaluate her surroundings thoroughly rather than wandering blindly through the Barren Lands.

It also looked like she'd engaged some sort of spell, too. I hadn't been able to read the words from her lips, but the way they'd moved reminded me of a Midnight Fae.

An interesting trick, as I hadn't realized she could even conduct magic.

But it also didn't surprise me.

There seemed to be a lot about Camillia that I didn't know. A lot that I wanted to learn, too.

Which was precisely the problem—I shouldn't want to know a damn thing about her.

Yet I couldn't stop thinking about her. I'd even given her some breakfast this morning before escorting her to the trials.

She's not mine.

I just felt obligated to help her as my prisoner.

However, Lucifer had raised a brow at that theory, then pointed out that I didn't treat the other prisoners that way.

But the other prisoners were Nightmare Fae who were dangerous beings that needed to be detained. They could also feed themselves.

Camillia... well, if she knew magic, she could

technically take care of herself. So maybe I'd misjudged that situation. Except it had felt right to help her. Like I was repaying a debt I didn't quite understand.

A debt to my past?

A debt to Emelyn?

Was this attraction to Camillia because I wanted to make amends for my previous wrongs? To try to fix something that could never actually be fixed?

To prevent history from repeating itself?

I swallowed, thinking back on the events that had led to Emelyn's death.

All the sneaking around had felt so forbidden and hot at the time. She'd been betrothed to the Midnight Fae Prince—a prince she'd despised. A prince who had actually taken another mate in secret himself.

A mate who had then uprooted Midnight Fae society and rid the world of the black plague known as Constantine Nacht.

But not in time to save Emelyn.

I swallowed more of my blood wine, wincing as I caught the telltale signs of *blame* crossing my mind. I didn't blame Aflora for acting too slowly. That wasn't fair. Nor did I blame her for the events that had led to Emelyn's death.

Constantine was to blame.

And he now lived in a tree, forever trapped in the middle of the real LethaForest.

His death hadn't brought back my parents or Emelyn, nor had it felt climactic or just. Mostly because nothing would ever help me overcome the anguish of my loss.

The snake-vines outside my door hissed, drawing my focus to the wood panel inside and disrupting my dark musings. Frowning, I set my glass down and started forward just as Shade walked through the wood with a grimace.

My eyebrows rose. "What the hell are you doing here?"

"Taming snakes, apparently," he muttered, brushing off some residual magic from his black cloak. It billowed around him all the way to his calves, the violet embroidery along the edges a marking of his inner power—Death Blood. I had several cloaks that matched, but I never wore them anymore.

Of course, the clasp at his throat was all his own—an intricate design boasting the magic of his mate-circle. The violet rose at the center pulsed with power as he slid his wand into an inner pocket.

He muttered some words, causing a plate of cookies to appear on my coffee table. "From my grandmother," he said. Not that I needed the explanation. "You've been avoiding my calls."

"I've been busy."

"Hmm," he hummed, wandering through my flat as though he had every right to be here. His icy gaze missed nothing as he took in the decor, only briefly flitting to the screen—which had automatically switched off when he'd entered. I wasn't sure if that was a result of the magic that powered the technology or if Lucifer had somehow felt Shade's presence. Perhaps both.

Regardless, it unnerved me because it meant I was being supervised, even here.

Which shouldn't surprise me.

Lucifer's trust had to be earned, and I'd only been working for him for a decade.

"I'm going to assume the cookies from Zen are why you're here," I said.

Shade nodded, his dark hair falling into his eyes. "She

said something cryptic about you needing a death stone for your date with the zombies."

I blinked at him. "My what?"

Shade lifted a broad shoulder and unsnapped his cloak to drape it over one of my dining chairs. "I don't pretend to understand her musings." He fished a jagged black rock from his pocket and set it on the table. "For your date."

My brow furrowed. "I have no idea what she's talking about, but thanks?"

His lips quirked up just enough to show amusement.

Then he strolled over to the bar to help himself to my open bottle of blood wine.

"Sure, make yourself at home," I drawled, setting down my own glass to go investigate the death stone. I was familiar with the magic but didn't understand why Zen thought I needed this. When a visit to the Netherworld Kingdom was required, I just engaged a portal.

Did she tell Shade about the Netherworld Kingdom? I wondered, glancing at him. It was something I hadn't known about until coming to work for Lucifer, and he'd been pretty clear about not sharing the information with anyone.

But Zen had lived a very long time.

And she knew a lot about everything.

It wouldn't surprise me if she knew about the zombie-like realm filled with dead Nightmare Fae.

Lucifer had only told me about it because he'd needed me to complete an errand there once. My Death Blood magic had made me the ideal candidate, so now whenever he needed something from that kingdom, he sent me.

It'd taken me a while to learn how to tame the beasts in that world, but I understood them better now.

I cleared my throat. "So. How are things?" I hedged, feeling awkward.

Shade and I had been best friends, once upon a time. However, he almost resembled a stranger to me now. Not because of anything he'd done, but because of my own need for distance.

I hadn't spoken to Seif, the third member of our old friendship triangle, much either over the years. Of course, Seif had his own responsibilities as the West Coast Regional Alpha, making him hard to keep in touch with.

But really, it was mostly me.

Hiding in a Midnight Fae paradigm in the Hell Fae Realm.

Lucifer was very particular about whom he allowed to visit and when, making it hard for anyone to reach me.

Shade had a pass since his grandmother had created this paradigm, but the dungeon was technically in Hell Fae territory more than the paradigm, so he was skirting the rules by shadowing down here.

Not that Shade ever obeyed authority.

"Aflora has decided to host a new version of the Blood Gala," Shade murmured. "She wants to use it as a way to bring everyone together to celebrate life."

I snorted. "Life. Of course. I suppose she is still the Earth Fae Queen as well."

Shade narrowed his gaze a bit. "And my mate."

"Yes, I'm aware."

"Then you may want to watch your tone."

I folded my arms. "You waltzed into my den uninvited, Shade. Now you're telling me about an event we both know I have no desire to attend. What do you really want?"

"To check up on my friend?" he suggested. "To make sure you're still alive?"

"Clearly, I am."

"But are you living?" he pressed, placing his glass of

untouched wine on the bar and facing me fully. "You've been hiding in this paradigm for a decade, trying to run from your past. That doesn't make it any less present, Ajax."

"When did you become your grandmother?"

"Probably when I had a child," he replied without missing a beat. "It's a surreal change, truly, but that doesn't make me any less concerned for you."

"I'm fine."

"Are you?" he arched a dark brow. "My grandmother seems to feel otherwise."

"And what do you feel?" I wondered aloud as I strolled over to my couch to relax into the leather seat again. My gaze flicked to the screen, but it was still dark. *Fuck. I hope Camillia is all right.*

The pull on my heart had me frowning.

Maybe this distraction from Shade is what I need. I shouldn't care what happens to her. She's just a candidate, right?

"I think death is painful," Shade replied, joining me on the couch and leaving his wine behind. "I think you're trying to cope and this paradigm is helping you hide from that pain. Which I understand and respect. That's why I don't intrude often." He looked at me. *Really* looked at me. "Just don't mistake that lack of intrusion for a sign that I don't care. Because I do. We may have grown apart, but you're still a brother to me, A."

It was on the tip of my tongue to nag him about getting sentimental on me.

But something about his words unsettled me too deeply to form a sarcastic retort.

I found myself swallowing and nodding instead, then muttered a spell to call my wine glass to my hand and took several healthy sips.

He followed suit, his nose scrunching at the flavor.

"Not to your liking?" I asked, attempting to distract from the moment that had just worked its way between us.

"It's a bit sour," he replied, frowning at it.

"You're addicted to your mate."

"Among other things," he replied, his lips twitching again. "But yes, I tend to only drink from her. Sometimes Kols."

I grunted. "Talk about *sour*."

"He's come a long way since you knew him last." Shade almost sounded fond of the former Midnight Fae Prince—the same one Emelyn had been engaged to—causing something to stir in my chest.

So much had changed in Shade's world.

I supposed a lot had changed in mine, too. Just in an entirely different manner.

He was living the dream.

Meanwhile, I hunted disobedient Nightmare Fae and imprisoned them.

How darkly fitting.

"I think things are about to change, A," Shade mused softly. "It just depends what path you choose." He glanced back at the table. "I suggest using that stone. But we'll see what you do."

I frowned at him. "Riddles?"

He shrugged and took another sip of his wine before setting it aside. "Just advice." His icy gaze met mine, a hint of emotion lurking in his expression. An emotion I couldn't quite define. "I look forward to our next wine date," he told me. "Hopefully without the snakes."

He stood, causing me to gape at him. "That's it? Stop by with some cookies and a death stone, lay some riddles at my feet, and leave?"

"You're not ready to talk to me yet," he replied, meeting my gaze with a hint of amusement in his eyes.

"And that's fine. But we'll meet again soon." He cocked his head. "Try not to bite her without permission. If I learned anything from my queen, it's that females don't particularly enjoy having their choices taken from them."

"Bite who?"

"I think we both know the answer to that," he replied with a coy grin.

Then the bastard disappeared in a puff of dark smoke that had the snake-vines hissing again outside my door.

I sighed and shook my head. "Cryptic jackass."

He always did shit like this, dropping by with a few random riddles and fucking off again.

But I couldn't quite keep the smile from forming on my lips.

Because something about that brought back pleasant memories of when he'd done this to others in our past.

He'd done it to me, too. Creating games I used to love to play.

I just wasn't sure I had the energy to engage in this new puzzle.

Not with Camillia on my mind.

Camillia. I reached for the remote, but the screen flickered back to life without me having to touch it.

Definitely watching me, I thought, glancing around. *Or at least a supervision spell of some kind.*

Lucifer would probably ask me about Shade's visit later.

Running a hand over my face, I sighed, then brought the wine back to my lips.

Only to frown at the darkness in front of me.

What am I looking at? Everything was pitch black, but the numbers were still displayed on the screen, so the device was definitely on.

I swapped the glass for the remote, searching for

another candidate's number. The girl was running toward the border crossing, her jaw set in a determined line.

"That's not what it looks like," I said to the screen.

Something she realized the second she crossed the border.

Causing the screen to go black once more.

My teeth clenched as I went back to Camillia's number. *Dark.*

I found another candidate, still alive and running. Selected several more, noting that only a handful of them were black. Then I went back to the girl who had crossed the boundary—still dark.

Just like Camillia.

Fuck. I jumped to my feet. "*Fuck.*"

That could only mean one thing.

Camillia hadn't made it.

She... she'd *failed*.

My heart stopped, my head swiveling back and forth in denial. "No." *No.* Not Camillia. She couldn't... She was...

I swallowed.

Everything inside me protested this reality, the fact that she was *gone*.

"No fucking way," I said, wanting to punch a hole through the screen. Except it wasn't tangible, the mirage technology making it resemble a translucent space that allowed video play. "*No.*"

Camillia was too strong to just... just *die*.

But Emelyn was strong, too, a dark voice whispered. *And she's dead.*

Because I hadn't been able to save her.

Yet I'd possessed every opportunity imaginable to save Camillia. And I hadn't. I'd just offered some food and information. I'd fucking *taunted* her.

I threaded my fingers through my hair and began to pull. "*Fuck!*"

I should have tried harder.

I shouldn't have let myself become attached.

I should have *helped* her.

I wasn't supposed to fucking care!

The snake-vines hissed, agitated by my mounting fury. I couldn't stop cursing. I couldn't stop pacing. I couldn't stop *hating*.

So much anger. So much fucking pain. A new nightmare.

I failed her. I failed Emelyn. And now I failed Cami.

My knees gave out as I fell to the floor, my lungs no longer knowing how to breathe. Yet I tried to scream anyway. To yell. To rant. To beat the shit out of the stone beneath me.

It did nothing for me.

It just hurt me more.

Fuck. Fuck. Fuck!

She's gone.

Camillia's gone.

And I'm the one who captured her. I'm the one who did this to her. I'm the one who killed her.

I grabbed my hair again, my past and my present converging to spin my reality out of control. I could hardly breathe. I could hardly even *think*.

Az wasn't here to ground me.

Shade had left me here with his fucking cryptic statements.

I was alone. Just the way I wanted.

But some soft part of me didn't want it this way at all.

That soft part of me throbbed, panging with loss.

This is why I don't want to care. Why I don't want to feel.

Yet I seemed incapable of achieving even that.

Because I'm a failure.

I always fail.

And now… now I've failed someone who could have meant something. Someone who deserved so much better.

I'm sorry, Camillia. "So fucking sorry."

CAMI

HELL FAE RULE #7: When You Can't Win a Fight, Run into the Shadows.

Except, as I quickly scanned the area, I didn't see any sort of shadow or a single place to hide.

Only lava pits.

And the illuminated path.

And, of course, a scattering of enraged Centaurs trying to maul us all.

Running straight into the crowd of females, I opted for safety in numbers.

The Centaurs roared in unison as they kept on my tail. One glance over my shoulder assured me I wasn't going to outrun these assholes.

Fuck, they're fast.

I was stronger than my mortal counterparts, but I was still half-human. That meant I couldn't keep up this burst of speed for very long.

Sucking in another gulp of stale, heated air, my lungs

struggled to process the oxygen from the environment. What little there was of it.

I considered using one of Melek's spells to alter the composition of the atmosphere around me but decided against it.

He was probably hoping I'd be desperate enough to make use of his help. He seemed to be using me as some sort of pawn in a game between him and the most powerful fae I'd ever met.

And Lucifer was not someone I wanted to piss off, something I had already somehow managed to do by just existing. Well, maybe because I'd seen through his mirage. But that had been a result of Melek's interference.

I didn't want to repeat that mistake now.

So no spells.

Just running.

Except… hmm… Is that…?

A shimmering magic hummed through the air, something similar to the one I'd noticed in the arena. *A mirage…? What's it hiding?*

I started toward it on instinct, my feet moving across the jagged landscape as I tried not to stumble in my inappropriate running shoes. With my luck, the heel would wedge itself in the rocks and cause me to trip and fall.

But I couldn't worry about that now. I had to push. To run. To escape the horde of snarling beasts behind me.

A group of warrior-like females lurked near the shimmering magic, their weapons flashing beneath the bright suns. Their toned muscles revealed that they were definitely in shape as they faced the Centaurs with their blades and bows drawn.

I ran right for them and ducked as they took fire at the Centaurs chasing after me.

"My weapon isn't working!" one girl shouted as she fired her pistol over and over at a Centaur.

I noted that the creature had a white aura around it. The being snorted at me and then at her with disdain before moving on, making me frown.

I wasn't the one who'd chased him.

Nor was I the one to fire at him.

Yet he snorted at me like I was beneath his hoof?

How unreal, I marveled, ducking again as more weapons fired over my head toward the group of Centaurs.

"There's another!" someone shouted, sniping one of the creatures between its red eyes.

It didn't even have time to release a death cry. It simply thudded over dead, its massive body crashing to the ground, its black aura fading.

At least some of them can be killed.

The thought seemed to register with the others in his group, because many of them paused to consider the girls ahead of them. I took advantage of their distraction to keep running while processing the varying auras.

It seemed those with darker signatures could be killed.

The others could not.

I filed that information away as I darted up toward the candidates decked out with gear. "Hey!"

I spotted a familiar silver-haired fae with obsidian irises.

Feyre.

She frowned at me as another shoved herself into my face. "*Hey* yourself. We are the Elites, and we aren't taking any new recruits, so get out of our way or we'll *make* you get out of our way." She ended her statement with a snap of her fingers right in my face.

Well, that was quite the speech.

I raised an eyebrow at the female with slick, tied-back

black hair. A red streak ran down the middle, giving her a punkish appearance that I found begrudgingly cool.

Glancing at Feyre again, I gave her a look that I hoped said, *And who is this bitch?*

We weren't exactly friends, but we had met.

Of course, that meeting had ended with her throwing a dagger at me. So, yeah, we were definitely not friends at all. Just acquaintances at best.

However, her lips quirked up a little on the side.

But she didn't make a move to help me.

Not surprising.

The punk chick snapped her fingers again, making me decide to name her "Queen Bitch" since no one wanted to provide an introduction.

Definitely not welcome here, then.

"Move on before I make you move on," she threatened.

Throwing my hands up, I took two steps backward. "Not looking for allies or a problem. Just looking for the exit."

The female narrowed her eyes at me, then snorted. "Good luck. If we can't find it, then I highly doubt a scrawny Halfling like you can."

That made my teeth grind together.

Scrawny Halfling? Really?

A Centaur pawed the ground a few feet away, just behind one of the lava pits.

Then it walked right through the fiery liquid without even flinching.

Fuck, these Centaurs are intense.

Queen Bitch turned toward him, a weapon falling into her hand as she analyzed his trajectory. Without the lava pit, he had a straight path toward us.

Well, us and another group of girls.

However, that group was quite different from the *Elites* —whatever the fuck *that* meant—as they all wore the white T-shirt and black pants uniform, and they didn't appear to have any weapons.

They also looked terrified.

There was a clear divide here between those prepared for the trial and those just trying to survive.

Queen Bitch led the group of "prepared" members, something she proved now by pulling an object from her bag to toss near the other group of women.

A loud pop exploded, earning the Centaur's attention.

My lips parted. *Did that bitch really just intentionally use other candidates as a shield?*

"Come on, Feyre," Queen Bitch snapped. "Let's find the trick to this trial. You take the south. I'll take the north."

Feyre frowned at the group of females now cornered by the salivating Centaur and a lava pit. They were huddling together, true fear etched into their expressions.

"*Feyre,*" Queen Bitch growled.

A single glance toward me held all the information I needed to know about Feyre.

She didn't like Queen Bitch any more than I did, but for some baffling reason, she tucked her chin to her chest and headed in the direction that I assumed was south.

A scream distracted me as the Centaur impaled one of the brides, making my blood boil.

I'm not getting involved.

I'm not going to do it.

Hell Fae Rule #6: Only Look Out for Yourself—No One Else.

I gritted my teeth as I repeated the rule three more times. Then I slipped around Queen Bitch, dipped my hand into her bag, and took one of the bombs.

Another girl screamed, causing my jaw to clench.

Yeah, fuck the rules, I thought, throwing the device at the ground near my feet.

"What the hell?!" Queen Bitch screeched as the blast redirected a herd of Centaurs straight toward us.

Shoving my way through the Elites, I left their screams in my wake as the Centaurs plowed onward without mercy. *Right over the lava pit.*

All of these Centaurs possessed black auras, their red eyes gleaming with madness with those shadows distorting their other features. And their horns were stained with blood.

The shimmering magic in the air made me wonder if this was all a mirage.

Or if Lucifer was done being merciful, thus making this a reality.

The screams of dying candidates suggested it was the latter. Or maybe none of this had ever been a mirage and the magic I sensed was something else entirely.

Regardless, we needed to *run.*

The Elites were hot on my tail, sprinting along the landscape and shoving one another out of the way. One of them caught my side, knocking me into a sharp rock. It spun me around, forcing me to take in the carnage in my wake.

Blood soaked into the ground, and Hell seemed to greedily suck up the moisture. I couldn't take my gaze away from the broken body lying underneath a trample of hooves.

Then the Centaurs did something strange. They began to fight over the corpse.

The massive beasts hurled their full body weight against one another. Their antlers slammed together, sending a massive clash ringing across the landscape.

While the other candidates took the opportunity to run

down the illuminated path, I crouched behind a rock and watched the scene unfold with a mixture of fascination and horror.

The hum in the air was stronger now.

What's going on?

I should run. I knew I should run. But I couldn't seem to stop watching. The Centaurs were no longer chasing. They were too busy *brawling*.

More magic warmed the atmosphere, causing my nose to twitch with the need to sneeze.

Then the girl on the ground split into two, similar to when I had seen Lucifer both standing and giving his speech but, at the same time, sitting and looking bored.

He hadn't seemed to appreciate that I'd been able to see through his enchantment.

So I doubted he would be all that pleased with what I could see unraveling before me now.

Because the entire landscape was unfolding before my eyes.

A gruesome scene of a slaughtered female.

And another of the ground swirling around a perfectly unharmed female. She wasn't broken into pieces or even bloody. At least, not this version of her.

Instead, she looked confused and disoriented.

A Centaur wrapped his arms around her and held her against his chest. He'd been the one fighting seconds ago. But he appeared to have won.

The girl stared up at him when a long, pink tongue slithered out from the shadows that hid his face and grazed her cheek.

She… giggled.

She fucking giggled?

The Centaur seemed pleased with her response of being licked in the face and pulled her onto his back as if she were riding a horse. He offered his long mane for her to hold on to and she took it, a look of bewilderment crossing her face.

A white aura glowed around the Centaur, and the shadows around his face briefly fleeted, revealing handsome features. His red eyes were still menacing, but I inexplicably knew that this was one of the good ones.

Well, maybe *good* wasn't the right term. There was still something I was missing.

The circular wave of murky power at their feet yawned open, and the girl screamed as they dropped into the darkness.

What the actual fuck?

With the white-aura Centaur and candidate gone, there wasn't anything to distract the remaining herd.

A sea of red eyes swiveled toward me.

I'd clearly overstayed my welcome in search of answers.

Cursing, I glanced down the long stretch of the illuminated path that was my only escape route. A group of brides in the front were nearly at the end, a location I had noticed the Elites avoided. It looked like some kind of finish line, and I wondered if the Centaurs wouldn't be able to cross over, like some sort of barrier or force field.

My questions were immediately answered when the first group of females jumped over the break in the ground.

Only to plummet down an invisible cliff.

Chills swept up my spine.

It may look like a border crossing.

Don't fall for it.

The Centaurs snorted, drawing my attention back to them as they slowly surrounded me.

They seemed at home in this horribly heated landscape, as if they breathed fire on a daily basis.

And ate girls for dinner. Creepy-as-fuck assholes.

I definitely wouldn't be giggling if they taste-tested me for dinner.

But something nagged at me. I couldn't help but feel like the Hellbeasts were a key to the trials, something I was supposed to learn or figure out.

Perhaps it had something to do with their auras. So far I'd seen white and black, and the black ones had been pretty unfriendly and attacked unprovoked.

The white-aura ones had only attacked in response to aggression, which, if someone had shot a gun at me, I'd probably attack, too. I couldn't blame them.

Maybe I could negotiate.

Because these Centaurs all had white auras.

"So, uh, what do you guys do around here for sport?" I asked, trying my best to give a smile as I opened my palms in an unthreatening motion.

The Centaur closest to me released a bull-like snort that didn't sound very friendly.

"You like to charge things?" I surmised. "That sounds like, uh, fun." I knelt, grabbing one of the broken stones. It burned against my palm, having absorbed the realm's heat, but I wouldn't be holding on to it for long.

"Have you guys tried jousting?" I asked conversationally. "You don't even need horses. You can just run with sticks or something." I hesitantly laughed.

They didn't.

I couldn't see their faces, but a few of them tilted their shadowed heads sideways.

I slid backward in a slow retreat, only to thump against something hard and heated.

Glancing up, I found I'd stumbled against the front legs

of one of the Centaurs. He leered down at me, ash puffing from his face, insinuating he was preparing to maul me.

But he wasn't, not yet. I seemed to intrigue him.

Keep talking, Cami.

"What about games of catch? I mean, you do have arms. Here, let me show you." I demonstrated by hurling my arm back and throwing the stone as hard as I could. It sailed through the air, missing all of the Centaurs, but I wasn't aiming for any of them.

The rock landed far off of the illuminated path, disappearing a moment later into the center of a lava pit.

Only, it didn't burn.

A distinct clattering noise sounded a moment later as if the rock had hit something hard.

Interesting.

Is that why they walked through the lava without flinching?

Is it all a mirage?

That would imply that the thick hum in the air was doing more than casting mirages over the supply pedestals and the fallen candidates.

The entire landscape was enchanted.

Which suggested the illuminated path was too obvious; it probably led to death. Hence the girls falling off the cliff. Or I assumed they had, anyway. That was what it had looked like when they'd disappeared.

The supply pedestals had also been a decoy meant to distract us.

Meanwhile, the true escape hid in plain sight.

In the form of the lava pits, I thought, considering the nearest one. Some of them might be real. But others might be portals. It would be fitting, considering we'd fallen through the ground to arrive here, too.

I would have to test them with rocks.

Assuming I could manage to make my way toward one.

Unfortunately, the Centaurs appeared rather displeased by my rock-throwing game. They were all snarling, their hooves stomping against the ground.

Ducking, I skirted backward through the horse legs behind me. He growled in response. Then I did the same to his buddy, attempting to escape their little entrapment without actually attacking them.

One of them shrieked as a dagger landed in its side from a passing girl.

Beatrix.

She was heading toward the path again, a snarl in her features that made the other Centaurs hiss and chase after her, leaving their fallen member behind.

It screeched in pain beside me, crashing to the ground and releasing the most god-awful sound of pain.

My brow came down. *But he has a white aura.*

The weapons hadn't been able to hurt the others with white auras.

So why had this one been hurt? Because she'd stabbed him while walking by him?

I wasn't sure, but I felt an inkling of pity for him as he writhed on the ground and tried to stand again.

The other Centaurs were chasing down the brides at full speed. Some they hooked under their arms and disappeared into the shadows they seemed fond of creating.

I didn't even want to know where they were taking them.

A scream from the left showed one of the Elites shoving a girl into a lava pit, making my eyes round. *Well, that's one way to test a theory...* I wasn't sure how they'd figured it out. Maybe they'd seen me throw the rock.

Regardless, they were using other candidates rather than inanimate objects to try the portal.

Lovely.

The creature keened beside me, his hand curling around the blade with a hiss. It sizzled in response, making him groan as he released the knife, the metal seeming to burn him.

The wound didn't appear to be fatal.

However, it clearly hurt.

The dark mist wavered around his face, and his panicked red eyes blinked.

"Hey," I said softly, reaching out a hand in offering. "Can I help?" The weapon hadn't hurt Beatrix, so it likely wouldn't hurt me.

But the Centaur might.

He bucked at me in response, nearly catching me in the head with a hoof.

"Okay, okay." I held my hands up in front of me.

There was something to these Hellbeasts that I was missing, and maybe if I could learn to understand them, I'd figure out what they really wanted.

Biting my lip, I considered one of Melek's spells that I could use to extract the blade. He'd taught me spells to manipulate my environment and to create shade, as well as food.

That meant I could technically create a change in pressure around the blade. It wouldn't use much magic, and it would be enough to extract it.

Maybe.

Hopefully.

Concentrating, I whispered the words under my breath that Melek had taught me. I didn't want to use his help, but I couldn't just leave this creature on the ground like this.

The Centaur made a guttural sound as the blade fell out and clanked against the hard ground.

Another herd of the creatures broke through the lava

pits, looking angry. I spotted a few arrows sticking out of their chests.

Seemed like they'd met Queen Bitch and it hadn't gone well.

They growled when they saw me and charged.

The Centaur with the white aura stumbled to his feet. As I had predicted, his wound quickly closed once the dagger had been extracted. He lowered his antlers.

But not at me.

"*Go,*" he growled, his voice low.

I blinked.

So they can speak...

No time to consider that more, not with his buddies charging toward me.

I darted toward the lava pit I'd thrown my rock into.

Closed my eyes.

And jumped.

TYPHOS

RARE SILENCE DESCENDED over the nightclub as the bride candidates ventured through the various lava pits.

My sinful home of debauchery and drinks had been morphed into a theater of sorts, with various Hell Fae sprawled out in black booths with translucent screens hovering over their tables.

Typically, those platforms were designated for holograms of feminine dancers—holograms my men could turn corporeal and use for their benefit as they wished.

Well, corporeal to an extent, anyway.

Virtual reality had worked wonders for placating the males of my kingdom, giving them ways to indulge their needs without having to leave the safety of the underworld.

It wasn't enough for everyone, thus some Hell Fae had chosen to leave in pursuit of their own mates. However, most of those mates were not allowed safe passage through my gates.

The source was very selective. Only a handful of females had ever been granted entry into my kingdom, all of whom were tied to powerful male Hell Fae. Which likely explained the source accepting their presence.

But it was definitely not the norm.

Hence, the unique atmosphere in the club tonight.

Danger lurked among these walls, anticipation, too, as the men engaged in a different game of sorts. One with the ultimate prize waiting for them at the end.

A prize they could keep. Unlike the holograms that weren't actually real.

But they certainly felt real when the right devices were engaged.

Not that I'd tried them myself. I had Melek for my pleasurable pursuits.

However, I did fancy the Hellfire Spirits—a drink that put any fae or mortal concoction to shame. A drink I now held in my hand as I wandered through the club to observe my subjects.

The space was large enough to house all eligible Hell Fae males who held stakes in the trials. And almost all of them were here.

Including Melek.

My magic powered the displays they all watched, providing me with a much-needed outlet for the power flourishing in my veins. I also lent my energy to empower the glorious ring of fire near the center of the club. The circle spanned around the central area I typically reserved for my throne on the raised platform.

I often sat there to observe my Hell Fae and make myself available for their questions and requests.

But I didn't sit there today.

I just kept it lit to provide lighting in the club while they all observed their choice candidates in the trials.

The first test was not difficult—at least by my standards. Mirages were simple to create, and they were easy to see through if one was observant enough. It didn't require magic. Only intuition.

Intuition that Camillia De La Croix seemed to possess in spades.

I watched her on the screen while sipping my Hellfire drink. Melek sat before me, aware of my presence at his back.

He calmly set his own drink on the volcanic stone table, but I sensed his agitation.

That sensation seemed to claw at the atmosphere in the room as others cursed when their candidates made choices that either disqualified them from the main events or caused them to perish indefinitely.

I didn't pity the potential brides.

If anything, I envied them.

They lived in the moment. They knew only the fight to survive. Many of them were being given the chance to prove themselves—a chance I'd never had.

And those who blindly fled would be treated like cattle.

Slaughtered.

Or eaten.

Finishing my drink, I crunched down on a piece of ice. It instantly melted on my tongue against my ruthless heat.

A curse sounded from a nearby table. I didn't bother looking. The whole point of this arrangement was to ensure my Hell Fae chose the right candidates. That required learning on behalf of my men and the females involved.

Quality mattered here.

Not quantity.

Something many of my men were learning a lesson about now, as they'd divided their gifts among several candidates rather than focusing on one.

Perhaps they would make better decisions during the next round.

I reached around Melek to set my glass beside his and rested my head on his shoulder while he observed Candidate Sixty-Six. "Has she used any of your gifts?" I asked softly, wondering what other intangible items he might have given her. *Not that many could compare to a mating bond.*

His gaze narrowed as though he'd heard my thought. Maybe he had. But his response was to my question regarding gifts. "No."

"Is that why you're irritated?" I asked softly, kissing his throat.

"Not really, no."

"Liar," I whispered, nibbling his earlobe.

"She used a spell to heal a Centaur," he replied as I rounded the booth to slide in beside him.

"And that bothers you?" Because I'd found it rather admirable. Shocking, too, as I hadn't realized she could use magic.

And oddly... *endearing.*

She'd approached everything with a discerning eye, taking in her surroundings before making decisions, and even trying to befriend the Centaurs—which had made me chuckle a little.

As though my Nightmare Fae wanted to chase *rocks.*

It would have been demeaning if I hadn't found it so damn adorable.

No one else that I'd observed had tried that approach. Of course, I hadn't watched many of the others. I'd been more intrigued by Melek's reactions than the actual candidates, and Camillia had been the only one he seemed interested in observing.

Given he'd mate-bonded her at the first level, I wasn't surprised by his choice.

But it did leave me curious enough to watch her with him.

I'd never seen him so serious, his expression etched in stone as he observed her through the first trial. "I gave her that knowledge for herself, yet she chose to use it to help another."

"And that upsets you?"

His lips curled down. "No. It actually quite pleases me."

"Oh? Is that why you're frowning?"

He glanced at me. "I'm merely confused as to why she's rejecting the knowledge I gifted her."

Ah. So his pride was wounded because the female had rejected his version of a gift. "Perhaps she doesn't want to use magic as a crutch," I suggested.

He pondered that for a moment. "Perhaps." His focus returned to the darkened screen. "How long will this last?"

"Until this part of the trial is complete." The girls who had found the lava pit portals would continue to spin until every female made her respective move.

"They're all going to be dizzy," Melek remarked calmly.

"Which should make the maze all that much more fun." Or it would end quickly with a bunch of unconscious candidates.

I supposed we would see soon.

"Did you gift her a spell to help with headaches?" I wondered aloud.

He gave me a knowing look. "You just want to know what spells I shared with her."

I shrugged. "I'm more curious to know how you knew she could use spells to begin with." It wasn't something many fae could do, let alone a Halfling. Her soul wasn't connected to the Hell Fae Source, which meant she had to tap into the power inside her own spirit—an ability most fae didn't possess.

Melek's eyes glimmered with secrets. "She's special, Ty."

"If she has your interest, then she's more than just special," I replied.

He brushed his knuckles along my jaw, his expression warming. "As are you."

Any other day, I would have scoffed at the statement and rolled my eyes. But hearing them now meant something to me. I caught his hand and pressed a kiss to his inner wrist, thanking him without words.

He held my gaze for a beat. "I only gave her atmospheric spells, mostly to help with temperature and creating food. The way she healed that Centaur wasn't what I'd meant for her to do, but it certainly said a lot about her character."

"It did," I conceded.

"So maybe she'll be able to pull the wind around her to help keep her stable when she finishes falling." He lifted his shoulders. "Or she'll continue to ignore my gifts."

I pressed another kiss to his wrist, releasing him. "Time will tell."

"Indeed." He picked up his glass again, whispering an enchantment to refill it. He'd conjured the drink originally as well, choosing to use his magic over requesting any sort of service.

"Sponsors are permitted private booths, you know," I said conversationally as I started playing with the screen. "You don't have to lurk in the corner and manage your own drinks. We do have staff for that."

"Am I technically a sponsor?" he asked, his eyes

dancing across the images as I started scrolling to find someone else to observe while we waited for this portion to end.

"I don't know. Are you?" I glanced at him.

He lifted a shoulder. "I'm undecided."

I considered him for a long moment, noting that the agitation wafting off of him wasn't due to irritation so much as a result of his underlying concern for the girl.

"Melek." His multicolored eyes met mine. "You realize I would give her to you, yes?" I'd already said this more than once, but I vocalized it again, just to drive the point home. "Then you wouldn't have to worry about her."

"I'm not worried." His tone confirmed he meant it, yet that underlying note of agitation continued to permeate the air between us. I knew my prince well. He might not think he was worried, but deep down, he cared whether the girl lived or died. And something told me it wasn't just because of what it would do to his soul if she perished.

"I need to see what she can do before I decide how to proceed," he added after a beat of silence.

"With the mating?" I questioned, my gaze returning to the screens in time to watch one of the candidates slip onto another Centaur's back. They seemed to be finding several potential brides. *Good.*

"With everything," Melek replied cryptically.

"Hmm," I hummed. "More games."

He merely smiled in response, then took over the remote to turn off the screen as one of my Hellhounds approached with a gold tablet in his hands.

I arched a brow. "The royal lieutenants are not supposed to report until the end of the trial."

"Some are sending in mid-term reports," he replied, his voice gruff.

Melek chuckled beside me. "I think they're eager, my lord." He reached for the tablet. "Thank you, Payan."

The Hellhound dipped his chin, then slowly backed away as Melek set the tablet between us on the table. My drink refilled in the next instant, my prince having whispered a spell to replenish the cup just like he'd done with his own.

"Let's see how things are going, hmm?" he mused, his palm falling to my thigh to allow me to take charge of the tablet.

"Another game?" I asked as his touch started to drift upward.

"Is seduction a game?" he countered.

"With you?" I met his multicolored gaze. "Always."

His lips curled. "Then it's one you enjoy." His finger drifted over my zipper and the growing arousal beneath. "Engage the tablet, my king. I wish to see how your kingdom is faring."

"Always reminding me of my duty," I murmured, both irritated and amused. Because I wasn't the one distracted by these trials, as evidenced by his gaze flicking toward some of the other tables to check on their screens.

I didn't call him out on that distraction, instead choosing to open the message on the tablet from King Zul.

20 passed, 4 casualties. They're being escorted to their quarters now.

I keyed back a quick reply saying to keep me updated.

Then my personal device buzzed against my wrist.

"Someone's popular," Melek purred, his finger still tracing my zipper in a teasing caress.

I grunted and pulled up my sleeve to read the message etched across my skin.

Only I could see the messages that appeared in my DNA. It was one of the many unique technologies I had gathered through my deals over the years with various species of fae and non-fae.

Candidate Sixty-Six's parents appear to be out of realm. I've tried a few different ways to locate them, all of which have failed. It's as though they've disappeared entirely.

I frowned.

"Not in the mood today, my king?" Melek asked, his touch searing my skin even through my pants.

"You know I'm always in the mood for you," I said, tapping on my arm as I scrawled out a reply to Azazel.

Return home.

If he couldn't find her parents through his usual means, then we would have to try a different method—by using the Hell Fae Source. Her father might not be under my contract anymore, but his soul still connected to his birthright through me.

I would find him.

Then I'd send Az after him.

But it would have to wait until after today's trial, and potentially the next one, as I had a lot of power to expel over the next week.

"Are you all right?" Melek's fingers stilled against me.

"Yes. Just surprised." Az was a powerful seeker. Evading him was a difficult feat, one very few could accomplish. It raised several more red flags where Camillia De la Croix was concerned. *I really need to learn more about this girl.*

The golden tablet buzzed again, this time with a message from King Stallus.

19 potential mates. 7 casualties.

It was a good number, and while casualties were to be expected, a twenty-two percent fail rate was acceptable. My prior disappointment lifted, making me roll back my shoulders.

I tilted the tablet toward Melek and he nodded.

Then the main screen flared to life once more as the next phase began, causing his touch to flinch against my now-throbbing shaft.

Whatever this female was, she'd definitely captured my prince's attention.

Which meant she now had mine, too.

A fate that would likely lead to her doom.

MELEK

THERE YOU ARE, little angel, I thought as her dirty-blonde ponytail flickered into view. I couldn't see her well, the tunnel around her quite dark. But it was enough of her silhouette for me to recognize her.

Of course, the number flashing on the screen confirmed her identity, too.

I resisted the urge to stroke said figure as she looked around, clearly trying to find her eyesight.

"At least she's standing up," I mused aloud, thinking of how dizzy she had to be after however many minutes of constant falling.

"In heels, too," Typhos replied.

"Yes, because you didn't allow her to change."

"You could have given her a spell for clothing."

"Hmm," I hummed. "Maybe I preferred the dress, after all." It was rather revealing, the kind of fabric one dreams of peeling off a woman. "I chose to help her with nourishment instead." The heat made her clothing irrelevant. She'd honestly be better off running naked through the trials.

Of course, that would detract from a future trial where that would actually be a requirement.

So her dress would do for now.

"As did Ajax," Ty mused.

Yes. As did Ajax, I echoed with an internal smile.

The Midnight Fae had played right into my hands last night, going to check on her and then providing her with gifts of food. He'd even shrouded her in a cooling spell, one that had likely followed her into her first trial.

A ring of fire formed around Ty's glass beside me, his power igniting as he attempted to add a dangerous element to his preferred drink. I watched his throat work as he swallowed some of the fiery liquid, his control resolute.

Yet I sensed the slight fracture inside him, the imperfection that required my constant repair.

The source had grown exponentially over the years, pushing more and more energy into Typhos. He managed it well on the surface, but I sensed the toll it took on his soul to keep everything in balance.

He wouldn't admit it out loud.

But that was all right.

I knew the truth. And I would fix him. In time.

My focus returned to the screen once more as Camillia slowly inched forward, her stance and pace telling me she was listening carefully to her surroundings.

Good girl, I thought. *But you could create a light.*

Since I'd given her a spell for that.

Of course, she wasn't using it.

Because she didn't trust me.

Yet she'd readily repeated the bonding spell.

That was what confused me—why had she accepted that gift and not the knowledge? Did she not believe I would protect her? Because even now I could feel my soul pushing energy her way to keep her safe. Protecting her in the dark. Pulsing life through her veins.

Why are you ignoring such an obvious spell? I wondered at her. *Just create some fire, little angel. Use it to guide you.*

Alas, she just continued to feel her way through the maze, her silhouette only visible to my eyes because of the enhanced technology following her.

Ty's palm went to my thigh, his fingers squeezing. "You're still tense."

"Am I?" I relaxed into his side, my head lying on his shoulder while I continued to watch the darkened screen. "Perhaps you can help me with that."

He ran his fingers along the inner seam of my dress pants, following it upward to my groin. "You still owe me six nights, little prince," he whispered against my ear.

I shivered, the words heating my blood. "That I do, my lord." We might have had a moment last night after my bonding Cami, but that didn't mean I would renege on my deal with Ty.

If anything, I would likely find a way to extend it.

I always did enjoy having him inside me, something I sensed he needed a reminder of now more than ever.

"Consider this a warm-up round," I suggested softly, spreading my thighs for easier access.

He reached forward to enlarge Camillia's screen, making it take up more of the table space. I'd kept it small to hide my interest from the others, but a shimmer of magic cascaded around us like a curtain, creating a private little viewing booth for me and Ty.

"If you won't accept one of the sponsorship booths, I'll just create one for you," Ty said, his lips touching my neck. "And I'll personally ensure your every need is met."

My stomach clenched. "Mmm, I do like the way that sounds, my king."

"I know you do," he replied, his palm skating over my zipper on his way up to my belt. "Keep your eyes on the screen, Melek. Tell me what she's doing."

"It's still dark, my lord."

"Not for long," he whispered, his fingers deftly unfastening the buckle before popping open the button at the top of my pants.

His warmth surrounded me, his spicy scent reminding me of burning cinnamon, making me sigh. I loved this male more than words could express. Which was why I'd put everything on the line for him.

He saw my mating to Cami as an affront to our connection.

What he didn't realize was that I'd chosen her for us.

These trials were very much for the Hell Fae who desired mates, but they were so much more than that to me.

The moment Cami had picked up that book in the library, she'd become ours.

I just hoped she lived up to her potential and proved my suspicions correct.

She appeared to be doing an admirable job now as she continued to feel her way through the tunnels, searching for any sign of life.

I relayed that detail to Ty as he nuzzled my collarbone. The zipper of my pants hummed through the booth as he pulled it down, revealing my hardening length.

His fingertips grazed my sensitive skin, his teeth nibbling on the button of my shirt to pop it open.

My heartbeat echoed in my ears as he continued his ministrations downward, parting my dress shirt one button at a time. "And now?" he asked, his mouth dancing along the top of my abdomen.

"Still dark," I said, my eyes glued to the screen as his hot breath caressed me.

This wasn't at all what he'd requested with his deal.

But I understood that would come *after*.

This was Ty's version of an apology. A way for him to put himself at my mercy while he sought forgiveness for doubting me.

I'd forgiven him the moment I'd seen him on the podium today.

However, that didn't matter.

He needed to secure his place in my soul, remind me who owned me, who owned *him*, what we meant to one another.

This wasn't about jealousy, though.

I knew he spoke the truth when he said I could have Cami.

He wouldn't deny me the pleasure of her touch; he'd merely request to join.

No, this was about proving to me that we were still a team. That while he might wear the title of *King*, I was very much his equal.

I threaded my fingers through his long, thick hair, loving the way it felt against my palm. It wasn't a way to direct him—I would never dream of telling this man what to do—just a way to hold him. To tell him I understood. To give him absolute power to do whatever the fuck he desired.

And right now, it seemed he wanted my cock in his mouth.

Because he desired my pleasure.

My cum.

My essence down his throat.

Another reminder for us both that we belonged together. *Always*.

A flash of light captured my focus as Cami's beautiful features finally graced the screen. "Mmm, she looks tired. But still stunning. And that dress of hers is ready to fall off entirely." Not that it had really been on to begin with. "There's the barest hint of rose along her breasts, telling me her nipples are pretty little rosebuds." Which made my mouth water for her.

Ty slid to the floor to kneel between my thighs. "The kind of nipples you want to tease with your tongue?" he asked before drawing his own tongue around the crown of my cock.

"Yes," I hissed, my grip slipping from his hair to slide beneath the long lengths to grasp his nape. "I almost want to request that she always compete in that dress." Because it was fucking delicious on her, practically painted onto her curves and leaving nothing to the imagination.

Especially as the strips along her tits started to move.

"Definitely pert little rosy tips," I confirmed before she could tug the dress back into place. "She doesn't like to show them off, though."

"I can make it so she doesn't have a choice. Just say the words, little prince." He spoke the words against my shaft, then swallowed me down to the back of his throat in the next instant, momentarily making me forget what the fuck we were even talking about.

Then the camera zoomed in on Camillia's face, showing the beads of sweat dripping down her skin. "The tunnels are making her hot," I said, my voice more guttural now that Ty had truly begun the job of torturing me. "The thin air seems to be impacting her breathing." Something I noted as her chest moved in rapid pants, her full lips parted in a way that reminded me of sex.

She would absolutely look like that beneath me— blushing, panting, sweating, and *moaning*.

Have any Minotaurs scented her yet? Ty asked into my mind, his mouth too busy to murmur the question aloud.

I lifted my hand to draw my fingers along the translucent screen, searching around Camillia's still form. The sudden light seemed to have shocked her into observing her surroundings once more. Which was a problem because those torches served as a beacon—one the Minotaurs would use to find her.

"Not yet," I said. "But they will soon."

Ty hummed in agreement against my cock, the vibration going straight to my balls.

"*Fuck*," I breathed, my head falling back on a groan I couldn't quite swallow.

Focus on the screen, Ty reminded me, his teeth grazing my skin in stark warning.

I squeezed the back of his neck but did as he commanded, my gaze finding Camillia once more. "There are several scrapes on her hands and arms," I gritted out, both in response to the delectable way he hollowed his cheeks around me and my irritation over seeing her injured. "I gave her spells that could help her with the temperature problem. She's clearly not using them."

Will you punish her for not accepting your gifts? he asked me softly. *Tie her up with your ropes, perhaps?*

My abdomen clenched at the image his words painted —Camillia bound and helpless in my silky hemp ropes. "I would leave her breasts free to play with those sweet little nipples," I confided, my gaze instantly returning to her breasts. "I'd lace another one between her thighs so every time she fidgeted, it would graze her clit, leaving her weeping for more." My focus shifted to the fabric flirting with her long legs, the slits revealing toned muscles as she began to move again.

Seeing the glimpses of pale skin made me want to rip the dress off of her, to explore what lay beneath.

But oh, that was a treat for another day.

My hips flexed as Ty pulled me exceptionally into his throat, ensuring I felt his control, his command, his *presence*.

"She's..." I trailed off, swallowing as sweat broke out across my skin. "She's running now. Scrambling over the stones. Rushing down the path." *Fuck.* I was so close to exploding, yet I refused to do it now. Refused to do it when she was still fleeing for her life. "She chose a smaller tunnel." It came out on a rasp of sound, my orgasm mounting both from the expert skill of Ty's mouth and the adrenaline thundering through my veins.

Run, Cami. Run.

But she'd been wise in her choice.

The Minotaurs were large creatures that wouldn't be able to pursue her in those tight corridors.

Which suggested she knew they were nearby.

Unfortunately, however, the smaller tunnels were still very much part of the game. They were all part of the elaborate maze the Minotaurs had created for their potential mates.

Has she found any of their gifts yet? Ty asked, his pace slowing as he withdrew all the way to the tip. *Do you think she'll accept one?*

"I don't know," I breathed, arching once more as he took me all the way to the base. "And she's going the wrong way." I knew the maze because I'd seen the plans when the Minotaur King had shared them with Ty.

That doesn't mean anything, Ty replied. "She could still find her way," he added aloud, his lips brushing my damp head.

"Yes." It came out on an exhale of air as he continued

237

his sensual torment by sliding his hand into my pants to cup my balls.

My head nearly fell back, but Camillia had just reached another crossroads, her exhausted features capturing my attention once more. She appeared utterly worn out, yet determined, her gray eyes reminding me of glittering metal. The torch had followed her, serving as the beacon it was to the Minotaurs tracking her movements.

"She's just reached the point where she can correct her mistake," I told Ty, my tone still deep with sensual need. "The quadrant crossing."

A need he stoked by dragging his teeth along the bottom of my shaft.

He knew exactly which point I meant, the four-way path that led in completely different directions. She didn't need to use any magic to find the right path, but she did need to use her senses and her wit.

She knelt on one knee and ran her fingers over the pebbles on the ground. The walls shook again as the Minotaur roared, but she ignored it and instead focused on the task at hand.

I relayed the details to Ty while adding, *Good girl*, in my mind. *Good fucking girl. Fuck...*

Ty was increasing his movements now that she'd neared the end.

He wanted me to explode with her victory, to feel as though I was standing right beside her, celebrating with her. All the while reminding me with his mouth whom I belonged to.

Cami sniffed the air, making my muscles tighten even more, the anticipation of her success mingling with Ty's expert mouth.

Yes, that's it, I thought, speaking to Ty, but also speaking to Cami. *Keep going.*

Cami leaned into one of the tunnels and closed her eyes as her nostrils flared.

The Minotaur would have left food as his gift, as they enjoyed cooking when in human form. However, when a female visited a Minotaur, she was usually on the menu.

Cami would have to find the food to prove herself worthy of the meal, regardless.

Like a mouse in a maze, Ty mused into my mind. *Searching for the cheese.*

I swallowed, my skin clammy with a combination of nerves and delayed gratification.

Are you going to give me a meal, little prince? Ty asked silkily. *Give me something to swallow for you?*

"*Fuck*," I panted, watching as Cami took off down the correct path. My heart raced in a combination of victory and need, leaving me breathless.

I curled one hand into a fist against the volcanic stone table, my opposite one holding on to Ty as though he possessed the meaning of life.

He took me deep once more as several screams filled the nightclub, candidates losing their lives to the hungry Minotaurs. It was meant to distract me from the potential death circling Cami as she raced down the tunnel. There was still one more break in the path, one that would serve as her final test.

"How long has she been in the tunnels?" I asked Ty, noting the extreme fatigue slowing her down. I knew his magic could move time differently, making that initial part of her wandering through the inky maze far longer than it had appeared to me.

At least three hours, he whispered into my mind.

"That's cruel," I told him.

He sank his teeth into my base, making me jump. *I am cruel, little prince. You know this.*

Sadist, I hissed back at him, my back nearly bowing off the leather cushion behind me.

Masochist, he returned.

I swallowed. He wasn't wrong. But I didn't mind playing both roles, something I reminded him of as I dug my nails into his neck.

Camillia's face lit up on the screen once more, her gaze still holding that steely glint to it as she evaluated the wider tunnels—tunnels that were large enough for the Minotaurs to move through.

She could try using a spell to manipulate the wind and blow light in all three directions to find her escape, but she clearly didn't want to use anything I'd given her.

Thus, the secret to this one would require faith.

That was the whole purpose of the first trial, though. To test each candidate's endurance and emotional intelligence.

My heart dropped as Camillia started down the wrong path. *Shit.*

MELEK

Ty stilled. *What is it?*

She's going the wrong way. If she continued that way, she would disappoint the Minotaur hunting her.

And a disappointed Minotaur tended to use his teeth.

"*Camillia,*" I said, my jaw tight.

She paused as if she could hear me, and given that we were bonded, maybe on some level she could.

Ty used his teeth again, warning me not to interfere too badly. But then he laved the tender skin with his tongue, soothing away the pain in the next minute.

Now who's playing games? I asked him as goose bumps pebbled down my arms.

The intensity of watching Camillia, of needing her to succeed, coupled with Ty's expert mouth, was quickly bringing me to the brink of madness.

I couldn't tell if I wanted to shout in frustration or come or do some manner of both at the same time.

Except…

"She's…" I narrowed my gaze, noting the blister on her lip as she sucked it between her teeth. "Fuck, she just needs to use that damn spell." Why wouldn't she cool herself? But at least she seemed to be battling her decision.

Every path she'd chosen thus far had been founded on logic. This one she'd clearly chosen blindly. It might have seemed like a fifty-fifty chance, but these final tunnels were spelled.

If she didn't know how to overcome the spell, she'd be lost and eventually become dinner to a Minotaur.

She slowly crept back to the crossway again, her gaze darting from side to side. That tattered dress slipped again, revealing her breast entirely and drawing a groan from me. "Her tits are fucking perfect, Ty," I told him, losing myself to the sensations again. "And she's... she's scenting the air again."

Searching for the cheese, he murmured. *Such a good little mouse.*

Yes, I agreed. *Yes.*

Because fuck, he was slaying me, his pace having picked up once more, matching the thudding rhythm of my heart, and demanding I stop delaying the inevitable.

As though Camillia could sense my impatience, my *need* for this torment to end, she dropped her torch and let it sputter out.

Yes, I repeated. *She's figuring it out, Ty. She's... she's... almost... there...*

Only a fine glimmer remained, which was exactly the amount of light Camillia needed to be able to see the real tunnels around her.

"Another mirage," she whispered, her voice carrying through the screen.

Ty stilled, his midnight irises lifting to mine.

Then she started down the correct path, her steps sure. "She's figured it out. She's—"

Ty's fiery essence flickered across his tongue as he

swallowed me all the way down, the subtle burn stealing the breath from my lungs. *Feed me, little prince. Give me everything.*

Fuck... He'd been teasing me before, allowing me to build to this moment, to focus on Camillia while she navigated the tunnels to find her freedom.

However, he wasn't teasing now.

He was *demanding*.

And I had no choice but to obey.

Camillia was still running, her body darkened once more, yet her silhouette showed every curve, every long, lean line, every tantalizing sway.

I could picture her naked.

See those beautiful tits with her rosy little buds.

Imagine my tongue tracing every inch on my way down to the dessert waiting for me between her thighs.

Ty would watch me taste her. He'd probably tell me what to do. Make me tease her, bring her to the edge, only to draw back and force her to watch him fuck me while leaving her without pleasure.

Only to then take her between us and utterly blow her mind.

It would be glorious.

Perfect.

Necessary.

Ty's power would flourish through her, through *us*, completing a mating he didn't even realize he craved.

I lost myself to the fantasy, lost myself to the sensation of his mouth around me, lost myself to the victory of Cami reaching the end.

And exploded down Ty's throat on a roar everyone in the club could hear.

I didn't care.

My king had done this to me.

My king drew out the pleasure like a fucking avalanche of sensation, causing my limbs to vibrate so intensely that I went ethereal for a brief moment. Feathers. No feathers. Feathers again.

And then I died a little.

Blissful agony.

Gorgeous completion.

An orgasm that rippled and pulsed and breathed new life into my very soul.

So fucking intense.

So damn perfect.

So gloriously regal.

Ty prowled up my body, his hungry gaze predatory as he captured my mouth in a kiss meant to destroy.

But the sound of Cami's sweet voice trickled around us as she said, "Hello," to the Minotaur waiting for her at the end of the tunnel.

I held my breath, the final test flickering across the screen. Ty moved his mouth to my neck, allowing me to watch over his broad shoulder.

The Minotaur was in human form yet said nothing as he offered his hand.

Camillia took it without hesitation.

Then he bent to run his tongue over her knuckles while she watched, her gaze curious. She didn't flinch, just observed.

He released a low noise, one that had her cocking her head. Then ever so slowly, he released her and straightened once more, his bored expression causing my shoulders to fall in relief. "He doesn't like the way she tastes."

Ty wrapped his palm around my still-hard shaft, giving it a stroke. "I bet she'll like the way *you* taste," he said, his teeth skimming my ear. "Maybe you should feed her later."

"It's technically within the rules," I replied, my breath

catching as he gave me a firm stroke. It didn't matter that I'd just come down his throat; I would always be ready for more with Ty.

I nearly pulled him to me for a kiss, but Camillia's scream had my gaze flying to the screen just in time to see her disappearing through another portal.

"She passed," Ty whispered, his focus on me, not on the screen.

"She did," I replied.

"How does that make you feel?" he asked.

"Pleased," I admitted. "And irritated." Because she'd done it without my help. Which was probably for the best, but I would have liked to hear her whisper more of my shared spells.

Ty chuckled, his hands going to my hips as he started to tug my pants downward. "Irritated because she denied your gifts?" The screen disappeared while he spoke, but the curtain of magic remained.

"Yes."

He used his body to push the table back behind him a bit, clearly wishing for more room for whatever he intended to do to me next—an action he proceeded to demonstrate in the next breath as he whirled us around to bend me over the table.

"It's for the best, little prince," he informed me softly as he finished removing my pants. "You won't be able to help her in the next trial."

My brow furrowed. "With the Sirens?"

His palms ran over my ass, then the whisper of clothing followed as he unfastened his pants. He wouldn't remove them. Not here. Not in the club.

No, he'd fuck me like this by just releasing his cock.

And given the way he was going, he intended to take me raw.

To make me *bleed*, just as he'd threatened last night.

My pulse picked up with excitement. I adored a little pain with my pleasure, something my king knew very well.

Others would see this as torture, maybe even gasp at the punishment.

Not me. Not *us*.

This was how we fucked.

And I loved every minute of it.

However, his comment confused me. "Why can't I help with the Sirens?"

"Because the Sirens are no longer part of the next trial." He palmed my ass again, spreading me as the head of his thick shaft touched my back entrance.

There was a hint of lubrication against his skin, just enough to ensure he didn't truly hurt me. He'd use his powers to keep this fluid, to ease me into his roughness and make me come again all over this volcanic stone.

I'm sending them to the Netherworld Kingdom instead, he whispered into my mind.

The heat flowing through my veins turned to ice. *What?*

Your candidate will have to prove herself there, little prince, he continued. *Because it's the one place you can't go. The one place your tricks won't work.* He leaned over me, the head of his cock pushing inside me as he moved. *You're not the only one who knows how to play these games.*

He thrust inside, drawing a growl from my throat.

Your move, little prince, he added as I began to pant. *Better make it good.*

Fuck...

That is what I'm doing, yes. He kissed the throbbing vein on my neck, his dark amusement palpable as he took my ass with an abandon I felt all the way to my fucking soul.

He could accept me taking a mate.

However, he was going to make us both work for it. To

prove the worthiness of the match and convince him of the rightness of this path.

It was a move that had my lips curling. Because I knew exactly what pawn to shift into place next.

Ty might be a master strategist. But I was his equal for a reason.

And this was a game I fully intended to win.

For both of us.

CAMI

"ARE YOU FUCKING KIDDING ME?" I breathed, my throat dry.

What a cheap fucking trick! Portaling me back to my cell right as I finally found the feast waiting for me at the end of the tunnel.

I growled, furious and starving, the scent of roast beef still tainting my nostrils.

I'd even let that Hell Fae lick my fingers—a really strange reaction to shaking hands, but what-the-fuck-ever. I was hungry. He had food. I would have lain on the ground and done anything he'd asked for a taste of that beautiful meal.

But no.

The floor had opened up and swallowed me whole.

Sending me back to this shitty place with the ratty rug and enchanted furniture.

So much for white auras meaning nice Hellbeasts, I thought, collapsing on the rug. That Hell Fae had boasted a pristine aura, one I thought had made him safe.

But one wave of his hand had sent me right back here.

To my damn cell.

My stomach rumbled with hunger, my vision blurring as tears threatened to take over.

Fuck off, I snapped, swiping at the treacherous little droplets. *I am not crying. Not today.*

Holding a hand to my middle, I groaned as I curled up on the ratty mat in the center of the cell, hating my life.

Well, at least I'm alive.

Although, it had cost me almost all of my reserves to keep breathing. Fighting my way through a bunch of Centaurs, not to mention Elite bitches, had been bad enough before I'd damn well nearly suffocated in the tunnels.

It was the heat that had drained me. The inhospitable landscape was not meant to be endured for extended periods, or even short ones, without magic.

I should have caved.

I should have used Melek's spells.

But I couldn't bring myself to do it.

Because I hadn't wanted to risk angering the Hell Fae King.

Shuddering, I closed my eyes and inhaled sharply, the need for air taking hold and squeezing my lungs. Only, the dungeon atmosphere wasn't much better, and it still smelled like a barn in here.

Ugh.

What I wouldn't give for a cool shower right now.

Some food.

A nap.

Well, while I was wishing for things, I wished I was in my apartment back home sleeping off a hangover, not trapped in this fucked-up game of survival.

But I wasn't in my apartment complaining to my

friends about the lack of desirable male specimens in the city.

Because my father had traded my soul to the literal devil.

Fuck.

I curled tighter into a ball, my body protesting every movement and causing my insides to riot with hunger. My head pounded. My throat barely worked. My lungs burned.

Everything spun, too. Probably from those fucking portals. This last one had lasted for… for… oh, I didn't know how long. I'd lost count around a thousand. But I'd been spinning forever, all the while salivating for that feast, only to end up in this dungeon several seconds, minutes, *hours*, later.

Just like the portal that had taken me from the Centaurs down to the maze.

It'd been torture.

Especially this last round in the spinning portal because I hadn't known where I would end up next. Part of me had worried I'd be dropped right into a Siren tank or something worse.

I was strong and could endure a lot, but my muscles were maxed out. It felt as though I'd run ten marathons. Maybe I had. And I had absolutely no concept of how long it all had taken. Nor did I care, not with my body shivering violently and sweating at the same time.

"Going to nap already?" a silky voice asked, causing my stomach to twist in a whole new way.

Forcing my eyes open, I met the multicolored gaze of a male specimen who most definitely was *desirable*.

Melek's angelic features made him almost too perfect, apart from the hint of ink peeking out at me around his wrists. It left me wondering what tattoos lurked beneath his clothes again, as I'd only seen subtle hints of it before.

His beautiful perfection almost seemed like a dream.

Maybe it was.

Maybe I'm dead.

That would explain all the loose buttons of his shirt, revealing part of his chest.

And his bedroom-like hair with those thick waves tousled messily around his ears, almost as though he'd just been fucked.

Hmm.

My gaze trailed down his neck to the hint of a dark design on his chest, the ink a stark contrast against his pristine, pale skin.

It seemed oddly appropriate, what with his perfection being a façade and all. His soul was as dark as those of the Hellbeasts I'd come across.

Well, not exactly. I actually couldn't really read his aura. *Interesting.*

His lips curved upward as he redid the shirt's buttons, hiding his tattoos from me and making my gaze narrow. He'd obviously done that on purpose, ensuring I saw his mark. Although, I had no idea why. But it seemed rather clear that Melek enjoyed his games.

"I'm not in the mood to play right now," I told him honestly, my voice a rasp of sound. "So if you don't mind…" I closed my eyes again, preparing to nap. Or maybe just shut him out.

Shut them *all* out.

Everything.

Just… just rest.

Find a way to stop trembling. Calm my muscles. *Relax.*

Except that didn't feel possible. Instead, I curled my fingers into fists and dug my nails into my palms. The pain helped ground me in the present, giving me the ability to draw in a deep, hot breath. My insides rebelled at the putrid stench, but my lungs accepted the temporary reprieve.

However, my stomach rumbled like a disgruntled lion. *Loudly.*

Melek openly laughed, his amusement making me want to curl even deeper into myself. I hated him. I hated *all* of them.

He was amused by my exhaustion and starvation.

What a charming trait.

"Fuck off," I muttered at him, thankful for my closed eyes. His attractiveness made me dizzy and stupid. With my eyes closed, I could *see* him for who he really was—a monster.

Which made it much easier not to fall for his deadly charm.

"Well," he drawled softly. "If you're not going to use my spells to make your own meal, how about you take this one instead?"

The sound of metal sliding across concrete grated against my ears, followed by the sound of bars clanking.

He's in my cell.

My nose twitched as he set something down beside me.

Beef. Not the roasted kind from the trial, but... I sniffed. *Steak.*

I opened one eye to peer at the tray of food he'd slid over to me. *Mashed potatoes. Steak. A pile of green vegetables. And a massive jug of water.*

Melek knelt so that he was at eye level with me, and I noticed he'd also brought the book from my dorm room—the one I'd taken from the library.

Melek considered me for a moment. "You only used one of my spells today. Why?"

I narrowed my eyes. It should be fucking obvious to him that after he gave me that damn necklace, everything went south.

His gifts caused trouble, and I was *not* falling for it again.

But his question elicited another thought that angered me even more—*he watched the trials*.

My glare intensified. *All* the Hell Fae had probably watched today's events, enjoying the sick and twisted events that ripped some of the girls apart. They got off on watching innocents die for their own fucked-up amusement.

"Cami?" he asked, true concern in his voice as he set the book down on the rug beside the tray. "Why didn't you use my gifts today?"

"You're seriously asking me that?" I meant for my voice to hold a touch of anger, but it just came out as a hoarse sound. How dare he insult me by asking as if he didn't already know why I'd refused his gifts.

Anger thundered through my veins, forcing me out of my ball and into a crawling position that soon led to me rising to my feet. It was a process—one I hated was so slow—but fuck if I was going to lie next to his tempting tray of food and let him feed me like some sort of pet.

Except I swayed and nearly fell, which completely defeated the purpose of standing, as it led to me leaning into Melek—who caught me deftly with his hands.

He guided me over to the couch, and I found myself praying that spell had returned.

Only nothing happened as he sat me down on it.

Nothing other than him joining me.

"I believe the humans have a term for this," he said conversationally, sweeping his hand through the air to magically call the tray to his lap. "It's called *hangry*."

"I'm not hangry," I growled as my stomach rumbled in clear disagreement.

Melek sighed, his expression losing its humor. "Please eat, Camillia."

I glared at him, but I took note of his polite request.

I doubted many heard Melek say *please*.

"You need your strength," he continued. "Especially since you don't have a proper source to pull energy from." His gaze flickered with curiosity then. "Is that why you denied my gifts? Because of the toll they take on your spirit?"

I blinked at him. I was starting to wonder if he was really this dense or still fucking with me.

But the genuine interest in his features had me leaning toward the former.

"The last time I used something from you," I started slowly, "I ended up here." I pointed at the cell around me. "Which you claimed was *my* fault for using the talisman. So why the hell would I use one of your spells?"

Now it was his turn to blink. "Oh." He relaxed against the couch. "I see."

I stared at him.

Then looked down at the food on his lap.

It really did appear quite appetizing.

But I was hesitant to accept anything from him.

"Lucifer already hates me." As evidenced by the way his midnight gaze had run over me earlier. "This is hard enough without that added difficulty." Because there was no way I could negotiate my freedom if the Hell Fae King despised me.

"He doesn't hate you, Cami," Melek murmured, his expression shifting into something akin to understanding. "You intrigue him. There's a difference."

"I don't want to *intrigue* him."

Melek considered me for a long moment, then slid the tray from his lap to mine. "All Hell Fae are allowed to give their preferred candidate three gifts. I am not allowed to give you anything tangible—a punishment I'm serving for the talisman—except for food. Which means you are very much allowed to eat this meal."

My brow furrowed. "A punishment for the talisman?"

His lips curled to reveal those beautiful dimples. "You are not the only one who was punished for that gift, Cami." He canted his head. "Though, I do think you have received the harsher sentence. I'll see what I can do to fix it."

Gratitude almost left my mouth, except I knew better than to accept words so easily.

Hell Fae Rule #8: If It Sounds Too Good to Be True, It Probably Is.

"In exchange for what?" I asked him, my voice still a rasp. My aching throat was practically begging me to shut up and just accept the water. But I couldn't. Not until I understood his terms.

His gaze practically sparkled, proving I was right to ask. "Accept my gift of food and water, and I will do something to fix your accommodations. Specifically, I will ensure air-conditioning and a proper bed. But only if you eat all the food on that tray and drink all the water in that jug."

I frowned. "That's it?"

"That's it," he repeated.

I squinted at him, another potential ploy coming to mind. "Is the tray bespelled to keep producing food and water?" Because I wouldn't put it past him to play an evil trick like that on me—forcing me to eat until I was sick, just to say I'd failed and he wouldn't be changing my accommodations.

"I'm not sure if I'm thrilled by your expert questioning or insulted by your lack of faith," he mused, his irises glimmering with approval rather than annoyance. "Eat all the food presently on the plate—that you can see right this second. Drink all the water presently in the jug—that you can also see right this second. And I will find you a comfortable bed to sleep in, and proper air to breathe, for at least the next three nights."

"Why three nights?"

"Because your next trial will begin on the fourth day, and I can't guarantee what will happen then." A hint of wariness overtook his features. "It's also a trial where my version of spells won't help you." A fork appeared in his hand, and he held it out for me. "Please accept my bargain and eat, Cami."

I sighed. "There's really not a choice."

"On the contrary, this entire game centers around choice and understanding." Melek snapped his fingers, calling the book to his lap. "Being able to see others as their true selves and *choosing* to accept them is the heart of Hell Fae kind."

I pondered over that statement as I grabbed the water, taking several gulps and groaning at the cool impact against my throat.

"I can refill that for you, but only if you want me to," Melek said when I finally finished drinking. Over half the contents were already gone, and I hadn't even touched my food.

"Yes, please," I whispered, aware that this might be a break in our deal, or potentially force me to drink more, but I doubted I would have trouble finishing another full jug.

He whispered some words, loud enough for me to memorize them, and the container hummed with magic. I took another sip from the now-full bottle, then set it down to start on my steak.

Melek read quietly beside me while I ate, the pages of the book depicting the various Nightmare Fae and their mating rituals.

I followed along, my eyes automatically translating the words on the page while my mouth salivated over the delicious meal.

Minotaurs court their mates through feasts, I read, my eyebrows coming down. *They lure their intendeds into mazes, tempting them with fresh meats and savory cheeses, then gift them the foods at the end. But only if the mate tastes right.*

My eyebrows rose as I forced myself to swallow my mashed potatoes. "Is that why that guy licked my hand? To see if I was his mate?"

"Not his mate, necessarily. But compatible for Minotaurs, yes." He flipped the page again, this time revealing the mating rituals for Centaurs.

Compatible mates can see through the smoky exterior, to the handsome features beneath. When that happens, the males duel, the winner earning the right to lick his chosen candidate.

"That's why there were two of them," I whispered, thinking of the giggling girl in the field. "She was being ripped apart, but not."

"A mirage." Melek glanced at me. "You can see through them."

"Not all the time."

"But sometimes," he clarified. "That's a very rare trait, Cami. One that will serve you well in these trials."

I snorted. "These death trials, you mean." *Except...* As I glanced down at the book to read more about the Centaurs, I realized that wasn't entirely true. "*Mate* trials."

"Indeed they are." His focus returned to the book.

"But some do die, unfortunately. The unworthy ones, anyway."

"Yet candidates like Beatrix and Queen Bitch survive," I muttered.

"Who?" he asked, those pretty eyes glinting up at me.

I shook my head. "Just some *friends* I made in the trials."

He appeared interested for a beat, then went back to the book to reveal the next page about Nagas and their chosen mates. "It seems the book just wants to talk about Nightmare Fae tonight. Perhaps it's a sign that you should study them, to better understand the heart of Hell Fae kind, hmm?"

He closed the cover and set it aside, then rotated toward me on the couch to watch as I finished eating. He seemed rather fascinated by the display, making me wonder if he had some sort of food fetish.

The tray disappeared with my final bite, leaving me with just the water jug. "It'll keep refilling automatically for you now," he explained softly. "That should keep you hydrated while I work on your upgraded accommodations."

He relaxed against the couch, his gaze capturing and holding mine.

"I know you feel this is all unfair and you may not agree with the purpose, but one day I think you'll understand it." He reached over to brush his knuckles against my cheek. "The Hell Fae Source is selective because the core inside of it has been severely wounded. It will take a special fae to heal that wound."

I stared at him. "Lucifer kidnapped six hundred and sixty-six women, all of whom are being forced to fight to the death in some sort of bizarre mating ritual for monsters. I'm not sure I'll ever understand that."

"Not all of the women were kidnapped, Cami. Actually, many of them *want* to be here." He lifted his ankle to his opposite knee, his arm stretching out on the couch behind me. "Lucifer left it up to the parents to prepare their daughters. Just as he left the terms of the deals up to them, too. He's merely collecting what he's owed, not for himself, but for his people."

"So you're telling me to blame my parents, not Lucifer." Something I'd already deduced. But I still held the Hell Fae King responsible for the trials and how callously he viewed our lives.

Although, apparently, most of what I saw today was some sort of fucked-up mating ritual, not actual death.

But I wasn't sure that made any of it better.

"I'm saying to keep your eyes open, Cami. You may be surprised by what you see. For nothing is as it seems here. Not even me."

"So you're hiding a monstrous side?" I asked, arching a brow. "Do you turn into a Manticore or a Centaur or something else lethal?"

"Something else lethal," he confirmed, grinning cheekily. "But some call me angelic, not monstrous. Perhaps even Virtuous." He winked and pushed away from the couch to stand. "You might want to wait for me on the floor, just in case that spell reignites. I don't have control over it, and while it hasn't come back yet, I suspect it will at some point. As I said, nothing is what it seems in this place."

He picked up the book to set it on the rug.

"I'll leave that for you, in case you want to do some light reading." He straightened again, his hand running down his light-colored shirt to smooth out the wrinkles. "You did well today, Cami." His lips curled as he started toward the cell, the door seeming to automatically open for him. "I'll be back soon."

With that, he left me to wonder if he truly meant what he'd said.

Any and all of it.

Time would tell.

Until then, I took his advice and slid off of the couch to join the book on the ratty rug.

I was too exhausted to read, so I used the leather as a pillow instead. And opted for a nap on the floor.

Ajax

I NEEDED AZ.

Because none of these fucking Nightmare Fae were giving me the fight I truly craved.

A fight that would *end* my misery.

Which I supposed meant I craved death. Maybe I did. Maybe I was just a masochist that craved pain. I really didn't fucking know.

All I did know was that these assholes weren't giving me what I needed—a bloody fucking fight.

Growling, I headed back to the dungeons, done chasing Nightmare Fae through the LethaForest. They were all assholes, their dark souls thriving on my anger.

Yet none of them seemed capable of making me truly bleed.

Hell, the burning thwomp had done a better job of flaming my ass than the two Centaurs who'd attempted to spear me with their horns.

Maybe I'd set Clarence free, just to give him another round in the LethaForest.

Yes, I decided. *That's exactly what I'm going to do.*

That fucker would love a chance to try to kick my ass. I should have thought of that before running out here, but I'd been so distraught after Cami's screen went black that I hadn't thought much beyond needing fresh air.

Which had led me to rounding up troublemakers outside.

And demanding they fight me.

Some had refused.

Others had been eager to face the Warden.

But none of them had been good enough.

None of them were *Az*.

I'd considered shooting him a message, to ask him when he'd be back. But that had felt needy. And I didn't want to explain why I wanted him here. He'd figure it out soon enough when he realized Camillia was dead.

My blood iced over, my jaw aching from clenching it so hard.

I hadn't been able to finish watching the games. I'd turned off the screen and left.

Lucifer would be pissed, especially if he needed me for something.

But I couldn't just sit there and keep watching. Not while knowing a girl had died because of me.

Because I'd brought her to this fate.

Personally.

After she'd proved herself to be more capable than every other candidate.

And now she's dead.

I was wrong. Last night hadn't been enough to absolve myself of my guilt. I'd helped her, yes. But it had been a half-hearted attempt.

"You can underestimate me all you want, but I will survive this. And I will not become a bride. I choose my fate, and no one will ever take that away from me."

Well, she'd been right about one thing—she wouldn't become a bride.

I stepped through the LethaForest portal and entered my dungeon quarters, furious and frustrated all over again.

Definitely seeking out Clarence, I decided, moving through my living area toward my front door.

Only to hear whistling coming from my bedroom.

My brow furrowed. *What the fuck?*

I followed the irritating sound to find Melek standing over my bed with his hands on his hips. "Now, if I give you fresh linen, that's a tangible gift to you only, yes?"

"What the hell are you doing in here?" I demanded.

His multicolored irises looked bluer today as he met my gaze. "I really am beginning to question your ability to hear me, dear Warden. Have you been spending too much time with the Sirens?"

I gaped at him. "Get the fuck out of my room."

His expression shifted from polite concern to severe lines, the look one I'd never seen on him before. "I am giving you a gift." He pointed at the black comforter and silky sheets. "These are the highest quality imaginable. And I added some pillows. *You're welcome.*"

He sauntered out of my room and into the living area, then backpedaled into my bathroom.

I followed him, flabbergasted by his presence. "What are you doing?"

"Giving *you* some hygiene projects. If you were to share them, that would be *your* prerogative, thereby making them a gift from you to the other person. Thus, I am not breaking any rules."

My brow crumpled in confusion as he whispered spells and added several bottles of shampoo, conditioner, body wash, and other items to my bathroom. He even conjured some toothbrushes.

Then he walked by me in the doorway and headed to my kitchen area off the living room.

And stocked my fridge.

"Perfect," he murmured. "Very accommodating, yes?"

"Sure." I folded my arms. "Should I be expecting company?" Because I couldn't think of any other reason for his bizarre behavior.

"Yes." He clasped his hands in front of him. "Which reminds me, I have several favors to ask."

"Oh, do you?" I feigned interest. "Too bad I don't care." It was probably the rudest thing I'd ever said to him, but I wasn't in the mood. "I have a Centaur to piss off. Excuse me."

I started toward the door.

"I may not be the king, but I am his prince. It would be unwise to dismiss me in this manner, *Death Blood*. Particularly as you are our guest, hmm?"

My fingers curled into fists as I turned toward him. "In a Midnight Fae paradigm. But sure. Send me away."

"I could," he threatened, power emanating from those two words alone. "But I need you." He calmed in the next instant, his expression softening once more.

It was then that I realized he'd been displaying immense power. A subtle reminder of his position and the very "other" energy that swarmed his dangerous aura.

That he could switch it on and off so quickly was just a further indicator of his unnatural power.

I had no idea what kind of abomination Melek truly was, but he clearly possessed some lethal talents.

Talents I really didn't want to test right now.

Because in my current state, I might just let him well and truly hurt me.

Which is probably what I deserve, I thought darkly.

Melek frowned as though he'd heard all that. Or

perhaps he saw the grim fate lurking in my features. "What do you want, Melek?" I asked, and even I could hear the exhaustion in my tone.

"It's not really what I want," he said softly. "It's what Camillia needs."

I frowned. "Camillia?"

He nodded. "Her cell accommodations are inadequate after the day she's endured. I would like her to stay here. Where you can keep her safe."

My lips moved but words failed me. "Camillia?" I repeated again, sounding like an idiot.

"Indeed," Melek replied. "But she needs more than just improved accommodations. She needs training for the next trial. Training that I can't provide."

"Training," I echoed, struggling to process his words. *Have I fallen into a weird alternate reality? Is a Paradox Fae fucking with timelines?*

Melek nodded. "Ty told me the next trial is in the Netherworld Kingdom. It's the one place I can't go. And I'm worried Cami won't survive it."

But she didn't survive the first trial, right? "Camillia's dead."

Melek scowled. "Well, that's not the spirit I'm looking for, Warden. I want you to teach her about the Corpse Fae in preparation. You're a Death Blood. You're ideal to help. And if she's staying here with you already, then…" He shrugged as though to complete the sentence with whatever obvious phrase he felt existed there.

"But she's *dead*."

"No, Warden. She is not going to die. Because you're going to help by training her." His expression turned severe again. "I thought you might do this as a result of whatever friendship you two created last night. But if that's not enough reason for you, then name your price and we'll strike a deal."

"You don't understand. She's already dead. I saw it. On the screen. She *died*."

Melek's eyebrows lifted. "On the screen? What screen?"

I pointed to the one in my living area. "That one. She died during the Centaur trial. It went black." A not-so-subtle choke swallowed that last word, making it barely audible. But I'd obviously said enough, as understanding overtook his expression.

"Oh, the portal period," he said, waving it away. "Yes. Ty made them spin for a while. It's part of why Cami is so exhausted. And her trek through the Minotaur maze."

"Minotaur maze?"

"Yes. The second half of today's trial." He gave me a curious look. "Did you miss it?"

"I… I didn't watch everything…" I trailed off, his words starting to form a new reality in my mind. "Cami's here?"

"No. She's in her cell. But I would like her to be here." He gave me another one of those concerned looks. "Seriously, Ajax. Have you spent too much time around the Sirens? They have a penchant for mind games. Dreadful creatures. Glorious, too."

Of course Melek would insult them and praise them in the same breath.

But that didn't matter.

Only his comments about Camillia did. "She's alive and you want her to sleep here."

"Yes," he replied slowly. "I've mentioned that at least twice now."

"And you want me to train her for the next trial."

"As a gift, please, yes. Unless you think training is a tangible gift, then… then I would prefer *you* give her that knowledge. Just as you can *share* the items you've recently acquired." He smiled. "I've given her nothing other than food, which is allowed within the parameters of the deal."

I had no idea what "deal" he was referring to, nor did I really care.

Because he'd just confirmed that Camillia was alive.

And he'd given me cause for a second chance.

A chance to truly help her. A chance to make things right.

It was a dangerous reality. A potentially lethal twist of fate. But I couldn't deny the pounding in my heart or the need to see this through. "I'll help her." The statement wasn't just for Melek, but for me as well.

It would be risky to attach myself to her.

But I accepted that risk over losing her again.

This was the second chance I'd never had with Emelyn. A second chance I wouldn't deny myself now. Not when I had the opportunity to finally do something right.

"She's in her cell?"

"She is," Melek confirmed. "Shall I bring her here?" He held out his palm. "It's a simple spell, and I would be doing it for you, not her. Which again does not break the deal."

His obsession with this deal must be important, but my focus remained on Camillia. "Bring her here." Not because I didn't want to go to her myself, but because it was a faster method that would either prove all of this was true or quickly morph into a realistic nightmare to remind me of her death.

Melek grinned. "I'll settle her in your bed."

He started toward the bedroom, words humming under his breath. His magic differed from mine, his spells in a language that sounded similar to the one Midnight Fae used for spells. And yet it was vastly different at the same time. Still lyrical, almost like a song. Just unique phrases that I couldn't understand.

But whatever he'd said had worked.

Because Camillia was asleep in my bed by the time I reached my bedroom door.

"I suggest enchanting the snake-vines to keep guard and ensure she doesn't leave without permission. That way, she's still technically incarcerated," Melek murmured as he wandered over to tuck a strand of damp hair behind Camillia's ear.

She sighed in response, her breath the most beautiful sound I'd ever heard.

Because it proved she was alive.

Scratched and bruised—at least on the arms, which I could see outside of the blankets—but beautifully alive.

"I'll return to check on you," Melek whispered, his words seeming to be for Camillia as he bent to kiss her forehead. "Sweet dreams, little angel."

He stood then, his majestic gaze meeting mine.

"Take care of her, please. And teach her how to control the dead. Knowing Ty, she's going to need all the help she can get." He disappeared with the words, leaving me alone with the beauty on the bed.

I just stood and watched her for a long moment, content to hear her breathe. My vampiric senses homed in on her pulse, the healthy rhythm music to my ears.

Camillia is alive.

She survived.

And she's in my bed.

I should be throwing her back in her cell and erecting a thick, impenetrable wall between us. One that would protect my emotions and guard my soul.

But she'd already penetrated my spirit. Today had been

proof of that. So I either embraced this and helped her. Or cut her off and suffered the consequences.

After the day I'd endured, I couldn't stomach the notion of doing the latter.

Which left embracing this situation instead.

An irrational choice. Yet it felt like the right one.

So I changed into a pair of gray sweatpants.

And joined her in my bed.

She'd likely wake up confused. But I'd be there to explain this change when she did.

Then we'd discuss the next trial and go from there.

CAMI

So soft, I marveled, sighing in contentment.

Mint and the undertones of pine infiltrated my nose, the mingling scents providing a layer of security that allowed all my aching muscles to relax into the cloud beneath me.

I stretched with a groan, my bones seeming to pop from whatever exercise I'd done yesterday. Clearly, I'd pushed myself too hard.

How far did I run yes…? My thought trailed off, causing my brow to furrow. *Wait…*

My eyes flew open as yesterday's events slammed into my mind.

I sat up in an instant, then groaned again as my head spun from the action, and fell right back down.

Into a pillow.

There's a pillow beneath me.

What…?

I'd fallen asleep on the book. The rug. The cell.

Swallowing, I felt around beneath me, noting the plush

mattress and silky sheets. Melek had promised me new accommodations. And it seemed he'd delivered.

Except…

I squinted my eyes in the dimness, a flickering flame on the wall my only source of light.

I'm not alone. My eyes widened. *Is that…?* My lips parted. *Ajax.*

His eyes were closed, hiding those pretty blue-black irises from view. But a hell of a lot more of him was on display.

Because he was shirtless.

And wearing gray sweatpants.

All of which I could see reflected in the low lighting because he was sleeping on top of the covers, not beneath them.

Am I dreaming?

I ran my gaze over Ajax's flawless chest to his abdomen and the little trail of hair leading downward from his navel. *Certainly looks like a dream,* I thought, my teeth skimming my lower lip.

Which made me flinch from the soreness of my mouth.

Yeah, definitely not a dream.

Because if it were, my lips would be full and moist and ready to explore all those firm ridges with my tongue. But I was parched, my throat begging for more water.

I considered moving.

Maybe even *running*.

However, leaving the bed might wake Ajax up.

And then what?

Curling my fingers into the sheets, I tried to figure out how I'd ended up here. Melek had promised to improve my sleeping conditions, and while, yes, this was certainly an upgrade from my cell, he hadn't said anything about Ajax being in the new accommodations with me.

But I hadn't exactly stipulated that I be *alone* in a bed. I'd just agreed to something soft and warm, with a hint of cool air.

Which he'd more than delivered on.

Just with the added bonus of a shirtless Ajax.

Something I probably wouldn't have minded in a previous life. He was a stunning specimen of a male who I had no doubt could tempt me into sin between these sheets on a normal day.

But here? In this place?

No.

Not after yesterday's trial and everything these men had forced me to endure.

Of course, Ajax had actually tried to help me. And his assistance hadn't gotten me into any trouble. He'd been a bit of a dick, though.

At first, anyway.

Yesterday he'd been almost... *human.* His stoic front had returned when he'd left me on that field to embrace my fate, but between providing me with food and a Nightmare Fae lesson, he'd actually been rather nice.

Which probably made me moronic for somewhat forgiving his kidnapping.

But I also understood that the fae world didn't play by mortal rules. He was just doing his job.

A job that makes him a blind follower, I reminded myself as I attempted to stretch again.

More popping sounded, my body screaming at me for overdoing it yesterday.

Definitely not a dream, I muttered, a grumble of irritation leaving my mouth.

Ugh. This would take a while to recover from. Yet Melek had implied I would have another trial in a few days. *Fuck.*

I shuddered, my instinct to curl into a ball only dispelled by a pair of brilliant blue-black eyes.

Ajax.

My movements must have woken him up because he was staring at me now with a hint of wonder in his gaze.

I swallowed. *That's the kind of look that leads to trouble.*

Trouble I did not want.

No. That was a lie.

A sinful part of me absolutely wanted that kind of trouble.

A sinful part I was trying very hard to ignore.

A sinful part that warmed my veins as Ajax reached over to draw his thumb along my lower lip, his touch oddly comforting against the blister healing there. "I'm glad you're alive."

I shivered, his words seeming to touch my very soul.

"I'm sorry for doing this to you," he continued, his touch moving to my cheek and onward to tuck a strand of hair behind my ear. "I would tell you I didn't have a choice, but I fear that would be a lie. Because I absolutely chose this life. It afforded me a distance I very much craved. A distance I felt yesterday in a way I never anticipated."

My brow furrowed. "Distance?"

"From loved ones. Former friends. New friends." He pulled his hand away, his gaze intensifying. "You told me that you will choose your fate. Well, mine was chosen for me. So I responded by altering the path as much as fate would allow. Or so I thought, anyway. However, yesterday taught me that I didn't much care for the alternative life I've decided to pursue."

"Oh." I didn't really understand what he was saying or why he felt the need to tell me this, but it seemed to mean something important to him. And for whatever reason, it had led to him apologizing to me.

An apology I wasn't quite sure what to do with.

Because he was the reason for my capture in the sense that he'd come for me personally.

But my father was the true culprit here.

"You were just doing your job."

"A job I chose," he replied, his gaze falling to my mouth as he lifted his hand to touch me again, that sense of wonder escaping his features once again.

It was almost as though he needed to reassure himself that I lay beside him—an instinct I understood because I almost wanted to do the same to him, to see if he truly was shirtless on this bed. But I kept my hands to myself, mostly because I didn't trust my sinful side not to take over.

"But I chose this job as an escape. And when I thought you had died, I suddenly realized that there was no escape. The pain can be ignored, but it can't be forgotten."

"You…?" I trailed off, swallowing again. "You thought I *died*?"

"In the trial." His palm slid to the back of my neck, the touch intimate as his gaze captured mine. "I know a few details about what to expect because of what I've either overheard or been told, but I'm not a Hell Fae. I wasn't privy to the full details of how everything would be televised. Hell, I'm not even sure I was supposed to be watching. But it came on in my room… and your screen went dark."

The mention of the televised trials didn't anger me like it had last night.

Perhaps because of Ajax's tone or the words he'd chosen to use—they implied that he hadn't intended to observe. That he wasn't supposed to watch them, even.

And when he had, he hadn't enjoyed it.

Or that was what his tone had suggested when he'd commented on it going dark.

"I thought it meant you'd died," he added softly. "I... I didn't expect the feelings that evoked. And I left my rooms. So I had no idea that it was just the portal until I returned." His focus shifted to his thumb as he stroked the pulse point of my neck. "I shouldn't care. I shouldn't even have you here." His grip tensed a little with the word. "But it feels like a second chance."

"A second chance for what?" I asked, my voice almost a whisper. This all felt so intense. So *unreal*. I wasn't sure how to feel about it. How to even begin *processing* it. This new Ajax was nothing like the arrogant one who had captured me, or the asshole who had taunted me in the cells.

This version of him...

Terrified me.

Because he was almost personable. Almost likable. Almost too alluring.

He shook his head. "I don't even know, Cami. It's just something I'm refusing to ignore. You're alive and I want you to stay that way." His gaze met mine. "I can't free you. I can't even really help you. But I can try to train you."

His attention shifted downward to the scraps of my dress. They truly left nothing to the imagination, especially as I was lying on my side and my boobs were practically falling out of the top.

But I didn't dare move to fix it.

Mostly because I still didn't trust the sinful part of me not to do something stupid like purposefully remove the fabric.

"I can offer you a shower, too," he said, his voice thick as his gaze remained on my chest. It was almost like he could hear the temptress inside me purring suggestions in my ear. "Clothes as well," he added. "And food, too."

"And your bed?" I added, glancing around us. "Is that why I'm here?"

His dark hair fell into his eyes, making him even more enticing as his lips quirked up at one side. "Would you rather be on the cell floor?"

"I would rather you tell me what's happening here and why I'm suddenly in your room and not in the cell or in my dorm," I admitted honestly.

He considered me for a long moment. "Lucifer has not given permission to release you from the dungeon, but he didn't technically say you had to stay in a cell. So we opted for my room as an alternative."

We? "You and Melek?" I guessed.

He slid his hand away from my nape, returning it to his abdomen as he tucked his opposite arm under his head. "He seems to have taken a liking to you."

I mimicked his position and startled as I found the book beneath the pillow. When I glanced at it, Ajax frowned. "What is it?"

At first I thought he was asking me about the book, but when I lifted the pillow to reveal it, it was nowhere to be seen.

Strange.

I swore I'd just felt it there.

"N-nothing," I stammered, my brow furrowing as I tried to settle again.

Only to feel the book once more.

I peeked under the pillow to see its leather spine, but when I lifted the fabric away from it entirely, the book vanished.

Huh.

"Cami?" Ajax prompted, a hint of concern in his voice.

I shook my head, clearing it. "I… I can go back to my cell," I offered, uncertain of what else to say. "Melek likes his games. And I don't really want to play." Even if the bed was super comfortable.

Ajax's explanation also suggested this hadn't been approved or sanctioned by Lucifer.

Which meant I would likely end up in more trouble when he found out.

"It's for the best if I just go…" I started to roll from the bed, but my legs gave out as I tried to stand on them, and I found Ajax's sturdy arm wrapped around my middle. He dragged me back over the mattress, his heat a blanket of masculine warmth that set my blood on fire.

"How about you stay here," he said against my ear. "I can draw you a bath. Then you can clean up while I throw together some breakfast."

I shivered from both the warmth in his voice and the feel of him pressed up against me. "O-okay," I agreed, not at all feeling like myself.

Maybe this is a dream after all, I mused. *A heated fantasy fueled by the hot climate, perhaps.*

It would be so easy to move in his arms and kiss him, to take the fantasy to the next level.

But his heat left my back in the next instant as he maneuvered me back onto the bed, placing my head on the pillow and my shoulders against the mattress.

He stared down at me for a moment, his hands braced on the bed, caging me beneath him.

Several beats passed, his gaze going from my eyes to my lips, the intensity seeming to spiral into a dangerous vibration of forbidden desires.

My throat worked, making me wince again at the reminder of my time in the trials.

Ajax observed the motion, his own throat working. Then he reached over me to the nightstand and grabbed a bottle of water.

I nearly lifted my hand to take it from him.

But he was already unscrewing the cap and bringing it to my lips.

The blues in his irises darkened to match the black center as he watched me swallow, his chiseled cheekbones appearing that much sharper with the change.

Handsome seemed too bland a word to use for Ajax. He was so much more.

And not just because of his features, but because of the hint of his soul staring at me through his darkened gaze.

It was as though I could see the real him.

The tortured Ajax beneath the cocky veneer.

The heart that tried futilely not to beat yet couldn't seem to stop thriving.

So much seemed to pass between us, an odd sort of understanding snapping into place.

This was the true Ajax. The one who'd suffered incredible loss, the one who had given up on fate and choices and had decided to pursue his own path into the darkness to outrun his pain.

He let me see everything.

"Ajax…"

He watched my mouth as though he expected me to say more. And when I didn't, he set the bottle to the side, then slid off the bed. "I'll let you know when your bath is ready."

With those words, he left the room.

I stared at his bedroom for a moment, still stunned that this wasn't a dream.

I found this shift in Ajax's behavior to be immensely unsettling. Mostly because of what it evoked inside me. *Intrigue. Desire. Yearning.*

All things I could not afford to feel.

Not when I still wanted to escape.

Nothing about this is right, I reminded myself. *Even if my libido says otherwise.*

CAMI

The bathroom impressed me with the level of amenities fully stocked as if Ajax had been expecting me.

Although, he'd said *us*, so this was all probably Melek.

Still, I accepted the "gifts" because they were technically coming from Ajax. And so far, Ajax hadn't done anything except be straight with me.

He'd also poured me a bath, something that had not only earned him bonus points but had also helped me feel a bit more alive.

So much so that I'd even been able to shower afterward.

I'd kept the settings on cool to try to dispel the heat flushing across my skin, but it didn't help. Mostly because Ajax's kindness had merely stoked an already burning flame, one that refused to be extinguished, even by icy pellets from the showerhead.

I braced my palms against the wall, debating my next move.

There were definitely certain ways I could tend to the growing heat inside me, but I wanted to be stronger than the urges, to ignore that sinful burn and remind myself of my situation.

Yet a foreign part of me continued to whisper, *Human rules don't apply here. These are Hell Fae. They take what they want. And you're part Hell Fae, so why not indulge in that craving, hmm?*

I nearly growled, choosing instead to focus on my still-aching muscles and the pain yesterday had caused. It helped ground me a bit, forcing me to forget Ajax's kindness.

At least until the products on the sink reminded me of the "gifts" waiting for me. I used a few of them, including the comb and hair dryer. Then I tucked a towel around my body and nudged open the door to peek out at Ajax.

He stood in a little kitchen nook off his living area, still in those gray sweatpants. As though sensing my stare, or perhaps hearing the door open, he glanced back at me and ran his gaze over me with undisguised interest.

It seemed appropriate that he wouldn't bother hiding his intrigue; he'd been upfront about everything else, so why not this?

Unfortunately, that forwardness only made me burn hotter, not colder.

Sharing space with him like this was going to lead to a different trial entirely.

He cleared his throat. "I left some clothes for you in the bedroom."

"Thanks," I whispered, feeling oddly shy as I hurried toward his room.

A uniform waited for me on his bed, that same white T-shirt and black pants. No underwear.

Because of course I would be forced to still go commando, I thought, sighing.

Shutting the door behind me, I let my towel drop and

slipped into the clothes. It beat wearing a towel around his living area.

I ran my fingers through my hair and checked my appearance in the mirror against the back of his door.

He'd done something to the lighting to make it brighter in here, the flames having expanded across the upper parts of the wall. It reminded me of a modernized medieval castle, which was a bit of an oxymoron, yet somehow it worked.

Magic ran up my spine while I studied my reflection, making me roll my eyes. I rotated to see my name against my back again.

However, the enchantment kept shifting over my skin, the vibration causing the hairs along my arms to stand on end as the stars began to appear beneath *Camillia De la Croix*.

My brow furrowed. *Six stars?*

Then I recalled what Lucifer had said about stars before the trials, and my lips parted.

Power. Or that had been my interpretation of his words, anyway. He'd said we could either keep it for ourselves or share it with our intended mates. No question about my choice there.

But how had I started with three stars? Had others started with that many, too? I hadn't really paid attention that first day on my way to the library, as I'd been more concerned with the names.

My lips twisted to the side. *Maybe the book has something to say about stars*, I thought, heading back to the bed to pull the item out from under the pillows. "You know, you would be a lot easier to read with a table of contents," I told the book as I opened it to the first page.

It showed the same page from last night about the Nightmare Fae.

Which was odd since Melek had been reading from the middle of the book, not the beginning.

I tried opening it from the other end, just to see what it would do.

More Nightmare Fae.

I flipped through a few more illustrations of the various Nightmare Fae, then crossed another section on paradigms.

"I don't want to see this," I informed the book as I settled onto the bed and crossed my legs. "I'm curious about the stars." Maybe if I gathered enough of them, I could use the power to barter with Lucifer for my freedom.

I refused to accept my fate here, even if it included a sexy and shirtless Midnight Fae making breakfast in the other room.

"I need something useful," I murmured, speaking to the book as though it were a real entity. Which maybe it was. It certainly had a mind of its own—something it proceeded to prove as the pages morphed into something new.

My eyes widened as an illustration appeared without words displaying a mystical landscape littered with stones.

Wait, not stones.

Graves.

What the fuck is this book trying to show me?

A crest at the top suggested that this might be a kingdom of some sort, or a royal graveyard. The latter sent a chill down my spine.

Throwing myself back onto the pillows, I pressed my palms against my eyes. "Why is everything so fucking cryptic?"

"What's cryptic?" Ajax asked from the doorway, his gaze on my breasts.

Because, yeah. White shirt.

No bra.

Sigh. Males.

"The book I'm reading," I said, fighting the urge to cover my chest with my arms, particularly as his attention was making my nipples come out to say "hi" back to him.

"Book?" he asked, finally meeting my gaze. "What book?"

I motioned to the place on my lap. "Yeah, the…" I trailed off when I realized the book had vanished again.

Weird.

"Never mind," I said with a sigh, then I swung my legs over the edge of the bed to stand. Which, of course, drew his gaze downward again. "So how about that breakfast?" I asked, desperately needing to be away from the bed and that burning stare of his.

He cleared his throat as though he felt similarly and cocked his head toward the living room. "This way."

———

"You're full of surprises," I said around a mouthful of hash browns and egg with melted cheese.

"Because I know how to cook human food?" he asked as he sipped a mug of coffee that I suspected had blood in it. "Most Midnight Fae know human preferences."

Glancing up, I found him watching the pulse in my neck as I swallowed.

Yeah, I knew Midnight Fae preferences, too. And I was sure that I'd be a lot tastier than his blood coffee.

"I was going to say that it's surprising that you have the morning off," I lied. That hadn't been at all what I'd meant, but it seemed like a safer route than admitting how much he'd surprised me since waking up. "Aren't you the Warden?" I teased, hoping for a lighter tone that would dispel some of the residual intensity warming the air between us.

He gave me a pointed look. "Yes, and I'm doing that job right now by making sure my charge is protected."

"Protected?" I reiterated. It was a strange word to use for a prisoner.

"Yes, Prince Melek gave me orders to train you for the next trial, and that's exactly what I'm going to do."

I frowned because knowing that Melek was the cause for Ajax's behavior didn't sit right with me.

The prince played games, ones with fatal consequences if lost.

Although, Ajax was a bit more straightforward, and if he meant to prepare me for the next trial, I'd listen. His advice about the border crossing had been accurate, as had everything he'd told me about the Nightmare Fae. He also continued to be honest with me, something I suspected was a rarity around here.

"What sort of training?" I asked.

"You'll see," he replied, the response reminding me of Melek and making me frown.

Ajax was usually the candid one who didn't bother holding back. "How very cryptic of you. Taking pointers from *Prince Melek*?"

The Midnight Fae huffed a humorless laugh. "Not quite, little rebel." His blue-black irises ran over me, his expression sobering as he took in healing scrapes and yellowing bruises. Being half-fae had the benefit of enhanced healing. Unfortunately, there were likely many full-blooded-fae candidates who could heal even faster.

"I'm not elaborating because I think you need to take today to rest."

"My mind is fine," I promised him.

Apart from the heat-driven fantasy associated with your shirtless form, anyway, I thought, my cheeks warming.

"I want to know more about the training Melek requested." *There*. My voice sounded politely stern, not breathless or sultry.

"If you're going to become a Hell Fae, then you need to do a better job of living in the present. Focus on what you *need* right now and stop worrying about things you can't control." He rubbed his chin, then leaned back in his chair, causing his muscles to ripple enticingly. Then he cocked his brow and glanced pointedly at my plate.

Narrowing my gaze, I speared another bite and popped it into my mouth.

His answering smile seemed to say, *Good girl.*

Fine. I would eat.

Not just to satisfy him, but because it tasted good, too.

The fae really did know how to cook. He also ate fast, his food having disappeared long before I commented on his penchant for surprising me.

But he took his time with his coffee, his pupils flaring each time he sipped.

Definitely has blood in it.

Thankfully, he hadn't brought me a cup. Because ew.

I tossed the final bite into my mouth and made a show of chewing and swallowing. "Satisfied?" I asked.

His gaze ran over me again, finding my braless breasts. "Hardly."

I rolled my eyes, ignoring the innuendo there. "Can you tell me about the trial now?"

He still had that little amused look about him, one that promised sinful and wicked things. "That depends. Are there any other needs of yours that haven't been met yet?"

That made my heart skip a beat.

He couldn't possibly mean that the way it sounded. He just meant food and sleep. *Right?*

I cleared my throat. "Well, I'm still tired. But I can't sleep if I'm stressing about the unknown."

He considered that for a moment and shrugged. "Maybe you could try trusting me and my motives and just take today off. Chill. Relax. Do whatever you want within the confines of my rooms. Then tomorrow, we'll discuss the next trial."

That sent a glimmer of fire through my veins. "What reason have you given me to trust you?"

"None." He canted his head. "But trust has to start somewhere."

He stood and began clearing the table, letting those words play through my mind.

"I'm not keeping anything important from you," he said softly. "The next trial is just more Nightmare Fae battles. But the next one just so happens to be a specialty of mine. Which is why Melek requested my assistance. And since I like your spirit, I agreed."

He stepped up to my side and slid his fingers through mine to extract the fork from my hand. But he didn't immediately take the utensil, instead choosing to hold on to me as he leaned down.

"I need you at full health for me to properly train you. Thus, today is about relaxing." He extracted the fork. "We won't begin until all your needs are met. Understood?"

My thighs clenched, his words seeming to mean so much more than just an afternoon of rest.

Because now I was fairly certain he was insinuating something entirely different.

And I wasn't sure I wanted to say no.

But before I could reply, he put the dishes in the sink and rinsed them off. "I'm going to take a shower. I suggest you make yourself comfortable." He eyed the front doorway. "And I wouldn't try to leave if I were you. My snake-vines are spelled to keep you here where I can keep an eye on you."

"Fabulous," I grumbled. Although, I really had no desire to leave this room. Not until I recovered from yesterday, anyway.

Which made his "rest day" idea a good one.

He winked as though he could sense my acquiescence. Or maybe it was his response to my sarcastic comment.

It really didn't matter.

Not with the view of all those muscles flexing as he walked. He even had those two little dimples on his lower back, making his whole torso a work of art.

If only he'd lose those sweatpants, then I'd be given a full preview.

His thumbs hooked into the sides of them like he could hear my interest. Or perhaps he just felt my eyes on him. Either way, he was a fucking tease because he disappeared into the bathroom before he tugged down the gray sweats.

The shower started in the next instant, causing me to curl my fingers into my palms.

I *really* needed a distraction. Something to do. Something to keep me from trying to join the sexy Midnight Fae.

I should *not* be attracted to him.

And yet, my insides were positively on fire for him.

Not. Going. To. Happen.

I forced myself to move to his couch and focused on trying to turn on his screen. Surely Hell Fae had interesting movies.

Unless they were all related to brides battling each other to the death.

Are there replays of yesterday's events somewhere? I wondered, hitting random keys on his remote. *Maybe—*

A flurry of magic shimmered through the air as a tall male with dark hair and broad shoulders appeared out of thin air near the entryway.

Az.

His violet eyes went to the sound of the shower, his mouth quirking up at the sides in a sexy little grin.

My lips parted as he pulled off his shirt, revealing a ripped chest and abs—comparable to Ajax's physique— and started toward the hallway with his hand dropping to his belt as his shirt hit the floor.

I gaped at his back, just as hypnotized as I had been with Ajax.

Until he froze.

I gulped, that burning sensation inside me morphing into an inferno.

He turned to me, his hawklike gaze locking onto my overheated form.

Holy shit. I had no idea what was happening.

But yes, please. *Can I watch?* I nearly asked. I didn't really know *what* I wanted to watch, just that I wanted whatever the hell was coming.

His nostrils flared, his trajectory changing as he stalked toward me on the couch. "What the fuck are you doing in here?"

Az

My blood burned with need, my inner beast riding me hard.

I couldn't find Camillia De la Croix's father—a failure that irritated my Phoenix. Tracking was one of my beast's primary strengths. To have that strength belittled by an unsuccessful quest stirred a bout of aggression inside me that needed to be expelled.

Hence the reason I'd come for Ajax. He was the only being who seemed to be capable of handling my furious energy during sex. It didn't matter how much I gave him; he just absorbed the vivacity and accepted it into his soul, almost as though he were meant to be mine.

But my Phoenix didn't recognize him as his intended mate.

Because my Phoenix didn't recognize *anyone* as mate-worthy.

And not for a lack of me trying—I'd searched for someone to satisfy my animalistic spirit for nearly two millennia. My lack of success could be a result of my mixed heritage. Or maybe that being just didn't exist yet.

Typhos had become my necessary conduit, his spiritual bond providing me with the outlet I required to expel my abundance of power. But he didn't satiate my inner beast. Very few could.

Which made Ajax unique.

And very special to me indeed.

Oh, he'd erected a wall around himself, blocking out emotions and isolating his feelings behind an impenetrable shield. However, one day I'd shatter that barrier. I already knew how. I just didn't want to push him. Not too severely, anyway. I enjoyed finding clever ways to chip away at that solidified armor, forcing him to accept me in little bursts.

My Phoenix enjoyed the game, too.

It added a layer of satisfaction to the mix that only intensified our mutual gratification.

A gratification I needed right now due to the fury building inside.

A fury that heightened upon finding the *source* of my violent energy sitting on Ajax's couch. Her parents were why I felt this way.

I wanted to wrap my hand around her pretty little neck and demand she tell me *how* they'd evaded my Phoenix. No one escaped him. There were very few realms in existence where a soul could freely hide, and I doubted very much that her father was in one of those.

Which suggested he'd cast a very powerful spell.

A spell he should not have the means to cast.

Camillia De la Croix's stormy gray eyes widened as I stalked toward her, my question hanging angrily between us. *"What the fuck are you doing in here?"*

She swallowed, the movement drawing my eyes to that throat I yearned to strangle. So delicate and pretty. Feminine. *Biteable.*

Maybe I could throttle her while fucking her.

The delicious thought painted a dark image in my mind that had my Phoenix peeking out at her in astute evaluation. *Can she handle us?* he seemed to be asking, my energy source appraising hers.

My beast was hungry.

Pacing.

Needing.

And whatever he saw in Camillia De la Croix had my knees bending to join her on the couch, my hand moving to her hair without thought.

She hadn't spoken.

She hadn't even moved.

Perhaps aware that a true predator hunted her now.

I leaned forward to scent her. *Mmm*, my inner beast hummed in approval. *Evening roses. Petals falling in the night, stirred by a sinfully decadent wind.* I inhaled deeply, loving the way her arousal laced through her subtle perfume, giving it that sensuous layer.

She reminded me of Melek and Typhos. But softer. More sensual. *Feminine.*

I nuzzled her throat, stirring goose bumps along her flesh that I longed to chase with my tongue.

"*Azazel.*" Ajax's voice fluttered through my mind, drawing my predator toward him as I placed a claiming palm against Cami's flat stomach.

She was breathing quickly now, sending more of that delicious arousal into the air.

Desire. Heat. Yearning.

It made me want to lick her pulse and bite down.

Seeing Ajax standing only a few feet away, wet from his rushed shower with just a towel around his waist, had me growling in excitement.

"You got me a gift," my Phoenix purred, pleased with the feminine offering. Ajax and I hadn't seen to our needs the other day after sparring because other responsibilities had intruded on our playtime. It had left my animal unsated and hungry, a sensation only worsened by the failure of locating this girl's father.

Which made Camillia a very appropriate gift for my Phoenix.

An alluring one.

My gaze went to her perky tits, proudly displayed through the thin white fabric, her nipples beacons for my mouth.

"She's not a gift, Az." Ajax spoke calmly but with a hint of steel in his voice. "She's a bride candidate."

My Phoenix rumbled a little, liking the sound of that. It'd been a long time since a female had appealed to my beast, their fragility typically a turnoff. But my animal recognized the warrior lurking beneath her skin, her burning energy one he wanted to explore with his own.

"Why is she in your room?" I asked, leaning in to scent her again. I closed my eyes, her fragrance deepening my hunger. Part of me wanted to eat her. The other part wanted to *know* her.

I led with the latter part now, my palm gliding upward to cup her breast and stroke my thumb across her stiff peak. Her head fell back on a moan, her body curling into mine.

"Az." Ajax pushed the coffee table out of the way and reached for my wrist. "Release her."

"I don't think she wants me to," I murmured, my lips skimming her pulse.

"Fucking Phoenix," he snapped. "Stop mauling the candidate."

Camillia released a breathy little sound that had me chuckling against her neck. "Do you want me to stop *mauling* you, little warrior?" I asked, my thumb drawing a light circle around her taut nipple.

Her throat worked against my mouth as she tried to swallow. "N-no," she stammered, her own hand covering Ajax's against my wrist. She didn't try to help him pull me away; she applied pressure instead, delighting my inner beast.

"You're hypnotizing her," Ajax accused, a low growl in his voice. "If you want to fuck, you can fuck me. Let her go."

"I'm not hypnotizing her," I whispered, my lips skating up to her ear for a little nibble. "I'm merely unwrapping my gift."

"She's not a fucking gift!"

"Then why is she here?" I asked again. I didn't really care about the reason. She smelled absolutely divine, and I intended to taste her regardless of her reason for being here.

Right place, right time, and all that.

"Do you want to be my gift, little warrior?" I whispered against her ear, my palm slipping back down to her abdomen and to the hem of her shirt. "Because I think unwrapping you would be quite fun indeed."

I slid my thumb beneath the fabric to trace the soft skin of her stomach. Ajax attempted to pull my hand away again, causing the little warrior to dig her nails into his skin.

He grabbed a fistful of my hair with his opposite hand and yanked my head away from her neck.

I growled, my beast furious about having his treat taken from him.

"Az." Ajax sounded unbelievably calm again. "You can't take her in this mood."

On the contrary, I could absolutely take her in this

mood. And the way she whimpered told me she'd love every minute of it.

My Phoenix purred for her as I tried to return my face to her neck, but Ajax's grip in my hair held me back.

I met his burning gaze, the smoldering rims reminding me of blue fire. "Let. Go."

"No." He tightened his hold instead. "Use me. Not her."

My Phoenix evaluated the option, taking in the water droplets dancing down his torso and the towel at his waist. He was very tempting. Beautiful, too.

But he didn't smell as sweet as the morsel beside me.

"She's part human, Az." Ajax's tone remained soft, almost coaxing. "You'll kill her in this mood."

I cocked my head, stirring a stinging sensation from his hold on my hair. But I ignored it, my Phoenix considering his statement. A tendril of energy slipped out from my soul to gently prod at the female, curious. "No." The word left my mouth with a conviction I felt to my very core. "She's stronger than she looks." I could taste her power, that underlying vitality that marked her as far more than human.

I yanked away from Ajax's hold, my fingers going to her chin to drag her gaze to mine.

"What are you, little warrior?" I wondered aloud. "You certainly don't feel human at all."

Her tongue dampened her lower lip, her pupils large and dark and bleeding lust into her expression. "My father is a Hell Fae."

I narrowed my eyes. "Yes. I'm very aware of that." *With the power to evade my Phoenix.* My grasp on her turned brutal. "What is his heritage? What mix?"

She winced from my grip, her hand finding my wrist again. This time her fingers touched my skin rather than

Ajax's. He'd released me entirely but remained right before us, his protective energy exciting my Phoenix.

Because it told me he liked her.

He *wanted* her.

And I could see why.

She was powerful. Beautiful. *A fighter.*

Something she evidenced now by digging her nails into my skin in a manner similar to Ajax's just moments ago. "You're hurting me."

"Yes." My focus dropped to her mouth as she licked her lips again. "You like it." I could sense it in her scent, her interest a blossoming flower in the room that drugged my senses.

She dug her nails in more. "I don't like bruises."

"What do you like, then?" I asked, deciding that was more important than the other question. Mostly because my Phoenix wanted to know how to please her. A strange desire, as I rarely wanted to please anyone other than myself. But there was something about this female that had my animal intrigued, and I would never deny his urges.

I gentled my grip to demonstrate that I knew how to listen, causing her nostrils to flare in response.

She likes my acknowledgment, I thought. *Good.*

Ajax sighed. "Az. She's a candidate. She's not here for this."

My brow furrowed. "Then why is she here?"

No one had clarified that finer detail for me.

Not that I truly cared.

Her arousal spoke volumes. I'd scented it the moment I'd faced her, that alluring perfume drawing me to her like a Phoenix to a flame.

"The candidates are supposed to be with their benefactors for the rest period," I added, my thumb tracing her plump lower lip. "Does that mean you're hers?"

Because that would imply that playing was allowed and I very much wanted to play.

"Melek requested an upgrade to her accommodations and some training," Ajax explained through his teeth. "Stop using your Phoenix energy on her, Az."

My lips curled. "No." My Phoenix rather liked this little warrior, her power an allure I refused to ignore. "What are you?" I marveled again, searching her eyes. "What is your father a mix of?" *How did he evade me?* My grip threatened to tighten again, my irritation returning at the reminder of my failed mission.

Even now, I couldn't sense him. And I had a lock on his essence, my Phoenix still hunting despite Typhos telling me to return.

The moment his aura surfaced, I would go after him.

Yet Camillia's aura differed from his.

She tasted sweeter. Almost innocent in nature. Yet that mouth of hers was positively sinful. I wanted to kiss her. Devour her. *Fuck* her.

Yes, my Phoenix seemed to whisper. *Take her.*

"Az." Ajax's deep voice interrupted my focus, his whip of power wrapping around my neck like a noose. "Release her. I'm not going to ask you again."

My Phoenix hissed in response, my energy whipping out in protest, going straight to his soul.

He growled, my name a curse on his lips as he squeezed his magical hold around my throat. "*Now.*"

I released Camillia's chin and faced the angry Midnight Fae. "You do not tell me what to do."

"I do today."

I arched a brow. "You think you've earned that right?"

"She's not yours."

"She's not yours either," I pointed out. *She belongs to Melek now.* Of course, he was just using her for some sort of game. Or perhaps he intended to keep her. Regardless, I wanted her. So he would just have to share.

As would Ajax.

I pushed off the couch to step into Ajax's personal space and blasted him with more energy. His invisible grip around my neck tightened, cutting off my airflow. Then it fizzled around me in a burning wave of ash-like mist as he dissolved the spell into something else.

Something hot.

Something *enticing*.

My Phoenix perked up at the embers, approving of the heat and fiery kiss against my bare chest.

Ajax's nostrils flared, the blue rims of his gaze smoldering.

Angry arousal hummed in the air between us, his pulse an alluring sound to my sensitive ears. *This* was what I'd come here for—*him*. My outlet. My Ajax. The Midnight Fae who could take my aggression and give it back in kind.

Yes, yes.

He owed me from the other night.

Or maybe I owed him.

It didn't matter. He was mostly naked with droplets of water rolling over his skin. And I very much wanted to indulge myself in a drink.

Except that sweet scent…

I started turning back toward the couch, but a blast of power from Ajax had me grabbing him and shoving him up against a nearby wall. "You're going to pay for that, Death Blood."

"Good." He grabbed the back of my neck, his hips pressing into mine. "Make me bleed, Phoenix."

CAMI

Holy. Shit.

The aggression in the air was a drug to my senses, making me hot all over.

Or maybe that was a residual result of Az's touch.

Because *wow*.

He hadn't bothered with one-liners or suggestive words. He'd just taken what he wanted without a single concern of being denied.

His approach had almost felt primal, like he was being guided by some animalistic entity inside him rather than his own mind.

Even now, he appeared to be acting on instinct, his motions fluid and borderline savage.

I swallowed, the sight before me doing nothing to calm the fire raging inside me.

Ajax had lit the fuse.

Az had poured gasoline all over it.

And together, they had ignited an explosion of ecstasy that left me breathless and needy on the couch.

I couldn't move even if I wanted to.

My eyes were glued to their masculine forms only a few feet away. They were growling and pulsing with power, thickening the air with desire and violence. I could barely breathe, their potent energy drowning me in a sea of *need*.

My thighs clenched.

I shouldn't be drawn to them. I shouldn't be just sitting here watching. Hell, I shouldn't be here at all.

But I *was* here.

Because of the Hell Fae Trials. Because of the agreement between my father and Lucifer. Because Ajax had subdued me and taken me to this place.

Being attracted to my warden was wrong.

Yet I couldn't help it.

He wore that towel low on his hips, revealing every alluring inch of that sculpted torso.

And Az was shirtless, too.

Both of them panting. Both of them engaged in some sort of energy war that I could feel against my skin. It hummed through the room, causing the hairs along my arms to stand on end.

Anticipation flourished between them, their eventual path evident in the way they held one another.

They're going to fuck. Right here. Right in this room. Right in front of me.

Because Ajax had told Az to use him instead of me. He'd demanded he release me, saying something about his Phoenix energy and hypnotizing me.

Maybe he had.

Maybe that was why I felt so enamored with him now.

But part of me didn't care. I'd recognized something in his violet eyes, something I wanted to explore.

"*Fuck.*" Ajax's curse vibrated the pulse between my thighs, making me nearly whimper in response.

These men were dangerous to my senses, making me feel all out of sorts and a bit drunk.

I wasn't a virgin.

But never had anyone made me feel like this.

Nor had I ever seen two males embrace the way these men were now.

They're not human, I thought, delirious from their growing toxicity. *They're fae. Old fae.* At least Az was, anyway. Ajax seemed a little younger. But still older than me. More experienced. Powerful. *Sexual.*

I inhaled sharply, my lungs burning from my lack of oxygen.

I needed to escape this room. To hide. To find somewhere to safely exist while Ajax and Az saw this through.

Yet my legs wouldn't move.

If anything, my limbs grew heavier as the power dynamic between the two men shifted, Az's energy seeming to overwhelm Ajax's aura.

I couldn't see it so much as feel it, the two beings fighting with their fae gifts rather than with their fists.

It was sexy as fuck.

Hot as sin.

Addictive as hell.

I'd never been more aroused in my life, and they weren't even kissing yet. This was just their mental warm-up with Ajax testing Az's limits. He appeared to be losing now, but something told me it was purposeful, that he wanted to lose and submit to Az.

Perhaps that was their dynamic—Ajax submitting to Az.

I doubted either man would ever submit to me.

But that was okay. I preferred my partner to be strong in the bedroom.

Wait... I shouldn't be thinking like this. I should be running! Using their distraction to—

Oh.

My.

God.

They're kissing.

My eyes rounded, my heart skipping several beats as Az attacked Ajax with his mouth.

They were up against the wall by the couch, literally within touching distance, and making out with a ferocity I could feel branding my own skin.

Az grabbed Ajax's towel in the next breath, yanking it from his hips and grabbing the hot arousal beneath.

My lips parted at the sight of Ajax's cock in Az's fist. And the metal barbell at the end.

The one that went through the head of Ajax's shaft.

He's pierced.

He's pierced down there.

He's huge.

He's pulsing.

He's so fucking beautiful.

All the thoughts scrambled through my mind, wiping every ounce of sense from my being.

I want to lick him. I want to feel that barbell inside me. I want to join.

Az ran his thumb over Ajax's weeping slit, then brought the essence up to his own mouth to lick it off.

Ajax panted in response, his hungry eyes on Az.

"Do you want to taste him, little warrior?" Az asked, his darkened irises refocusing on me.

"Az," Ajax warned, some of that power igniting once more.

"You told me to fuck you, and I'm going to. But what about you? What about *her*?" Az didn't take his gaze off of me while he spoke, making me burn that much hotter for them.

Because his words were an invitation.

An invitation I should absolutely reject. These men were my captors. But fae lived by different rules.

And they weren't the actual reason for my imprisonment.

If anything, Ajax had tried to improve my accommodations. He'd been honest from the beginning, too.

And Az... I barely knew. Yet his straightforward approach left me breathless. He was the kind of man who could approach a woman in the bar, tell her he wanted to fuck, and have her naked in minutes.

If I were that woman, I'd say yes in a heartbeat.

Just like I wanted to do now.

"Leave her alone, Az." Ajax's fingers went to Az's pants to deftly undo the top button. "Go hide in my room, Cami."

Az grunted. "Like that'll save her." His beast-like gaze remained on me. "Want to play with us, little warrior?" He grabbed Ajax's shaft again and gave him a violent stroke, causing the other man to curse as he yanked down Az's zipper.

The animalistic aggression in the room darkened as Az lost his pants entirely, leaving both men naked with Az's focus still entirely on me.

Ajax grabbed him in a similar manner, demanding his attention. "Run, Cami."

I couldn't.

I couldn't entirely breathe, let alone move.

They were too hot. Too imposing. Too *consuming*. All my attention falling to their thick, pulsating arousals.

Az was longer and leaner than Ajax, which seemed

true to form, considering he had a few inches of height on Ajax, too.

But they were positively beautiful together. Virile. Inhuman. *Stunning*.

I swallowed, my brain fracturing beneath the enchantment of their embrace as Ajax leaned forward to nip menacingly at Az's throat.

Az responded by tightening his grip and eliciting a threatening growl from Ajax.

Energy vibrated in the room, the two men engaging in their powers and strength and fighting on a sensual level that was borderline savage. This was obviously how they preferred to play with each other, all violent undertones and sexual overtures.

And Az wanted me to join.

He still hadn't stopped studying me despite having Ajax's dick in his hand.

Something about that made me burn even hotter.

Because he didn't bother to hide how much he wanted me, his searing gaze running over me with clear interest. There were no false promises or coaxing platitudes, just a man expressing his desire.

Perhaps that was the fae way. Or maybe that was just Az.

"*Cami*," Ajax breathed, his head falling back as he finally looked at me with his heated blue-black gaze. "If you stay there…" He broke off on another curse as Az twisted his hand upward and swiped at the precum trickling from his head again.

But he didn't bring his thumb to his own lips this time.

Instead, he lifted his hand toward me as an offering.

A beckoning.

A physical invitation since I hadn't yet responded to the verbal one.

My stomach clenched, my mouth watering for a taste.

I leaned toward him as though he controlled me via a string, my lips parting automatically to accept the offering. It was as though Az held out the air I needed to breathe, the sustenance I required to *live*.

My mouth closed around his thumb, the decadent flavor stroking my taste buds and stirring a moan from deep within.

Ajax. Az. Ambrosia.

The salty essence went straight to my soul, setting my blood on fire with a blazing need that I could no longer ignore.

Maybe it was several days of adrenaline and near-death experiences that had led to this moment.

Maybe it was exhaustion from residing in literal Hell.

Maybe it was being around two inhuman males, two *fae*, that set my libido on fire.

Or maybe it was just fate.

Regardless, I followed Az's hand as he started to pull back, my lips refusing to release him, my tongue needing more.

He drew me up to my feet, easily leading me beyond the couch to join them by the wall. "*Fuck*," Ajax breathed. "You've enthralled her."

A different term from the one he'd used earlier —*hypnotizing*. And he spoke as though it was already done, that his hypnotic spell had been upgraded to enthrallment.

Az smiled, the curl of his lips positively predatory and lacking a single ounce of remorse. "No. Her inner warrior is leading her, not me."

Inner warrior? I repeated, considering the term. I wasn't sure I agreed because I felt pretty enthralled by him and his hypnotic now-black irises. They reminded me of inky pools of velvety need, the glint intense and all-consuming.

I wanted to drown in him. In *them*.

Az's thumb left my mouth, leaving me shaking beside him. "Ajax doesn't think you want this," he murmured. "Prove him wrong, Cami. Kiss him. Touch him. *Lick* him."

I shivered, the words, drawing my focus to the Midnight Fae. He almost appeared pained, his expression radiating his inner conflict. He wanted to tell me to run. But part of him also seemed to want me to kneel, to *lick* him just like Az had said.

I wasn't sure how exactly I knew that.

Instinct, maybe.

The glint of lust in his eyes, perhaps.

But that knowledge made me feel strong, *desired*, and capable of so much more.

Ajax wanted me to run. To hide. To let Az and him fuck while leaving me alone in his bedroom without any sort of outlet for all the pain and anguish and *need* building up inside me.

No.

I refused.

They were both naked. Sexy as sin. The ultimate fantasy standing before me in a display of alluring muscular perfection.

Ajax's pupils dilated as he met my gaze, that earlier burn between us reigniting in an instant and engulfing me in fresh flames.

I wanted him.

I knew it was wrong. I knew none of this should be happening. And I still intended to find a way out of these trials.

But playing with Az and Ajax didn't commit me to them. It would just soothe one of my many aches. Perhaps even make this whole experience somewhat worth the trouble.

Well, that seemed like a stretch.

However, I didn't want to think about it anymore.

I wanted to lose myself in their touch, see to this ache between my thighs, and *prove* to Ajax that I wanted this.

Yes, yes, I thought, taking a small step toward him. *Prove to Ajax that I want this. Show him I'm not enthralled.*

That was what Az had told me to do.

That was what I *wanted* to do.

Kiss him. Touch him. Lick him.

Ajax's nostrils flared, his throat working. "Cami, you don't have to do this."

"I know," I whispered, my fingers reaching forward of their own accord to *touch* him. Just his chest, the smooth center of his breastbone, because I didn't trust myself to stroke him anywhere else. Not with his piercing below. *I should lick him there*, I thought. *I should go to my knees and kiss him, then lick them... right... there...*

My knees started to bend, almost as though my mind were no longer my own.

I glanced back at Az, wondering if he was the one driving my motions, treating me like some sort of aroused puppet that he could mentally control. His dark eyes ensnared me once more, the obsidian depths making my lips part and my nipples harden to painful peaks.

Oh God...

I was utterly enraptured by them, their lustful toxicity driving me onward and erasing all thought from my mind.

Az's palm curled around the back of my neck, his thumb stroking my pulse as he leaned in to press a soft kiss to my lips. I parted for him automatically, wanting more.

But he guided my mouth away from his.

And toward Ajax.

Pushing me into the Midnight Fae with a gentle force that had me obeying on instinct.

Ajax growled, the vibration rumbling my lips.

"Kiss her," Az whispered. "She wants you to."

"I'm going to fucking kill you," Ajax threatened, his words eliciting a tremble from deep within. Because I wasn't sure if he meant that statement for me or for Az, or perhaps even both of us.

But it didn't matter.

Because in the next breath, his lips captured mine.

And I forgot everything in a blink.

All that mattered was Ajax. His mouth. His tongue. His *taste*.

Warm. Hot. Decadence.

Masculine power.

Midnight perfection.

Az's grip on my neck tightened, reminding me of his presence, his lips against my ear. "Kiss him, Cami. *Really* kiss him."

I did.

I *was*.

But I wanted to make it better, more intense, more skilled, just to prove a point.

I gave myself entirely to Ajax, my arms encircling his neck as I slipped between him and Az. Heat bathed my front and back, both males allowing me to feel their matching arousals through my clothes.

Only for those clothes to begin vanishing.

Az's hands roamed my body, his grip leaving my neck to remove my pants. Ajax took care of my shirt, his fingers brushing my skin as he slowly peeled the fabric upward to reveal my stomach and then my breasts.

It all happened so quickly, my senses not even given time to realize their intent until I was naked between them, trapped between their muscular forms, and panting with a need that lit my veins on fire.

"She's perfect," Az whispered, his lips skimming my neck as he trailed his mouth upward to nibble on my earlobe. "Are you sure we can't fuck her, Ajax? Because she feels so soft and pretty." He bit down harshly, eliciting a gasp from my throat.

A gasp that Ajax swallowed on a growl as a trickle of warmth touched my skin.

"She bleeds sweetly, too," Az said, his tongue tracing the wound he'd created and leaving a subtle sting behind.

Then he reached around me to grab a fistful of Ajax's hair to yank his mouth away from mine and kiss him soundly.

Ajax stiffened against me, his hands going to my hips as he pulled me even closer to him, his cock a brand against my belly as he sucked my blood from Az's tongue.

The world spun around me, the scene so intensely erotic that I nearly passed out at the sight and feeling of being trapped between these two men.

Except Ajax's mouth claimed mine again in the next instant, grounding me against him as Az's lips returned to my neck.

This was all so much more than I'd anticipated.

So much more than I could ever have even dreamed about.

Part of me wondered if this was some sort of new trial, a way to see if a Hell Fae bride could handle the virility of their potential mates. And just the thought of that made me dizzy all over again.

Except Ajax and Az were there, their hands roaming over me with unveiled interest, their warmth branding my skin and demanding my open participation.

I lost myself to their touch, to their mouths, and their expert tongues.

Because they started *sharing*.

Ajax spun me to face Az, telling me to kiss him in a similar tone that Az had used before, and I obeyed. Because I didn't know what else to do. I was a slave to their passion, utterly consumed by their masculine claims, and enraptured by the moment.

Az's tongue was just as skilled as Ajax's, only with a hint of command in his movements. He wasn't the type of man to allow me to lead. He knew what he wanted and how he wanted it, which he proceeded to demonstrate with his mouth.

While Ajax seemed a bit more open to exploration, potentially even okay with shifting roles so long as he ended up on top in the end.

Two very different males.

But equally powerful, equally proficient, and equally hard.

I felt owned.

Possessed.

Marked as theirs.

Almost as though we didn't need any sort of claim to be mated.

A terrifying thought, one that fled the moment Az cupped my breast, his thumb massaging my nipple. Ajax's lips found my neck, his tongue teasing my pulse.

One bite, I reminded myself. *One bite and I'm his.*

It was the sort of thought that I should voice out loud, the word *stop* hanging on my tongue.

But he moved his lips to my shoulder, his palms sliding to my stomach and downward to the tops of my thighs. Exploring. Memorizing. *Indulging*.

Az's fingers threaded through my hair, my ponytail disappearing in a snap. And then he tugged, harsh enough to bring tears to my eyes. Tears he studied as he pulled away to scrutinize my features. His all-black eyes were positively feral, consumed by whatever beast rode his spirit.

A Phoenix, I thought. *He's a Phoenix Fae.*

But no ordinary Shifter Fae, no.

He was something *more*. Something full of energy and grace and absolute power. He could destroy me in a breath. He might even do just that now.

I seemed to be under some sort of evaluation, his animal deciding whether or not to proceed.

A subtle hum of power rolled over my skin, kissing my senses as he continued to stare me down. A warm burst followed, making me gasp at the way it flourished through my veins, seeming to go straight to the sensitive area between my thighs.

I clenched my legs, dampness pooling there in response.

And another zing of energy followed, going straight to my clit.

Fuck…

He wasn't even touching me. Not really. Just his thumb against my nipple and his lips a hairsbreadth away from mine.

But he was stroking me *inside* with his power.

I moaned as he did it a third time, my core throbbing with an intense need that had me leaning back against Ajax for support. His palms slid inward along my thighs, his fingertips brushing my slickening folds as he released a rumble of approval. "She likes your power."

"So do you," Az replied, making Ajax's cock jump against my lower back.

I swallowed, my mouth suddenly dry as another shock wave filtered through us both, causing my insides to burn and Ajax to pulse behind me. His mouth went to my throat again, his pant of need rivaling my own.

Whatever Az was doing to us was stoking our need and setting us both that much closer to the edge.

Without really touching us, I marveled again. *What the hell is this magic?*

I felt delirious. Spinning in a pool of need. Drowning in his dark gaze. *Throbbing* with power.

Az brushed his lips against mine, the barest hint of a smile curling his mouth. "I want to keep her."

"She's not ours," Ajax gritted out.

"I think I'll keep her anyway," Az mused, his nose brushing mine. "My Phoenix is quite taken with her. Perhaps even more than he is with you."

Ajax grunted. "I could use a break."

"Could you?" Az's dark eyes left mine to flick to the man behind me. "Want to run off to your room and leave us to play?"

"I could use a break from *you*," he clarified. "I'm not leaving her."

"Ah, so you do want her."

"I think that's pretty fucking obvious, isn't it?" Ajax pressed into my back as though he were drilling through me to reach Az, causing me to gasp. Because his action drove me that much closer to Az, pressing his own erection into my belly.

I don't know how I ended up between them. But I think I'll stay here forever, I thought dreamily. *I make a good Cami sandwich. Except they're the meat, not the bread.*

I nearly sighed in contentment.

But another wave of that addictive energy warmed my veins, eliciting a moan from me instead.

"How wet is she?" Az asked.

Ajax drew his fingers through my sex, his resulting groan making me light-headed. Rather than respond verbally, he lifted his hand to Az's mouth, similar to how Az had offered me his thumb.

Dark eyes captured mine as Az bent to lick my essence from Ajax's fingers. The smolder in his irises had me trembling, my legs tensing.

Ajax palmed my sex while his opposite hand went to my breast, his fingers still damp from Az's mouth, as he held me upright between them.

"She's delicious," Az said, his obsidian orbs going to Ajax. "I want to watch you fuck her with your tongue while I take your ass."

AJAX

THE IMAGE Az's words painted made my cock throb.

So crass.

So to the point.

So damn *wrong*.

I should stop this. I should demand that Cami run. But the scent of her interest, the feel of her *heat*, rendered me useless in this sensual assault.

Az's Phoenix had won.

All I could do now was control the fallout.

In this moment, I hated Az. I adored him. I wanted to punch him. I needed to worship him. It was such a conflict of interest, all of this so acutely inappropriate that I nearly grasped my ability to reject them once more.

But then Cami turned, giving me a full display of those gorgeous tits, flat stomach, and neatly trimmed mound.

And I was done.

It'd been a long time since I had truly touched a woman. She smelled so sweet and fresh, her arousal a beacon my tongue desired to explore.

I wanted her. I'd wanted her from the moment I'd laid

eyes on her in the Human Realm after watching her kick Payan's ass. She was fierce and strong and sexy as fuck.

Her eyes gleamed up at me now, her gaze reminding me of a Siren. So tempting and illustrious. A man would die for that look alone.

A sacrifice I might just make by touching her.

Because she wasn't mine.

She was a candidate under my care.

It felt as though I were taking advantage of her situation, taking her without true consent. But her mouth against mine *felt* consensual. Especially as she clasped the back of my neck and parted my lips with her tongue.

I grasped her hips once more, one of my palms sliding to her lower back to bring her closer to me, and welcomed her kiss by returning it with my own.

Somehow she knew I needed this.

Or perhaps it was all Az.

His Phoenix could compel, but he kept saying it wasn't him, that she wasn't hypnotized by his own desire. Az didn't lie. If he was manipulating this situation, he'd own it.

Which meant she wanted to be here.

Yet I sensed that hint of hypnotic energy in her gaze, not in a tangible or obvious sort of way, though. It was more like she'd lost herself in the sea of lust, her mind capitulating to ours as she gave us full access to her body.

The attraction was absolutely mutual.

I'd scented her interest before, my vampire-like senses picking up on her thrumming pulse and dilated pupils.

But attraction wasn't always enough.

Especially in a situation like this.

It was why I should pull away and demand again that Az take me in another room.

Except Cami's tongue held me captive against her.

She wrapped her arms around my shoulders, hugging me and pressing those perfect breasts against my chest. I groaned in response, her athletic form fitting mine so beautifully. She was small. Delicate. Yet incredibly strong. So fae-like and gorgeous.

I wanted to keep her.

I wanted to make her mine.

And having her blood in my system only made that desire more resolute.

I knew better than to bite her. I *wouldn't* bite her.

But I would indulge her.

I would taste her.

I would feel her come on my tongue.

Az crowded her back, his touch going to my hair before tracing along her arms and down her sides. Then he reached between us to find my throbbing shaft. He didn't grab me, just gently stroked it with one finger, teasing me while I kissed Cami.

She pressed against Az's hand, trapping his touch against my dick and eliciting a soft chuckle from him. "Our warrior wants more," he said, kissing her neck and wrapping his palm more firmly around me. "As do I."

Yes, I knew what he wanted.

He'd already outlined his intentions.

And Cami seemed to be confirming with her mouth that she wanted what Az had suggested.

I leaned into her, urging Az to take a step back as Cami reacted to my movements. Her tongue continued to dance with mine as I shifted forward again, her arms tightening their hold, suggesting she didn't want to let me go.

My palm remained against her lower back, loving the feel of her skin and the soft teasing brush of Az's arousal against my knuckles. I used my opposite hand to grasp his hip, pushing just enough to tell him what I wanted—a better position to meet his sexual demands.

Az took hold of Cami's waist, pulling her with him as he moved, taking my hint and leading us through the living area and into my bedroom.

Which had been where I'd told her to hide.

So I supposed that meant Az was right when he'd said that wouldn't save her.

Fuck, nothing would save her from us now.

It was dangerous and intoxicating and so undeniably wrong.

Yet I couldn't fight the attraction anymore. I didn't release her. I kissed her harder instead. And I followed her up onto my bed with my mouth on hers, crawling over her body as Az guided her to the mattress.

It was seamless.

Beautiful.

A sensual movement of fate.

I couldn't stop touching her. I couldn't stop kissing her. I couldn't stop *wanting* her.

She felt too perfect beneath me, her supple form melting into mine as I lay on top of her.

Warm. Wanting. Wicked.

She parted her legs for my hips, her dampness a wet kiss to my dick that had me throbbing for her. But I wanted to taste her first. I wanted to create the image Az had painted in my mind.

So I began a path downward, my lips kissing every inch of her on my way to her breasts. Az bent to take her mouth with his own, making me groan against her nipple. It was such an intensely erotic sight, watching him master her with his tongue.

We'd never shared a woman. Mostly because Az's

Phoenix was selective and I tended to avoid sexual entanglements.

But Cami surpassed all logic.

There was just something about her that I needed to know. To explore. To *taste*.

The reminder of my quest made my dick pulsate with need, my mouth salivating for her. But I finished my task of memorizing her tits first, taking her nipple into my mouth and sucking deep. Laving her. Nibbling. Careful not to *bite*.

Oh, but I wanted to sink my teeth into that creamy flesh.

Make her bleed.

Drink from her.

It was a pulsing craving that left me breathless.

Az released her, his all-black eyes meeting mine, his Phoenix clearly sensing my yearning. Because he knew me. He could read my energy. He could read every damn thing about me.

A blade appeared in Az's palm—one of the many that he could magically summon at will.

He pressed the sharp edge to Cami's breast and stirred a gasp from her throat. "Don't move, sweet warrior," he said, his opposite hand going to her throat. "I'm giving Ajax what he needs."

It was on the tip of my tongue to tell him to stop, to tell him this was too far, but he sliced across her skin in the next moment, eliciting a hiss from her lips.

Blood beaded along the path he'd created, the superficial cut just enough to draw her essence to the surface.

The blade disappeared with a whispered command from Az, and then he was kissing Cami again, soothing her pain with his mouth. She'd stiffened beneath me, her thighs tightening alongside mine.

I debated how to proceed, but her essence called to me, begging me to lick her.

And not just along her breast, but between her legs, too.

I started with the wound Az had created, comforting her with my tongue and groaning at her decadent flavor. So light. Sweet. *Addictive*.

My instincts roared in my skin, demanding I bite her once more, but I tamed my inner urges and licked her thoroughly instead before returning to her stiff peak. She moaned as I worshipped her tits, whatever sting the wound had created fleeing in favor of the pleasure Az and I provided her with.

Then I continued downward to the proof of her desire.

So wet. So hot. So *needy*.

Her clit was swollen, begging for my touch, and her slit glistened with warm interest.

I drew my tongue along her weeping seam, groaning at her alluring flavor. It was different from her blood, yet just as sweet, almost citrusy in its decadence.

Addictive, too.

Just like the rest of her.

"You were right, Az," I whispered against her flesh. "She tastes amazing."

"Mmm," he hummed, still kissing her.

I gripped her thighs to widen her legs even more and speared her with my tongue.

She jumped, her hands grabbing the comforter on either side of her hips and squeezing.

Az palmed her breast, holding her against the mattress as he continued to dominate her mouth while I acquainted myself with her sweet pussy.

She began to shake, the vestiges of an orgasm clearly close already. I drew my tongue upward, circling her clit before sucking the sensitive bud deep into my mouth, forcing her over that initial edge.

It'd been a while since I'd done something like this, but I knew how to drive a woman to madness.

And the evidence of that skill proceeded to make itself known as she screamed against Az's mouth.

A beautiful sound. One I intended to repeat. Which I told her without words as I continued my assault against her weeping cunt.

She trembled, her legs trying to close, but I wouldn't let them. She could take more. And I planned to give her more, too.

Az hushed her as she tried to protest. "Let the man do his job, Cami."

She panted. "I—"

"You can handle it," Az interjected. "And I want to see you come again." He leaned down to nip her lip while I watched from between her thighs. "And again." He laved her bottom lip. "*And again.*"

"Oh God…"

"Fae," he corrected softly. "Not gods."

I chuckled and she jolted in response. "You like that vibration, Camillia?"

She groaned, her eyes rolling back in her head.

"I think that's a yes." Az leaned down to capture her nipple between his teeth, biting down in a way I wished I could. But I didn't trust myself not to break the skin.

She jerked again, her knuckles turning white from grabbing the comforter so tightly. Then she moaned as he tongued her abused peak.

It seemed Az was right about her desiring a little pain with her pleasure. *Noted.*

Not that this will be happening again.

Maybe.

I shook the thoughts away, focusing on the present instead and the feral way Az moved along the bed. I knew what he intended to do, but he straddled Cami's torso instead, positioning his groin near her mouth.

"Suck me," he told her. "It'll help me fuck Ajax."

I swallowed, aware of how much he was going to make it hurt.

He wanted to make me bleed.

His Phoenix craved it.

And rather than truly harm Cami, he planned to take that aggression out on me. I wasn't sure where he'd been or what had set him off, but I'd *felt* his aggressive energy while in the shower. I'd immediately shut off the water, grabbed a towel, and rushed out to shield Cami from his intensity.

Except I hadn't been able to protect her entirely from his Phoenix, hence our current predicament. But at least I could save her from the eventual pain of Az's release.

He wasn't necessarily a sadist, but his Phoenix required an outlet. One that could handle the energy Az needed to expel.

I often served as that outlet, just as I would today.

But with the added benefit of Cami in the room.

And her sweetness in my mouth.

Cami released the blankets to grab Az, her nails biting into his hips as he pushed forward. I couldn't see it, my angle from between her legs preventing me from witnessing her reaction to having Az in her mouth. However, the tensing of his muscles told me he liked it, and the way his head tipped back on a groan suggested she'd pleased him more than he'd anticipated.

Because Az was always in control.

Always the one dominating from behind.

Yet whatever her tongue did to him now had him visibly shaking with passion.

"Fuck, Ajax," Az groaned. "She's an enchantress. I may need to revise my intentions."

He thrust forward, causing her to make a protesting sound. But the fresh wave of wetness between her thighs told me she liked his dominance. I understood because I did, too.

I circled her clit with my tongue again, worshipping her with my mouth and thanking her for taking care of Az.

He seemed ready to explode, his back and thighs and ass all tense as he drove into her. But he pulled away as a wave of energy thundered through the room.

Cami moaned, her hips leaving the bed. I pushed her back down with my palm against her lower abdomen.

Az moved away on shaky limbs, his Phoenix seeming to take over his features as he looked at me. I gave him a subtle nod, knowing what he needed. There wouldn't be time for prepping. He would take me raw, just as he often threatened to do, and I wasn't going to like it. But I would take it if it meant protecting Cami from his impending explosion.

Cami's chest rose and fell, her arousal and exertion palpable. He'd blasted her with just a hint of the energy he needed to release, leaving her breathless and pink. Or maybe that was her excitement. Regardless, I worked her with my mouth, driving her toward another release and watching as her eyes rolled back into her head.

"Make her come a third time," Az demanded as he positioned himself behind me. "I want to watch."

Cami tried to object while in the middle of her current orgasm, but the sound died behind Az's groan as he thrust into my ass. I cursed against her damp center, my insides *burning* from Az's assault. The wetness from her mouth had barely helped, but at least he hadn't gone in dry.

"*Fuck.*"

"That's my intention, yes," Az said, driving in and out of me without bothering to ease into the motion.

It was brutal. Vicious. And so very *Az*.

He wouldn't apologize later. It wasn't in his nature. But he would take care of me in his own way.

Cami blinked wide eyes at us, her cheeks turning red.

"Lick her," Az commanded, his voice gruff.

I muttered another curse as I fought to loosen my muscles, knowing it would help me accept his savagery. But it was hard when he just kept fucking me with abandon, the burn growing in ferocity with each carnal thrust.

Cami's fingers wove through my hair, her eyes meeting mine. Concern radiated from her. Concern that I wanted to replace with pleasure.

I gave her a long, sensual lick while she watched, my focus on her more than the rutting beast behind me. She swallowed, her nostrils flaring as the stirring of passion began to enter her expression once more.

I added my fingers to the mix, sliding two into her slick center and curling them upward to hit that spot deep inside that made all women groan.

Cami didn't disappoint, her resulting moan going straight to my balls.

My shaft pulsed, Az fucked, and Cami began to lift her hips against my mouth.

It was a beautiful dance of eroticism and animalistic intrigue, driving the two of them to pleasurable heights.

I watched, my heart beating rapidly, as bliss stole through Cami's features, making her look even more angelic, more beautiful, more *her*. She positively glowed, her expression one I would never forget as Az growled in my ear.

His Phoenix was fully in charge now, driving his every move, thrusting, thrusting, thrusting, until every sound he made was more beast than man.

Cami watched from beneath hooded eyes, her arousal a rapturous taste against my tongue as her inner walls clamped down around my fingers.

"*Now*," Az demanded, the word seeming to be for Cami as she fell apart on a cry of pleasure-induced pain. Her eyes were on me as she came, providing me with the stunning sight of her full climax, the heat of it scorching my insides as Az joined her in an eruption that branded my veins.

Power flooded through the room, the intense energy rippling through me before reaching Cami.

She quivered in response, feeling some of the aftershocks. But the majority of his intensity went into my spirit, where I absorbed it as I always did, the power feeding my own.

Az pulled out of me, flipping me onto my back as he took my shaft into his mouth, sucking and thanking me with his tongue. I groaned as I reached the back of his throat, his power still pouring into me as he swallowed around my head, demanding I join him in this blissful state of existence. I threaded my fingers through his hair, accepting his care and attention, but my eyes went to Cami, her pretty pink cheeks and swollen lips a sight that left me vibrating with a fierce craving. I wanted to be inside her, fucking her, feeling her orgasm around my dick like she had my fingers.

The image alone brought me that much closer.

And then Az laved the piercing in the head of my cock,

twisting it with his tongue in the way he knew I couldn't resist.

Sending me to the stars, forcing me to join them in the land of ecstasy and grace.

A strange sort of combination of names left my lips as I tumbled into oblivion, one that sounded a lot like "CamAz." I couldn't really say because my mind blacked out for a long moment as a pleasing thrum overwhelmed every inch of my being, killing me for a brief moment in time.

Darkness.

Throbbing.

Blissful.

Silence.

Underlined with quakes of vehemence and energetic strokes of vivacity as Az's mouth redefined the meaning of life.

He took every drop. *Sucking. Claiming. Swallowing.*

I floated in that state, loving the way it felt, and woke to the sensation of a damp cloth against my ass and Cami's delicious curves against my groin. *Spooning. Resting. Being taken care of by Az.*

This was his version of an apology.

His version of guarding those he cared about.

I never spoke during these moments.

I never acknowledged what this meant.

But something told me that one day soon, I would be forced to acknowledge what Az meant to me.

What Cami *could* mean to me.

Just not today.

Today… today we would rest.

And maybe play again.

Az kissed my shoulder, the touch so tender I closed my

eyes. Because I wasn't ready to embrace what it meant yet.

"Sleep," he whispered. "I'll be here."

I nodded, the only acknowledgment I ever gave during these moments.

He would be gone by the time I woke up.

But he would be there while I slept, just as he'd promised.

Only this time, it wasn't just me. It was Cami, too.

What would she do when we woke? How would she react?

I'd worry about it then.

For now, I held her. Enjoyed her. Cherished her.

While Az protected us.

And fell into a deep sleep.

MELEK

My LIPS CURLED at the sensation warming my veins. It would be so easy to engage my ethereal form and fly down to Ajax's dungeon. But I didn't want to intrude.

Instead, I reveled in the sensation of Cami's pleasure while lounging in bed, waiting for Ty. He would sense my need from the other room and come to me once he wrapped up his conversation with the Corpse Fae King.

Or *lieutenant*, as my love preferred to call them.

His league of Nightmare Fae Royals who managed their own realms. I preferred *Kings* since that was their true purpose and the formal titles they used within their realms.

But I supposed Ty was the only true leader as the Hell Fae King. It was his energy and connection to the Hell Fae Source that allowed the Nightmare Fae realms to prosper.

It also gave him the energy and ability to create his nightmarish forms to punish those who defied his deals.

I lounged against the pillows, not bothering to hide my sensual mood. Cami appeared to be enjoying herself immensely in Ajax's care. Part of me wanted to venture down there just to see exactly what he was doing to her.

No. Not just him, I thought, feeling a blast of Az's familiar energy through my link with Cami. *Them.*

Oh, now that is quite the twist, I mused, my lips curling even more. *Az has joined, hmm?*

I supposed that meant my plan was working even better than anticipated.

Az's Phoenix was notoriously selective. The fact that Cami appealed to him only further confirmed the rightness of this whole situation.

She belongs here.

She belongs with us.

Ty sauntered toward our bedroom with a glass of red wine in one hand and his tablet in the other, his eyebrow lifting as he found me naked in the bed on top of the sheets.

"You seem pleased," he murmured, leaning against the doorjamb and pausing to admire the view.

"Not nearly enough, my king," I told him, reaching down to give myself a lazy stroke. "Join me?"

He considered me as he took a long sip of his wine. "Only if you tell me what we're celebrating."

Always so smart, my Ty, I thought, grinning at him. "Camillia has finally accepted one of my gifts."

"Oh?" He pushed away from the door to wander toward me, his long legs graceful as he moved. "And which spell did she use?"

"Not a spell." I reached for his wine as he stopped beside the bed, taking a sip for myself. "Something else."

"Are you going to tell me what that something else is?"

"It's not tangible," I promised him.

He opened the drawer of the nightstand to set his tablet inside. "I believe we agreed that was for the first round before the initial trial. You're allowed three tangible gifts now." He glanced up at me. "Within reason, Melek."

"Am I?" I feigned innocence. "Maybe I'm not the one who chose to present her gifts for this round."

That gave him pause. "Someone else has chosen your candidate?"

I smiled. "Two someones, I think."

He straightened, instantly alert. "Who?"

I allowed my gaze to roam over his fit form. "Remove your clothes and I'll tell you."

"A deal?"

"A request," I countered. "Please."

He glanced down my body to my throbbing groin, his dark sapphire gaze pulsating with interest. "Only because you asked nicely." He pulled his shirt off first, revealing all those sharply carved lines and muscular ripples. His pants went next, leaving him clad in a pair of black briefs that he didn't touch as he joined me on the bed. Something told me I'd be removing those with my teeth soon.

That was fine.

I enjoyed exposing him in my own way.

He sat against the headboard, his long legs crossing at the ankles just like mine.

Then his palm went to my thigh, a touch meant to tease. "Who?" he repeated.

That single question was underlined with immense power, and it held an underlying meaning, too. If I asked him to remove the competition, he would. Just like he would bring Cami to me right now if I requested it.

But that wasn't how I wanted to play this game.

It wasn't about forcing Cami to choose us.

It was about proving to her where she belonged by way of putting all the pieces of the puzzle together.

Ajax was a powerful acquisition that I'd been after for a while. It didn't surprise me at all that Camillia De la Croix was the one to seduce him into the inner circle.

Well, perhaps not *fully* into the circle, anyway. He still lingered around the edge. But Cami would be the one to push him into the center and force him to take his place within this sphere of power.

It was only a matter of time.

I met Ty's burning gaze as I reached around him to set the now-empty wine glass on the nightstand. "Our Warden has chosen to upgrade her accommodations in the dungeon."

Both of Ty's eyebrows rose. "He *what?*"

"It's not against the rules," I informed him softly, my hand slipping over his to draw his touch up to where I desired him most.

"He's not a Hell Fae."

"No, but the dungeon is his territory. And if he wants to invite a prisoner into his quarters, it's his prerogative." There were no rules down there regarding intimacy with the Warden, mostly because they'd never been required before. Only a suicidal fae would think to entertain one of Ty's violent creations in the bedroom.

But Cami was a different entity entirely.

"You said there were two," Ty said, narrowing his gaze. "Who else?"

The way he asked told me he already knew. Likely because he would be able to feel Az's pleasure even more intensely than I could sense Cami's. And as Az's relationship with Ajax wasn't a secret to anyone, it would be fairly obvious who that second person was in this equation.

But I humored him by replying anyway. "It seems Az has decided to play. And he *is* a Hell Fae."

His jaw ticked. "I see."

I grinned. "Do you?" Because something told me he

didn't fully see the big picture yet at all. Which was okay. I would show him in time.

"Your gift to Cami was Ajax."

I contemplated that phrasing for a moment. "In a manner of speaking, yes." But I had meant the gift of comfort and pleasure that she experienced now as a result of Ajax's involvement. However, it was close enough to the truth to count.

That gift would continue when he started training her for the Netherworld Kingdom.

I suspected he would reserve tomorrow for that, as today had been about rejuvenating the soul and finding pleasure in each other's company.

A perfect way to spend a shared existence.

Which had me curling Ty's hand around my throbbing shaft. Because I very much wanted to indulge in that with him now.

"Is it her pleasure that has you aroused?" Ty asked softly, his thumb brushing the head of my cock. "Or is it your success at whatever game we're playing?"

"Both," I admitted honestly. "I'm very pleased with how the pieces are moving on the board. *And* I'm feeling the afterglow of her pleasure, as I'm sure you're feeling Az's."

Ty nodded. "His power is humming through me."

"Was it a large explosion?"

"Yes."

I smiled. "Good."

His lips didn't curl, his thumb instead teasing me with another soft stroke. "It means I have some power to expel."

"Oh?" I gazed innocently at him. "Would you like my assistance with that, my liege?"

"Always."

I leaned in to kiss him, but his grip on my shaft

tightened in warning. "You still owe me several days from our last bargain, Melek."

"Do I?" I cocked my head to the side. "Well. How would you like me, my lord?"

"On your knees."

"Kneeling or all fours?" Clarifying Ty's desires was always intimately important.

His lips finally twitched, some of his amusement shining through. "All fours."

"As I suspected," I mused. "Will you be punishing me?"

"I haven't yet decided."

"Have I displeased you in some way?" I asked, genuinely curious.

"You rarely displease me, little prince."

"That's not an answer, Ty." I cupped his jaw, my thumb tracing the dark stubble along his chin. "Are you displeased with me?"

"No," he replied, leaning into my touch. "Just curious as to what game we're really playing."

"If I told you that, it would no longer be a game."

"No, it would not," he agreed, kissing the palm of my hand. "But not everything in life needs to be a game, Melek."

"Perhaps not. But this does," I assured him. "To do anything else would belittle the prize at the end." And it would be a rather large prize indeed. One that would change all of our lives. "You trust me, yes?"

"I do." He leaned in to press his lips to mine. "With my life."

That was good. Because all of this was *for* his life. For his existence. To save him from himself. He just didn't realize it yet because he was too busy shouldering every burden himself. But I saw through him. I knew what he needed better than even he did. And I would give him this.

In the form of Camillia De la Croix.

She was the key to it all.

I just needed her to survive and *choose*.

"I love you, Ty," I whispered, holding his stunning gaze. "With all my being."

"I love you, too, little prince," he replied just as softly. "Now get on your hands and knees and let me show you how much."

My lips curled once more, my heart skipping a beat. "You say the sweetest things to me, my king."

He growled, his teeth sinking into my lower lip. "*Now*, Melek."

"As you wish, my lord."

CAMI

WARM.
Hot.
Male.

My senses came alive in an instant, my eyes flying open to find myself sequestered in the dark. *Ajax's room*, I recalled, recognizing my surroundings and recalling everything that had happened prior to falling asleep.

Az's hands.

Ajax's mouth.

Their combined touch.

Their intensity.

Their *need*.

My thighs clenched, my insides tingling with delicious memories.

Memories that seemed to come to life before my eyes as Az appeared beside the bed wearing nothing but a pair of black pants. He studied me for a moment, then squatted to bring himself down to my level and pressed a bottle of water to my lips.

I sat up just enough to drink, then lay down again.

Which caused the masculine arm around my waist to tighten, an action Az tracked with his gaze. "Ajax will wake soon," he told me softly. "And he's not going to like what happened."

I frowned. "He's not?"

Az shook his head, causing his dark hair to dance along his forehead. "This is going to make him feel. He'll do his best to push you away as a result."

"Oh." My brow furrowed. "So he's going to regret this?"

I wasn't sure how to feel about that. If anyone should regret what had happened, it was me.

These were my proverbial captors, after all.

Yet I couldn't deny how right it had all felt. Nor could I say I didn't want it to happen again.

Actually—I ran my gaze over Az's sculpted torso—*I very much want it to happen again.*

"He'll think he regrets it," Az murmured as he set the bottle aside and reached out to cup my cheek. "But it'll be a lie."

"Okay," I whispered.

He drew his thumb along my lower lip, his eyes tracking the movement.

My tongue reacted of its own volition, licking the path he'd just traced, absorbing the subtle flavor of magic left behind.

Power seemed to emanate from Az, his inner beast expelling massive quantities meant for other fae beings to absorb.

If I used all my reserves reciting the spells Melek had taught me, would Az be able to restore my energy levels? I wondered.

It was a dangerous thought, but a useful one. One I might be able to use to my advantage.

To survive.

Assuming I couldn't negotiate my way out of these bride games.

Or find a way to escape.

Do I even want to escape still?

Another dangerous thought.

One I tabled for now as I focused on Az and the intensity radiating from his heated expression.

"Don't let anything he says belittle what happened here today, Cami. And don't let his negativity fool you. Because this will be happening again, sweet warrior." He leaned forward to brush his lips against mine. "I vow it."

I shivered, his breath mingling with mine as he captured my mouth with his own, sealing the pledge with a searing kiss.

It seemed to brand me from the inside out, his tongue whispering promises against mine that I didn't fully understand. But I embraced him regardless, loving the way his power seemed to bleed into my essence, overwhelming my insides and reviving my world with new life.

By the time he pulled away, his irises were full-black again. "My Phoenix likes you." His voice was low and filled with caution. "Be good for Ajax. Do what he says. And don't push him too far. He's not ready for us yet."

"Us?" I repeated.

Az merely smiled and kissed me again, this time with the hint of a goodbye on his tongue. I wasn't sure how I knew that; perhaps I just felt it in the sweet way he took my mouth. But he proved my instincts right as he pulled away to stand once more. He drew his thumb along my lower lip. "You don't need to behave for Melek, though. Feel free to give him hell."

He winked and disappeared in a cloud of ash that dissolved before it hit the marble floor.

My lips parted, and I flew upward to touch the space

he'd just occupied, confused by his magic. But there was no trace of him. No energy signature. No tangible presence at all. Almost as though the ash hadn't actually been corporeal, just a burst of power that I'd somehow seen.

Wow, I marveled, my nipples tightening at the graceful display. Az resembled pure power, giving him a decadent flavor I longed to taste more of.

I'd been almost disappointed when he'd taken his cock away from my mouth, even though I'd been struggling to keep up with his brutal movements.

However, I'd *wanted* to be good enough for him. To be able to tame the beast inside him. To be the one to bring him to his knees.

It'd been a sinful desire, one I'd embraced as he'd fucked my mouth.

And I found myself very much anticipating our next experience.

Which was wrong, of course. Because I needed to be focused on escaping or finding a way out of these trials.

Unless I want to indulge in these gifts, I thought, considering my options.

Melek's spells.

Az's intriguing ability to expel power.

Ajax's useful information—which he had said he would provide more of for the next trial. However, I still didn't know what that meant or what the next trial would entail. Because he'd wanted to rest first.

While what we'd just done hadn't felt all that much like resting, I certainly felt more alive now. Refreshed. Not even sore.

Like I had slept for hours.

Wait... I frowned, searching for a clock. *Did those orgasms knock me out for hours?*

Because I felt like a brand-new Cami, not the broken

one from after the last trial.

I shifted my focus around the room, unable to find any indication of time.

It was on the tip of my tongue to ask Ajax, but I didn't want to wake him. However, when I glanced down, I found him staring up at me with an unreadable expression.

"What are you looking for?" he asked, sounding both tired and suspicious.

"Um, a clock," I admitted. "I'm wondering how long we've been out."

He eyed me for another long moment, then waved his hand with a murmured spell to show a sundial of some kind. No, not a sundial, a *moondial*.

"It's almost curfew," he said. "Not that you're allowed to go anywhere."

I looked at him. "Because I'm still in prison? Or because you don't want me to go anywhere?"

"Lucifer hasn't given you permission to leave," he replied, not exactly answering my question. Or at least not providing the answer I wanted to hear, anyway.

Because part of me had hoped he was the one who didn't want me to leave.

Which was wrong to an extent, as I shouldn't want him to want me here. Because I shouldn't want to be here.

Maybe it won't just be Ajax who is in denial about what just happened, I thought. Except I wasn't in denial. I'd enjoyed it. And I wanted to repeat it.

That was the wrong part of the equation.

However, I'd learned long ago that fretting about the negative never resulted in anything positive.

So I accepted what had happened. Accepted that I wouldn't mind a repeat. And accepted that I still wanted to leave.

Perhaps those items didn't correlate appropriately.

But that was an issue to think about another day, as I needed to focus on the next trial now.

"Does that mean our rest day is done?" I asked, unable to keep the hopeful note from my voice.

He thumbed through the moondial for a moment before nodding. "We can use after hours to train. It'll be easier to engage the death..." He trailed off, his brow furrowing. "*Fucking Shade.*" He sat up, the muscles of his abdomen flexing in an alluring manner that almost distracted me from his comment.

"Death? Shade?"

He shook his head. "An old friend. He brought me a death stone, and now I know why. Always meddling." He ran his fingers through his thick, dark hair, the strands falling in a manner that seemed appropriate for the bedroom.

Upon catching my gaze, his own eyes narrowed. "Look, Cami. This—"

"Was fun," I finished for him, not wanting to do this right now. "But I want to know more about this *death stone*, like what it's for and why we need it."

He studied me for a moment, then cleared his throat. "I still need a proper shower. Then we'll discuss."

I very nearly offered to join him to conserve water and to learn more, but he was already rolling out of the bed. "This isn't happening again," he said from the doorway without looking at me. "You're not my candidate."

I arched a brow. "Who said anything about being *your* candidate? I don't even want to be *a* candidate?"

He lifted his blue-black eyes to mine. "You're a Hell Fae Bride, Cami. That's not going to change."

"We'll see."

"Just because we fucked—"

"We didn't, actually," I interjected. "And that's not

what I meant. I told you, Ajax. I'll survive this. I'll find a way out."

He sighed. "You won't."

"I will," I corrected him. "And in the interim, I'll have some fun." I glanced pointedly at his bed and then at him. "Now go take your shower. I want to learn more about this *death stone*."

His jaw clenched, but he must have realized it was a futile argument because he left.

Which was good.

Because I almost suggested we have *fun* and then go play with the death stone.

An irrational plan. However, that didn't make it any less enticing.

I pinched my lips to the side. *Right.* I needed to ignore the ache between my thighs—one that had seemed to come alive the moment I'd woken up and found Az in the room—and focus on the trial.

On surviving.

On finding a way out of this hellish mess of fate.

I flopped back down and winced as my head landed on the book. Glancing sideways, I saw the telltale edge of the leather binding. "Where do you keep going?" I asked the text as I rolled to the pillow beside it—the one Ajax had just been using. It smelled like mint and pine, making me sigh in contentment.

Then the book opened to reveal an image of a bookshelf.

I blinked at it. "Is that where you go?" I startled. "Wait... you can understand me?"

Several pages fluttered, revealing an ancient language that seemed to morph into words I understood in the next instant.

I started reading, a piece of history unfolding before

my eyes.

Something about Virtuous Fae and the dismantling of a massive source of power. An image of Lucifer appeared, or someone who looked a lot like him with wings.

Wings that burned on the next page, stirring notes of smoke in the air that I could actually smell.

And leading to him falling from the clouds, his body broken without his feathers.

I pressed my fingers to my mouth, swallowing my gasp. The sight of Lucifer falling was horrific, his expression so unbelievably shattered that it broke my heart to watch him fall.

Someone had betrayed him.

Someone he loved.

Melek, I realized on the next page, his blondish-brown hair longer than he wore it now, his eyes colder than I'd ever seen them. A devious little smirk twisted his mouth, his angelic features radiating evil intent as he watched Lucifer fall.

"What are you showing me?" I whispered, swallowing as the next page appeared with a flash of light that momentarily blinded my vision. It almost felt as though I were there, being taken along for the ride, reliving whatever history this book intended to convey.

Stars appeared next, winking beacons of intensity that scattered through the sky.

The Fae Realms, the book read, showing me the varying types of fae that split from this bursting of the Source. "But how?" I asked, not understanding what it all meant. "What history is this?" Was it even real?

Lucifer appeared again, his bruised form kneeling on the ground, his back bloody and his eyes radiating a sorrow I felt deep in my soul.

Only, that sorrow morphed into an incredible fury that

made my heart race. I could actually feel the anger emanating from his dark blue gaze, drilling through my veins in molten waves of lava, burning me to my very soul.

His mouth parted on a scream that shook the earth, forcing me to cover my ears.

Immense power followed, a new bright spot revolving right before us, spinning, morphing, stirring into existence.

So hot.

So vivacious.

So *beautiful*.

I stared at it in awe, longing to touch the burning embers within.

So close, I marveled, reaching for the tendril of energy peeling away from the sphere. My spirit sighed as it touched me, wrapping around my wrist and up into my arm, soothing some wounded part of me.

More, my soul demanded. *Take. More.*

Yes, I agreed, reaching for another strand, only a flicker caught my eye, returning my focus to the original tendril.

It was no longer white.

But gray.

And turning black.

I frowned, my brow coming down. *What…?*

The blinding sphere before me jolted as though cringing away from the tendril I'd just absorbed, some part of the energy source seeming to weep at the loss.

I lowered my arms, confused by the rejection.

My soul urged me to proceed, to ignore the bleeding power. But something about it felt wrong. Like I shouldn't have stroked the brightness.

It's not mine, I thought, taking a step back.

Which had me frowning for an entirely different reason.

Because I wasn't sure how I'd ended up on my feet.

I'd been in bed, reading.

And now…

I spun around, my eyes blinking rapidly at the darkness spanning in every direction. Except for the fiery source. The ball. The one Lucifer had created upon his Fall.

What's going on? Where am I? What happened to the book?

I opened my mouth to call for it, only to realize I couldn't breathe.

Air didn't exist here.

And the source suddenly seemed infuriated by my presence.

It *burned*, humming and growing and forcing me several steps backward. I tried to apologize, but sound didn't exist here.

What's happening to me? I twisted and turned, searching for any way out.

But the sphere kept growing.

Faster now.

Forcing me to run.

Tears traced down my face, the wrongness of that tendril inside me twisting in my gut. *I don't belong here. I'm an intruder. An imposter. I need to run. Run. Run!*

Panicked, voiceless, airless, mindless.

I no longer understood reason.

Except for that niggling in my mind that wondered if this was some sort of trial. A new wave of testing. Perhaps Ajax had lied to me about taking his shower. Maybe he'd pushed me into the next phase.

Did I sleep for the whole rest period? Am I losing my mind? Is this all another mirage?

I paused then, my chest trying to move on a pant that didn't exist.

How am I still alive? I'd been running for what felt like minutes without the ability to breathe. *Something isn't right.*

I spun back to the light, sensing the fiery kiss of its fury as it engulfed me from head to toe, stroking hot embers across my skin and *melting* my insides.

My soul wept.

My heart skipped several beats.

And my eyes… my eyes ceased to be.

Too bright. Too hot. Too *intense*.

The world spun to life in an instant, the heat of the power scorching my skin and setting my spirit on literal fire.

I screamed. But no sound left my lips.

I'm dying, I realized. *This isn't a mirage at all. It's real!*

And I'd stepped right into the white-hot flames.

My legs gave out beneath me, sending me to the ground in a pose similar to what I'd seen Lucifer in just moments ago. On a page of a book that shouldn't be real.

Maybe I'd fallen asleep.

Maybe this was all just a nightmare.

All I could do now was supplicate, hope, and pray for mercy.

Apologies left my lips, none of them heard. But I felt them deep in my soul.

I tried to return the tendril, to expel it, to remove the foreign power.

It slowly drained from my veins, right along with my life, leaving me cold and alone and boneless.

In the middle of a bed.

Wait… My eyelashes fluttered, my gaze suddenly clearing to reveal the familiar settings of my college dorm room.

Allison's twin bed came into view, her fluffy blue quilt unmade and falling off the edge.

The actors on her posters seemed to stare at me, judging my sweaty, naked form.

Because I was unclothed.

And sticking to a comforter I didn't recognize.

I glanced at my desk to find foreign objects there as well. The partially opened wardrobe revealed skirts and blouses that I would never wear.

And the dresser at the foot of my bed had a makeup kit on top of it.

"What the…?" I sat up, my head spinning from a toxic mix of confusion and exhaustion.

Giggles in the hallway sounded, the noise so foreign in nature that I frowned. *Was it all just a bad dream? The Hell Fae Trials? The Source? This room?*

My mind couldn't compute the sequence of events or the strange sense of wrongness in this room.

Another mirage? Another test? Another trial? Another dream?

I shivered, ice drizzling through my veins. Nothing about this felt right. If anything, a sense of foreboding trickled down my spine.

I slipped from the bed, my legs weaker than normal. From my run? Was it real? Did I expel all my energy? Even my own powers?

I wrapped my arms around myself, feeling more vulnerable than I had in a very long time.

I needed clothes. No, I needed *food*. And water.

Oh God, water. I crept forward into the bathroom, my knees threatening to buckle with every step. It felt as though I hadn't moved in years. Which was strange. It'd been minutes since I'd fallen asleep reading, or whatever that had been.

But how am I here? I wondered as I finally reached the bathroom.

My fingers shook as I twisted the faucet, then I carefully bent to drink directly from it. The action left me feeling dizzy and all out of sorts.

However, the water sent a splash of soothing tranquility through my system.

So cleansing and pure.

I nearly hummed in approval.

Only, that sense of dread grew, ice slithering down my spine as a shimmer of magic touched my senses. I straightened, my gaze flying around the small bathroom, searching for the source.

But it wasn't in the room with me.

No.

The source was in the doorway.

In the form of two very pissed-off fae.

Ajax took in my nude state, his lips flattening at the sight.

And Az twirled a blade, his irises twin pools of obsidian fury.

Both men looked like they were about to eat me.

Or maybe even kill me.

I gulped, my throat aching despite the water I'd just sipped.

Ajax grabbed my arm and hauled me out of the bathroom before pushing me up against a nearby wall. He slammed his hands on either side of my head, trapping me in a cloud of his minty scent.

His irises resembled blue fire as he narrowed them at me, his lips almost close enough to touch mine. "You're in trouble now, Camillia." He sounded cold. Furious. Very unlike the Ajax of hours before.

"Yes," Az agreed, his voice just as livid. "'You evaded my Phoenix for thirty fucking days, and you're going to tell me how you did it. Right fucking now."

Cami's Story Continues with *Hell Fae Warden*

Hell Fae Warden

"Why am I naked and tied to a chair?"
Because you're in Hell, little rebel. *My* hell.

Camillia De la Croix isn't human.
She's a Halfling Hell Fae with a fiery spirit and a will that
refuses to break.

The rebellious beauty escaped my dungeon.
Fled Hell.
Then f*cked off to Fae only knows where.

Now I'm paying the price of her little jaunt around the fae
realms.
Because her antics earned us both the wrath of the Hell
Fae King.
He blames *me* for allowing her to escape.

If I don't find out how she managed her little field trip, I'll probably be shipped off to the Netherworld Kingdom to play with the Corpse Fae.

Fortunately, Hell Fae Commander Az wants the answer to this riddle just as badly as I do.
Prince Melek, too.
The three of us will break Camillia's resolve.
Then we'll throw her back into the Hell Fae Trials where she belongs.

You took advantage of my hospitality once, sweetheart.
It won't be happening again.
Now start talking, or I'll turn up the heat.
And this time, you won't be allowed to come.

USA Today Bestselling Author Lexi C. Foss loves to play in dark worlds, especially the ones that bite. She lives in Chapel Hill, North Carolina with her husband and their furry children. When not writing, she's busy crossing items off her travel bucket list, or chasing eclipses around the globe. She's quirky, consumes way too much coffee, and loves to swim.

Want access to the most up-to-date information for all of Lexi's books? Sign-up for her newsletter here.

Lexi also likes to hang out with readers on Facebook in her exclusive readers group - Join Here.

Where To Find Lexi:
www.LexiCFoss.com

Reverse Harem Paranormal Romance - Never Choose.

J.R. Thorn is a Reverse Harem Paranormal Romance Author who loves coffee, stormy weather, and heated discussions with her inner muse. She can often be found scribing her steamy stories in her writing cave far away from the prying eyes of her toddler, husband, and two vocal cats.

www.AuthorJRThorn.com